ON PLANET SWAMP, A LIFE SENTENCE ISN'T ALWAYS A LONG ONE . . .

Suddenly a cold current of water touched Renn's neck. He spun around, eyes probing the darkness. Nothing.

Just nerves. He turned back and clipped the cargo line to the sling. Something hit his lifeline with incredible force. The lifeline jerked him upwards and then let go as razor-sharp teeth sliced it in two. Looking up, Renn saw a huge mouthful of back-ward-curving teeth coming straight at him. Renn ducked behind an artifact and felt the water boil around him as the monstrous thing slid by. He tried to follow the thing's head and just barely escaped as it darted in from behind. Suddenly a huge coil of the thing's snake-like body materialized around his waist. As it began to tighten he saw the head turn on the end of a long serpentine neck and dart his way. He went for the force blade. Damn! It was out of reach below the fat coil of the hard flesh which was wrapped around his middle.

It was hard to breathe. Renn's vision began to blur . . .

Ace Books by William C. Dietz

WAR WORLD
FREEHOLD
IMPERIAL BOUNTY
PRISON PLANET

PRISON PLANET

William C. Dietz

ACE BOOKS, NEW YORK

This book is an Ace original edition,
and has never been previously published.

PRISON PLANET

An Ace Book/published by arrangement with
the author

PRINTING HISTORY
Ace edition/March 1989

ISBN: 0-441-67936-6

Ace Books are published by The Berkley Publishing Group,
200 Madison Avenue, New York, New York 10016.
The name "ACE" and the "A" logo are trademarks
belonging to Charters Communications, Inc.

PRINTED IN THE UNITED STATES OF AMERICA

10 9 8 7 6 5 4 3 2

*This one is for Robert and Carolyn Greene
in gratitude for their encouragement,
friendship, and youngest daughter*

PART ONE

Criminal

——— Chapter One ———

"Get a move on, monster meat . . . I haven't got all day." The guard grinned as he shoved Jonathan Renn through the lock and into the shuttle. Two more guards grabbed Renn and threw him down.

He hit the shuttle's durasteel deck with considerable force. It hurt but Renn was used to pain. That's because the guards used pain as a universal language. A language which never required translation and always got results. Plus, in the imperial order of things, their status was only slightly higher than that of the prisoners they guarded. The ability to inflict pain was an important expression of their superiority.

Renn understood all this but it didn't make him feel better. He shook his head to clear his vision. As things came back into focus he found himself looking straight down at a brass plate set into the deck. It read, ABANDON ALL HOPE YE WHO ENTER HERE. The guards laughed, and rough hands jerked him to his feet. The whole episode was part of their routine send-off. Well, screw them. He'd given up hope long ago.

At first he'd hoped that someone would discover his innocence, free him, and convey the emperor's heartfelt apologies. "Sorry old boy, horrible mistake, can't imagine how it happened, can I drive you home?"

Then the days turned into weeks, and weeks into months, and his fantasies of full exoneration gradually gave way to another, more realistic hope. Perhaps the Imperial Court would be lenient. Yes, he was innocent, but a suspended sentence wouldn't be too bad, at least he'd be free to get his hands on Shinto, and choke the truth out of him. Sure, others *could've* framed him but he knew Shinto had. And if they'd turn him loose he'd prove it. And why not? After all, he was a respectable businessman, with a clean record and friends in high places. "The court finds Citizen Jonathan Renn guilty as charged. However in light of his spotless record, obvious penitence, and impressive character witnesses, the court feels a degree of leniency is appropriate. We therefore sentence Citizen Renn to pay a fine of one thousand Imperials, suspended, providing he stays out of trouble for one standard year."

Then his trial came. It lasted fifteen minutes. His friends in high places never appeared, the evidence was overwhelming, and the judicial computer spent 3.5 seconds reaching a verdict. "For crimes against the empire Citizen Jonathan Renn is hereby sentenced to spend the rest of his natural life on an Imperial Prison Planet. The sentence shall commence immediately."

He appealed of course, and his case went before a panel of sentient judges at nine the next morning. After comparing stock portfolios, drinking coffee, and trading gossip for an hour they discussed Renn's case. Five minutes later they decided to support the lower court, and get together for lunch.

A prison robot with an electronic lisp delivered their decision a few minutes after that. "Thitizen Renn, I'm thorry to inform you that your appeal hath been denied and your thententh thtands. Would you like a cold drink?"

A few days later he and sixty-two other prisoners were packed aboard a shuttle and boosted up to a supply and transport ship. Even as they entered their tiny cells the ship was breaking out of earth orbit and preparing to enter hyperspace. A few hours later Renn felt the characteristic nausea which accompanies a shift into hyperspace and knew he was on his way. But to where? He didn't know, because he was a prisoner, and everybody knows you don't tell prisoners a damn thing.

Weeks passed, and the ship left hyperspace three times to orbit around three different worlds. Renn assumed they were prison planets. He hadn't paid much attention to prison planets in the past. After all, why should *he* care about the fate of the empire's criminals, deviates, and psychopaths? They deserved what they got didn't they? He grinned at the irony of it, and tried to remember what he'd read or heard about prison planets.

The concept had originated with the first emperor. Having won a long civil war, he'd built his empire on the shattered remains of an earlier confederacy, thereby uniting hundreds of human-occupied worlds. Afterwards, he faced the task of restoring civil order to planets which had spent years under military authority. While efficient, martial law is always onerous, and most worlds were eager to get rid of it. So when the war was over, most moved to establish approved forms of planetary government.

As the new governments were phased in, and the military governments were phased out, most planets experienced a sudden upsurge in crime. As a result, newly restructured court systems swung into action, convicted wrong-doers at a record pace, and stuffed them into already crowded prisons. "Build more prisons," the emperor's advisors told him, but he resisted the idea, knowing prisons were expensive, and easily used to symbolize governmental oppression, fancied or real. What's more, he felt an empire should offer its citizens a certain amount of consistency, and couldn't see how equitable prisons could be constructed on hundreds of different planets. So what was the answer?

The answer came, as many answers did, while the emperor lounging in the comfort of his daily stim bath. Of course! It was so obvious! Why hadn't he thought of it before? For a long time he'd been concerned about the many second- and third-rate planets, which though inside the sphere of his control, were unsettled. Such worlds made tempting targets for the neighboring Il Ronnian empire. As human and alien empires grew steadily towards each other, each did its best to establish footholds in the other's territory, and unoccupied worlds were especially tempting. So why not use some of those worlds as prisons? By doing so he could simultaneously get rid of the prisoners and make those particular planets less attractive to the Il Ronn.

The more the emperor thought about it the more he liked it. Although unpleasant, many of the worlds were not only capable of supporting human life, they also contained valuable resources. Suddenly the emperor saw a way to make the prison planets self-supporting as well! Once dirtside, the prisoners would be on their own. There would be no cells, no guards. They could settle for mere survival if they chose, or if they wanted something more, they could work for it. If they wanted off-planet technology, supplies, and products, they'd have to pay for them, and that meant producing something of value. What they produced would vary depending on the resources of their particular planet and the demands of the marketplace. Slouching back in his stim bath, the emperor smiled, and rewarded himself with another five minutes of relaxation.

The emperor wasted no time putting his idea into effect. The requisite planets were soon selected, surveyed, and evaluated. Experts from a variety of disciplines examined each planet's geology, mineral resources, major ecosystems, weather patterns, and more. From this knowledge they designed basic equipment packages, cured potential diseases, and chose which products the prisoners should produce.

Then, to discourage unauthorized arrivals and departures, automatic weapons systems were placed in orbit around each planet. Soon thereafter the first prisoners arrived and went to work. By now the first emperor had died, having passed the throne along to his son, but his prison system lived on, and showed every sign of continuing to do so.

So whenever the ship swung into orbit around a prison planet, Renn listened to the clanging of cell doors, the muffled shuffle of manacled prisoners, and wondered if they'd come for him this time. But they never did. Shuttles would come and go, the noises would gradually die away, and the whole thing would start over. Why certain prisoners were assigned to certain planets, and not others, remained a complete mystery. He'd even asked a guard once, and the guard beat him, not for asking the question, but because he didn't know the answer, either.

More weeks passed, each as featureless and nondescript as the one before, until suddenly and without warning, his cell door clanged open, his name was called, and he was marched down the gleaming corridor towards an unknown future. Now others watched *him* go, peeking through the ration slots in their cell doors, feeling a mixture of envy and pity.

He was half carried and half dragged through the shuttle's inner lock, down a corridor, and into the main cargo area. As the hatch cycle closed behind him, he looked around, screwing up his eyes against the harsh glare of the loading lights. They threw bright pools of greenish light onto the scarred surface of the deck. For a moment he thought he was alone, but then he heard the scrape of a boot on durasteel, and a guard stepped into a pool of light and dropped a large cylindrical bag near his feet. It hit with an audible thump. He beckoned Renn forward.

The guard's uniform hat threw a heavy black shadow down across his face, making it impossible to see his eyes, adding to his already ominous presence. Renn was still three feet away when a huge hand flashed out, grabbed a fistful of his coverall, and jerked him in close. Two quick blows rocked his head back and forth.

Renn tried to ignore the pain. He knew from experience that resistance brought only more pain. Nonetheless he wanted to hit back, and it took all his self-control not to do so. The guard's eyes were bright sparks in dark sockets. Thin lips were pulled back to reveal rows of yellowing teeth. As he spoke, the guard's fetid breath made Renn gag. "That's just to get your attention monster meat. My name's Murphy. Captain Murphy to you. Accordin' to Section Thirty Six, page forty, of the Imperial Prison Regs concernin' scum bags like you, I've gotta waste my valuable time briefin' you on your new home . . . the planet Swamp." Murphy grinned happily. "So pay attention . . . cause I'm only gonna say it once."

The guard reached into a shirt pocket and withdrew a hand-held holo projector. As he snapped it on a miniature planet popped into existence between them. It was about two feet in diameter and looked quite real. It had a slight axial tilt, and outside of the heavy cloud layer obscuring much of its surface, seemed otherwise unremarkable. A host of tiny automatic weapons platforms orbited around it along with a small globe. Renn wondered what it was.

Murphy nodded towards the holo. "That's where you're headed monster meat . . . and it's a real beaut. I won't bother you with a lot of boring stats on mass, luminosity, orbital eccentricity and stuff like that, cause it ain't gonna make a damn bit of difference to the likes of you. All *you* need to know is that Swamp has enough gravity to keep your ass there forever, an atmosphere you can breathe, and an ecosystem full of swamp monsters for you to kill. You kill 'em, skin 'em and sell 'em and you stay alive. Fail and you die. Even a scum bag like you oughtta be able to understand that. Questions?"

Experience had taught Renn that questions often led to abuse, even when invited, but he decided to take the chance. "Is that satellite a moon?"

Murphy laughed. "No, scum bag, it ain't no moon. It's a space station, full of eggheads with nothin' better to do than play grab ass, and stare at some stupid pus ball planet all day long. On those rare occasions when you can see the sky . . . look up and wave . . . maybe they'll take time out to piss on your head." The guard touched a button on the holo projector and the planet suddenly vanished. As he returned the device to his shirt pocket Murphy said, "Now the manual says I've gotta take you on a tour of your gear . . . it's amazin' they don't have me wipin' your nose too."

The guard bent over, released the seals on the black bag, and withdrew a neatly folded bundle. Straightening up he threw it at Renn. As Renn caught it he realized it was some sort of a one-piece suit. It was surprisingly heavy. Holding the suit by its shoulders he allowed it to unfold. It had lots of zippers and pockets, some of which had things in them, plus built in holsters for hand weapons. An environmental suit—for a rather unpleasant environment. Suddenly Renn began to have some very bad feelings about Swamp. As if reading his mind, Murphy grinned, and said, "It'll protect you from the elements, plus some of the smaller life forms. It ain't body armor . . . but it sure beats bare skin. Put it on."

Renn obeyed. As he put on the suit, and the heavy boots that went with it, Murphy continued to talk. He named each item as he plucked it from the black bag, explained its purpose, and showed how to use it. His voice had taken on the rhythmic singsong quality of someone who's given a lecture so many times he has it memorized. "This here's a Sanders-Hexon model 86 recoilless blast rifle . . . minus power pak naturally . . . wouldn't want you to shoot yourself in the toe aboard ship . . . which'll be your main armament. A bit dated . . . but not a bad piece if you take care of it. You also get a hand blaster and a slug gun . . . both unloaded of course . . . and a force blade for skinnin' all them monsters you're gonna kill. Then there's your collapsible shelter . . . same kind the marines use . . . first-aid kit . . . thirty days of emergency rats . . . you can also use 'em to poison swamp monsters . . . and a nifty array of solar cells . . . though God knows when you'll ever see the sun."

There was much more, but somewhere along the line, Renn stopped listening. He'd accepted his fate, but it had seemed distant somehow, and not entirely real. Now, as Murphy inventoried his supplies, he realized his situation was not only real, but much worse than anything he'd ever imagined. For one thing he was completely out of his element. Sure, he'd handled blasters and slug guns occasionally, but he'd never really mastered them. Like his father before him, Renn was a businessman. His weapons were law suits, option clauses, and delivery dates. Now those things were suddenly meaningless, and he was supposed to kill swamp monsters using a set of skills he didn't have. Maybe things could be worse . . . but he couldn't see how.

Marla snarled as the guard opened the door to her cell. The guard, a very unpleasant young man called "Zit," peered in rather cautiously and then entered. He was stupid, but not that stupid. Marla had inflicted a nasty slash on his right thigh only a few days before. It was still healing. So when he saw her muzzle was still strapped in place, a big grin split Zit's pock-marked face, and he grunted with satisfaction. "Come on you cyborg bitch . . . try it." He tapped the palm of his hand with the nerve lash.

Marla was sorely tempted to accept Zit's invitation. In

spite of their earlier run-in, she'd managed to conceal most of her special capabilities, and this seemed a poor time to reveal them. And Marla's capabilities were quite extraordinary. Although she looked like a rather large German Shepherd, Marla was much, much more. She weighed about two hundred pounds, had durasteel teeth and claws, enhanced infrared vision, multi-freq audio intercept, power-assisted musculature, and the full intelligence of a female human with a tested IQ of 125. Had she wished to, Marla could have popped the leather muzzle, and ripped Zit's throat regardless of the nerve lash. While emotionally satisfying, she knew it would also be pointless. The other guards would simply hunt her down and kill her. So Zit would live. Sublimating her anger, Marla forced herself to adopt a submissive posture and whined in the back of her throat. Though she was not really a dog, acting like one often worked to her advantage. Even when people knew Marla was a cyborg, she still looked like a dog, and no matter how hard they tried, they couldn't resist the urge to treat her the way she appeared. Zit was no exception.

"That's better bitch," Zit said nodding his satisfaction. "Now get your miserable flea-bitten ass out into the corridor."

Marla circled around Zit, her tail held between her legs, trying to exit the cell without giving him with an opening. It didn't work. As she scurried through the door he delivered a vicious kick to her left rear haunch. Limping, she preceded him down the gleaming corridor, glancing over her shoulder now and then to make sure she stayed well ahead of him. Meanwhile he provided occasional directions, such as "Right, bitch," and "Left, bitch."

Before long they left the ship via a guarded lock, and entered a shuttle. Marla was spared the ritual with the brass plate. Zit and his fellow guards assumed anything that looked like a dog couldn't read.

Marla's heart sank as she scurried down the next corridor. This was it, the final trip down to some godforsaken prison planet to spend the rest of her life—looking like a dog. Double punishment, it seemed to her.

She stopped in front of a closed hatch. In spite of her many special abilities, there were some things Marla just couldn't do. Opening hatches with her paws was one of them. Zit caught up, opened the hatch, and then kicked her into the shuttle's cargo hold. It was his last chance to demonstrate his superiority.

As she spun around, Marla was dimly aware of the two men, but most of her attention was centered on killing Zit. The last kick was one too many. Pain, plus her frustration and fear, combined to override the logical part of her mind. Gone were her good intentions and determination to maintain a low profile. She popped the muzzle and snapped at the closest part of Zit's anatomy. As luck would have it Zit's foot was coming forward in another kick. Marla's power-assisted jaws closed around his ankle and sliced through it like a knife through warm butter.

As his right foot hit the deck with a soft thump, Zit began to scream, spraying hot blood over Marla's face as he toppled over backwards.

Murphy pulled his stunner, flipped the setting to max, and fired. It hit Marla like a blow from an invisible club. She dropped like a rock as all her systems locked into a spasm.

Renn watched in amazement as Murphy calmly holstered his stunner, hit an alarm button on the nearest bulkhead, and proceeded to kick the dog's stunned body. Renn reacted without conscious thought. He jumped on Murphy's back, wrapped one arm around the guard's thick neck, and squeezed with all his strength. It was a waste of time. Reaching over his shoulder, Murphy ripped Renn loose, and proceeded to beat him senseless. Fortunately, the environmental suit absorbed a good deal of the punishment. Murphy was still pounding away when the ship's medics arrived and went to work on Zit.

Marla was conscious. Her nonorganic components had served to protect her brain and spinal cord from the full effects of the beam. It should have knocked her out. Still, she couldn't move. All she could do was watch Murphy beat Renn's unconscious body and curse him from the bottom of her heart.

Having stopped the worst of Zit's bleeding, the medics took a moment to haul Murphy off Renn's motionless body, and tried to calm him down.

Marla looked Renn over. There was blood all over his face, but his chest continued to rise and fall. At least he was alive.

While part of her mind considered the situation at hand, and wondered what kind of punishment Murphy would mete out, another part, a part she hadn't used in a long time, noticed Renn was good-looking. Ignoring the blood, she saw light brown hair and even features. The way Murphy had taken him apart, the idiot obviously knew nothing about hand-to-hand combat. But he had guts, by God, guts enough to fight for what he assumed was an abused dog. Something deep down in a hidden recess of her being softened, and then gave way entirely, causing the other part of her mind to groan in disgust. "You've got to be kidding, you a female cyberdog, falling for some incompetent clown who can't even throw a decent punch! Don't you have enough problems? All he'll do is cause you more pain. How stupid can you get?"

The hidden part of her sighed, and answered, "Very, very stupid I'm afraid."

Suddenly Murphy's voice came from somewhere behind her. She tried to turn, but nothing happened. His voice was tight with rage. "All right, all right, I'll leave him alone.

I still say I oughtta kill them both right now . . . but you're right . . . those clowns in Internal Affairs would go crazy . . . so I'll let Swamp do it for me. Strap 'em down . . . we're goin' dirtside."

Seconds later two medics picked her up, carried her across the hold, and dumped her into a cargo net. They were none too gentle, but thanks to Murphy's stunner, she couldn't feel a thing. Moments later Renn was dumped in beside her. He bounced a couple of times and then lay still. Although the net was designed for fragile cargo, and was suspended by a network of shock cords, it wasn't intended for living organisms. Apparently the ride down would be part of Murphy's punishment.

A few minutes later repellor beams pushed the shuttle out and away from the larger vessel. Seconds later it blasted down towards the planet below. The shuttle's pilot was a cheerful middle-aged woman nicknamed Aunt Sally. She had the pleasant easygoing manner of a favorite aunt. And her graying hair, lined face, and matronly figure did nothing to ruin the image. Matronly or not, Aunt Sally was one hot shuttle pilot, and everybody knew it. As she slipped the shuttle into a descending orbit, she lit a cigarillo, and watched Murphy out of the corner of her eye. He hated the damned things which was reason enough to smoke them. As she puffed the cigar into life Murphy wrinkled his nose. She knew he wanted to complain but didn't dare. Aunt Sally grinned. Screw him. He might be the captain of the guards, but this was *her* shuttle.

At first the descent wasn't too bad. But as time went on, and the effects of the stunner began to wear off, things got worse. Now more and more sensory input was making it through to Marla's brain, and she wished it wasn't. She'd always been prone to motion sickness . . . and her transformation into a cyborg hadn't lessened the problem. Each time the shuttle hit a new layer of air, it bucked violently, causing the shock-mounted cargo net to move every which way. It made her dizzy. Gritting her teeth, she fought the darkness that threatened to engulf her. Battle-trained Class III cyberdogs don't faint.

Meanwhile Renn groaned and tried to turn over. He was coming to.

"Good," she thought. "Because God knows what's waiting dirtside." Then the shuttle hit an air pocket, and seemed to drop like a rock, and a wave of blackness pulled Marla under.

At first Renn thought he'd passed from one nightmare into another. He could still see Murphy's huge fists coming at him and hear the meaty thump as they hit his face. It had continued long after he'd ceased to feel it, and ceased to care. Then came the welcome darkness of death. But now his peace had been shattered by a confusing mix of sensations. The pain he could understand—it might be part of death—but the motion didn't make sense at all. How could you feel motion if you were dead? Maybe he wasn't dead after all. The thought depressed him.

His eyes popped open. Damn. He was alive all right, if you could call laying next to a dead dog in a gyrating cargo net living. No, the dog was still warm, so maybe it was alive, too. The shuttle shuddered, and the whole cargo net swayed in sympathy. They were making an atmosphere landing. He'd made some tricky atmospheric landings himself, enough to know what they felt like, although he'd never made one in a cargo net before. He tried to sit up, but the combined forces of Swamp's gravity, and the shuttle's erratic motion, made that impossible. Besides it hurt like hell. Renn forced himself to relax and gather his strength. Ten to one he'd need it.

Aunt Sally blew out a thin stream of noxious gray smoke

and smiled. The shuttle was screaming over the swampy terrain at about 900 miles an hour just 300 feet off the ground. This was fun. Talk about a rush! They'd have her ass on any other planet. A globe-circling sonic boom doesn't improve your popularity. But if a few prisoners lose a little sleep . . . so what?

Below, an endless canopy of green flashed by, obscured now and then by broken clouds, and divided by a thousand channels of sluggish brown water. Just part of the endless equatorial swamps which gave the planet its name. Aunt Sally knew the planet had other, more attractive latitudes both north and south, but those were empty of the swamp monsters which fueled the planet's economy, and therefore empty of prisoners as well. Because even in the more pleasant latitudes you needed weapons, medical supplies, and a hundred other things to survive. And there was only one way to get them—hunt swamp monsters, or support those who did. She shivered. God help the poor bastards.

Aunt Sally scanned her readouts and gently cut power. The LZ was ninety standard miles ahead. As the ship slowed, she stubbed out the cigarillo, and grinned when Murphy heaved a sigh of relief.

Silently cursing the shuttle pilot, Murphy touched a series of keys and activated the shuttle's automatic weapons system. SOP for any prison planet, but especially Swamp. The place was home to some very hostile alien life forms, plus about a hundred thousand prisoners, all of whom wanted to leave. And even though the orbiting weapons platforms would burn any ships lifting without the proper codes, there were still prisoners willing to give it a try as had happened five years before. Two thousand of them had joined forces to ambush a supply shuttle. Murphy smiled at the thought. Home-made rocket launchers against ship's weapons. It was no contest. The shuttle's energy weapons cut them down in bloody swaths, started a forest fire around the LZ, and boiled the surrounding channels temporarily dry. When it was over and the ship lifted, only forty-seven prisoners were still alive, most of them badly wounded. Murphy sighed. He'd been on leave and missed the whole thing.

As the shuttle lost all forward motion, Aunt Sally's blunt fingers danced across the control panel, and they started dropping towards the surface. Outside, the ship's repellors made a loud screaming sound, and deep in the swamp something heard, and raised a massive head to answer in kind. Other things heard too, quickly slithering into turgid brown water, or scurrying deeper into lush vegetation. Thousands of insects took to the humid air. Each was the size of a small bird, and the combined sound of their wings filled the air with an ominous hum. Soon they filled the sky and threw a shadow across the land below.

As that shadow swept over them, a small group of men paused, and looked up with hungry eyes. Then without a word they resumed their march. They were tough, as mean as the swamp itself, and just as heartless. Their leader was a full seven feet tall. His giant strides set a mean pace, and the others hurried to keep up. But they didn't mind, because greenies didn't arrive every day, and when they did, it was easy pickings. To them a sonic boom was a call to action. An omen of good things to come. So they hurried forward while the swampy trail squished and sucked at the soles of their boots.

Moments later the shuttle thumped down onto the glazed surface of the LZ. In its own way the LZ was a high-tech work of art. Initial surveys had shown the spongy land wouldn't support anything heavier than a scout. So the Imperial Engineers had made a few changes. First, they set up a complex network of interlocking portable force-field generators. Each was situated to create an invisible cylinder of energy. One end of the cylinder rested on a small island

and the other reached a mile up into the sky. Having done this, they dropped a miniature hell bomb right down the middle of the invisible shaft. When the bomb went off, its energy was channelled straight up and down. The result was an island of fused rock and earth a quarter-mile across and a mile deep. *Voila*! A crude but serviceable landing zone.

So far, not even the combined effects of time, swamp, and weather had managed to damage the LZ's blackened surface. Wind-blown soil occasionally collected here and there, quickly giving birth to a fantastic variety of plant life. For a while lush foliage would grow, and then, when it became too thick, the next shuttle in would burn it off. Aunt Sally considered doing so on this trip, but decided it wasn't necessary quite yet. There was growth working its way in from the edges of the LZ, but there was still plenty of room in the middle, and that's where she set the shuttle down. Putting all systems on standby, she pulled out her knitting, and started a new row.

Marla regained consciousness as they pulled her from the cargo net. Although she had full sensory input her body was still paralyzed. Renn was nowhere to be seen so perhaps they'd taken him first. One man held her up, grunting at the effort involved, while another slipped a cargo sling under her stomach. Then each grabbed one end of the sling, lifted, and carried her towards the main cargo hatch. The hair on the back of her neck bristled as the sluggish breeze brought her the corrupt smell of the surrounding swamp. A growl formed deep in her throat and she carefully suppressed it. They'd love to stun her again.

When they reached the open hatch, Marla saw it was ten or fifteen feet to the ground, and there was no ladder in sight. The men began to swing her back and forth in concert. They were going to throw her out! Desperately she tried to regain motor control but felt no response. Damn!

Depending on how she hit, the fall could kill her. Suddenly Murphy was there laughing. "Bye bye bitch! Hope you can fly!"

And then she *was* flying. Flying and falling towards the hard surface below. She hit hard but felt no pain. Had she been lucky enough to land on something soft? Then she felt movement underneath her. "Damn! You're a heavy dog. That's the last time I'm catching you till you lose some weight." Suddenly Renn was standing over her. For the first time she realized he was a bit chubby.

She tried to say, "Look who's talking," but found herself making a growling sound instead. Anyway she didn't mean it. He'd obviously risked injury to break her fall.

Then she heard Murphy's laughter, and saw Renn turn in that direction. Her own head still refused to move.

Murphy stood framed in the cargo hatch, hands on hips, the large equipment bag on the deck beside him. Looking down he shook his head in mock sympathy. "In a few hours you'll be dead meat, scum bag, and the thought makes me sad, not because I like you, but because you deserve a few years on Swamp before you die." Murphy shrugged. "But them's the breaks. Here, I'll even leave your gear, not that you've got the slightest idea what to do with it." With that Murphy picked up the bag and threw it. It hit Renn in the chest and knocked him over backwards. Murphy was still laughing as the cargo hatch cycled closed.

As Renn got up, the ship lifted on screaming repellors, danced to the far side of the LZ, and blasted towards the sky. As Aunt Sally fed power to the main drives, she lit another cigarillo, and grinned. By the time Murphy reached the control room it would be full of smoke.

Chapter Two

Renn watched the shuttle lift with mixed emotions. Unpleasant though it was, the prison shuttle was a connection with the past and everything familiar. As it dwindled to a spark of light, and then vanished altogether, he knew there was no turning back. But at least he was free! He'd make a new start, find a way off this damned pus ball, and get the bastards who'd framed him. Wouldn't they be surprised when he showed up to even the score!

As quickly as the fantasy came it was gone, replaced by the stark reality of the brooding swamp, the humid air which settled over him like a cloak, and the strange noises all around. The dog made a sound deep in its throat and he knelt by its side. He gave it a reassuring pat on the head, and said, "Take it easy boy . . . you'll be OK . . . it takes awhile for the effects to wear off. That bastard Murphy must have set his stunner for max."

"You idiot!" Marla thought desperately, trying to speak but producing a whimper instead. "I'm not a dog, not a boy, and not nearly as stupid as you are. Can't you hear them? Damn, they sound like a herd of elephants . . . and the smell . . . my God they stink! Break out a weapon and load it. Do something for God's sake!"

But Renn didn't do anything. He didn't have her amplified hearing, enhanced sense of smell, or experience in dealing with physical danger. So when the men stepped out of the dense undergrowth a few seconds later he wasn't ready. There were five of them, all dressed in hand-sewn leather. They seemed to fade into the thick green vegetation behind them. All were heavily armed. One was seven feet tall, and so intimidating his weapons seemed superfluous. His huge frame was topped with a big, bony head, a blade-like nose, long greasy hair, and a single eye. It gleamed with malevolence. Not stupid malevolence, but intelligent malevolence, the kind that chooses evil over good because it seems like the most logical decision. Shiny metal filled the giant's other eye socket, flashing in the broken sunlight, and showing Renn a picture of himself. It didn't look good. When the giant spoke, his voice was surprisingly cultured.

"Well, well," he said, turning to his friends. "What have we here gentlemen? A newcomer it would seem. A newcomer and his pet dog. How touching. I never thought I'd see the day when prisoners were allowed to bring pets . . . but," he said, turning to Renn, "we are forgetting our manners. Welcome to Swamp stranger. For somewhat obvious reasons I am called 'Cyclops.' While not the name my mother and father chose, it is in keeping with the culture of this planet, and has a somewhat intimidating quality. The four gentlemen behind me are variously known as the Blaster, Knife, Trap, and the Scuz."

Renn nodded and smiled. "It's a pleasure gentlemen. Great set of names. You should open a law firm."

When Cyclops laughed the sound was cold and harsh. It sent a chill down Renn's spine. "Oh that's a good one isn't gentlemen? The stranger has a sense of humor. I like that. Tell me stranger, how do you like our planet so far? I hope our informal spaceport and somewhat shabby appearance do not offend you?"

Not sure of how to handle this strange combination of threat and civility, Renn tried to smile. "No of course not, I . . ."

"Then you agree we look shabby?" Cyclops interrupted.

"Why no," Renn replied, "I just meant that . . ."

"He thinks we look shabby," Cyclops said sadly turning to his men, all of whom did their best to look offended. "He has only been on our beautiful planet for a few minutes, and he is already criticizing the way we dress, and the condition of our only spaceport. It makes me sad. Does it make you sad, too?"

"Renn watched helplessly, as the other four took turns saying that they felt sad. Cyclops was obviously playing with him.

Cyclops nodded, holding up one hand for silence. "I hear you gentlemen, and understand your unhappiness, but hark, for I bring you glad tidings!"

The other four did their best to look interested.

"I feel certain that out new citizen mentions our shabbiness only because he intends to remedy it! Yes, that must be it!" Whirling back towards Renn, Cyclops said, "That is correct is it not? In that bag you have fine raiments to improve our appearance? Small conveniences with which to improve the quality of our lives?"

Marla groaned internally, and struggled against the lingering effects of the stun beam, but it was hopeless. Although the effects of the stunner were wearing off, she was still far short of full mobility, and nothing less would get the job done against five armed opponents. "Give 'em the bag," she said, almost croaking it out, but growling instead. "Now's no time to fight. They've got you outnumbered and out-classed. Just give 'em what they want." She managed to raise her head slightly, her eyes seeking his, hoping he'd somehow receive her thoughts via mental telepathy. One look made her groan and slump back. The fool was getting ready to fight. It showed in the tense way he held his body and the determination on his face.

Cyclops saw it, too, and smiled. It would be more fun this way.

Renn gulped back his fear. "Look, Cyclops, or whatever your name is, why don't we just cut the crap. You intend to steal my equipment. You're armed, plus there's five of you, and only one of me. Its too bad you haven't got the guts for a fair fight."

"A fair fight!" Marla wailed inside her self. "If you had a rocket launcher he'd still win! Give 'em the bag!"

Cyclops rubbed his chin as if considering Renn's challenge. Then he turned to his companions. "Well gentlemen, what do you think? The stranger wants to give us his many gifts, but begs the honor of personal combat first. What say you?"

Not too surprisingly, the other four all agreed that personal combat sounded like a good idea. Turning back to Renn, Cyclops shrugged, as if to say, "Well there you are, what can I do but comply?"

As Cyclops made a production out of laying down his weapons, Renn went through a series of warming-up exercises, much to the amusement of Blaster, Knife, Trap, and the Scuz.

Marla felt proud and sad at the same time. Proud that Renn had the guts to fight, and sad, knowing the certain outcome.

Renn knew he must be a ludicrous sight, dancing around and shadowboxing, but it was better than standing still, and besides, if his plan worked he'd have the last laugh. It was a desperate plan, and one which he knew had little chance of success. Nonetheless, it was better than nothing. At least he hoped it was.

Having unloaded all his personal weapons, and laid them out neatly on the surface of the LZ, Cyclops smiled, and flexed his fingers. "Come and get it stranger."

And Renn did. Putting his head down he charged straight at the giant, hitting him in the stomach, and bowling him over. The maneuver caught Cyclops completely by surprise. As he fell, he took Blaster and the Scuz down with him.

Meanwhile Renn rolled sideways, and scrabbled among the weapons Cyclops had placed on the ground. One was a

.50 caliber semi-automatic handgun. It was a weapon with which Renn was slightly familiar. If he could just get hold of it, Renn was reasonably sure he could release the safety, and fire it. The rest would be a matter of luck. And there it was, just beyond the end of his fingertips, if he could reach it. . . . Just as his fingers closed around the cool plastic, there was an explosion of pain, followed by—nothing.

He opened his eyes to total darkness. Was he blind? Or dead, and confined to some corner of hell so remote, so desolate, that light never reached it? Suddenly two red eyes came at him out of the dark and he tried to move, to escape, but a jagged lance of pain held him pinned where he was. And then, when it seemed the red-eyed monster would lunge for his jugular, it stopped, and he heard an unfamiliar female voice. "What the hell are you doing? Can't leave you for a moment . . . now stop that and lie down. You're not ready to go anywhere yet."

Suddenly a cold wet nose brushed his cheek, and a furry head nudged him down. He heaved a sigh of relief. It wasn't some sort of monster after all . . . it was the dog. The dog! The dog was talking! He tried to sit up but once again the pain drove him back down. Now he could make out a faint outline of the dog's head and shoulders against the cold light of the stars.

"Oh, I get it," Marla said apologetically and sitting back on her haunches. "You just discovered I'm not your average mutt. Sorry about that. You've been coming and going for quite a while. I didn't realize you were here for keeps this time."

When Renn spoke his voice sounded strange in his own ears. "Then you're for real . . . a talking dog?"

"Sort of," Marla agreed. "Actually I'm a female cyber-dog, trained for security work."

"Cyberdog?" Renn asked dully. "Some sort of cyborg?"

"That's right," Marla answered. "But we can play 'what's a cute little cyborg like you doing in a place like this' later. Right now we've got some more pressing problems . . . like your head for example."

Renn reached up to touch his head. His fingers came away sticky. He couldn't see . . . but he knew what it was. Blood. "What the hell happened anyway?"

He heard a soft chuckle. "You tried to knock One-Eye down and kill him with his own gun. One of his friends shot you. Knife I think . . . or was it Trap? Anyway the slug only grazed the side of your head, but it made one helluva mess, so they left you for dead. They talked about shooting me, but decided to save the ammo. Said I'd make a nice snack for some swamp monster." She laughed. "Not unless swamp monsters like steel and plastic."

"So they left?"

"Yup. And took your gear with them. They've been gone for three hours and twenty-six minutes."

"Three hours and twenty-six minutes?"

"Being a cyborg has some advantages . . . including a built-in chronometer with time lapse and the works."

"Oh," Renn replied stupidly, his next comment forgotten as something big screamed a long way off, and was answered from someplace nearby.

"And that's our other problem," Marla said calmly. "While we're waiting for you to recover, various things would like to have us for dinner. I've killed two smaller carnivores in the last couple of hours . Night feeders most likely, attracted by the smell of your blood."

Renn thought about that for a moment. For reasons he couldn't fathom he had a very unusual friend. One who'd already risked her life on his behalf. He should be pulling his share of the load instead of lying around like so much dead meat. Suddenly he had an idea. Patting his pockets, he discovered they still had things in them, and wondered why Cyclops and his friends hadn't stripped him of the suit itself. "They didn't search me?"

"No," she replied. "What'd they miss, a collapsible field hospital?"

"No," he said smiling in spite of the pain, "something almost as good. A survival kit. And most survival kits come with a lighter. I wonder if that undergrowth is flammable."

"Not bad for a head case," Marla conceded. "Let's find out." While he went through his pockets trying to figure out which packet was the survival kit, Marla disappeared into the night. She returned a number of times, dragging various kinds of vegetation in her teeth. Meanwhile he managed to find the survival kit and the lighter it contained.

"OK," Renn said, "let's give it a try. There's no point in you working your tail off if this stuff won't burn."

"Tail off? Is that your idea of a joke, chubs?" Renn was taken aback by the hostility in her voice.

"No . . . it's just a figure of speech. I meant no offense."

"Well all right," Marla growled self-consciously. "It was probably my fault anyway. I'm a bit oversensitive sometimes."

"Think nothing of it," Renn replied lightly. "Let's see if this stuff burns." After about ten minutes of experimentation, they found three varieties of vegetation that refused to burn at all. A fourth gave off such a horrible stench that Marla had to haul it away, and the fifth burned with a bright crackling flame.

Thus encouraged, Marla gathered more of the fire plant, and they soon had a respectable bonfire. Although Marla kept watch, the fire seemed to have the desired effect: no more carnivores ventured near.

Renn had also discovered a small first-aid kit tucked away in one of his pockets, and used it to clean his lacerated scalp, and cover it with a dressing. He also took some broad spectrum antibiotics plus a couple of painkillers. They both stared into the fire for awhile, each curious about the other, but afraid to ask. Then the painkillers took effect, and Renn found himself becoming drowsy. Although the night was not especially cold, the warmth of the fire felt good, and before he knew it, he had drifted off to sleep.

It was still night when he awoke. In front of him the fire burned bright, surrounding him in a dancing orange glow, and revealing that his companion still kept watch. She was curled up beside him, her eyes on the fire.

He watched her for awhile, wishing he could reach out and pet her, but unsure of how she might react. What was it like in a dog's body, he wondered? Not very pleasant he supposed. She certainly didn't like it. Renn wondered what she'd looked like before her transformation into whatever she was. He pictured her as a brunette, with shoulder-length hair, a pretty face, and a slim figure, probably because that was the kind of woman he liked best. Renn found himself wishing he'd known her then. He felt sure he'd have liked her. God knows he owed her a lot. Not many people would've stayed to help him. He decided to break the silence. "Thank you."

She turned to look at him with her big brown eyes. Her lips pulled back from her teeth in a parody of a human smile. "You're welcome, but it's I who should thank you."

"For what?"

"You tried to defend me aboard the shuttle, and frankly, it's been a long time since anyone tried to protect me from anything."

Renn shrugged. "It just seemed like the right thing to do, although I didn't do it very well, and it hardly compares with fighting alien carnivores and the like. By the way, I'm Jonathan Renn." He held out his hand and then jerked it back. "Sorry."

She laughed. "Well don't be. It shows you think of me as a person and not a dog. I apologize for what I said earlier. I get stupid sometimes. My name's Marla. Marla Marie Mendez. Here, shake." Sitting up she held out a paw.

Leaning on one elbow, Renn accepted her paw and shook it. "Pleased to meet you Marla Marie Mendez. Like you said earlier, what's a nice cyborg like you doing in a place like this?"

She looked into the fire. "What you really mean is, why did I become a cyborg? And what did I do to wind up here?"

Renn started to speak but she interrupted. "No, that's OK, it's a perfectly reasonable question. I'll tackle it in two parts." She paused for a moment, as if gathering her thoughts, and then began.

"When I was twenty years old—let's see, that's about four standard years ago now—I was injured in a very bad air car accident. My boyfriend and I were coming home from a skiing trip. He fell asleep at the controls. You know how they work, you release your grip on the stick, the autopilot comes on, and an alarm goes off. Anyway that's what's supposed to happen, only it didn't. There was some kind of malfunction. As a result we hit an eighty-story condo complex at about eighty miles an hour. Fortunately, it was under construction so we didn't kill anyone besides ourselves. My boyfriend was pronounced brain-dead at the scene, but they decided I had a chance, and rushed me to a hospital. He was in the front, I was asleep in the back, and apparently that small difference saved my life. Two days later I came to. I couldn't see, but I could hear in a distorted sort of way, and talk, at least if I felt like talking. I heard a voice, a kind voice, that sounded as if it were far, far away. It asked me questions and I answered. Then it went away and I drifted off to sleep. But soon it was back. Sometimes it asked me questions about how I felt, or what I was thinking, and sometimes it just kept me company. It said that while my injuries were quite severe, the doctors were doing everything they could, and that everything would turn out just fine. It went on like that for a long time. Months in fact. Then the voice came for one last time. I knew it was the same voice, but it was different somehow, sadder, and sort of hollow. It said my injuries were so severe the doctors couldn't save my biological body. The voice was sorry, but there was nothing anyone could do, and I must face up to it. The voice said I had three options. . . ."

Marla paused here, and though she made no sound, Renn felt certain she was close to tears. Without thinking he reached out to pet her, running his hand down the soft fur on her back, feeling the shudder that ran through her body. "Marla, there's no need . . . "

She cut him off, her voice tight with emotion. "Yes, there *is* a need. I *want* you to know. As I was saying, there were three options. I could opt for self-authorized euthanasia, I could continue my present existence, which I learned was nothing more than a brain and spinal cord in a computer-monitored nutrient bath, or I could become a cyborg. Well, it didn't take me long to decide on number three."

"I'm glad you did," Renn said softly stroking her back. She looked back over her shoulder and he saw something that might have been gratitude in her eyes. Then she returned her gaze to the fire and continued her story.

"There was only one problem. It costs a lot of money to construct a cyborg body. You can't mass-produce them. Each one is custom engineered for the person who occupies and uses it . . . and I was broke. On top of that, the insurance money was all gone, and while the government might stake me to a life-long nutrient bath, they wouldn't pay for a cyborg body. And since my father was killed fighting the pirates in the Battle of Hell, and my mother disappeared out along the frontier shortly thereafter, there was no family to bail me out."

"She just disappeared?"

Marla laughed. "Yeah, Mom wasn't the matronly type. I suspect she's keeping some prospector warm at night. Anyway, the voice told me there was a way. Certain large companies are willing to pay for the creation of a cyborg body, provided that you indenture yourself to them for a certain number of years, and provided that you accept the kind of body they're willing to construct."

"Don't tell me, let me guess," Renn said. "The kind of body they're willing to construct matches the task they have in mind."

"Exactly," Marla agreed. "And that's how I wound up as a cyberdog. A company called 'Intersystems Incorporated,' had need of some very special security guards. Guards with human intelligence, because security work takes a certain amount of smarts, a comfortable appearance, because nobody wants an ugly looking autoguard hanging around all the time, a capacity for physical violence, since that provides an effective deterrent, and complete trustworthiness, because any other kind of guard isn't worth much, and these particular guards would have access to the company's most sensitive data banks."

"Wait a minute," Renn interjected. "Intelligence is a given, the dog-image is comfortable, and allows for the possibility of violence, but I don't see why it makes you more trustworthy around the company secrets."

"This is why," Marla replied holding up a paw. "Ever tried to operate a computer keyboard using one of these babies? Take my word for it . . . don't bother."

Both were silent for a moment, and then Renn said, "You've had some tough breaks, that's for sure. OK, that's how you wound up as a cyberdog, but what about the rest? What brought you here?"

She grinned, revealing a pink tongue and rows of white teeth. "I'm a thief. My original period of indenture was for ten years. At the end of that time I could leave Intersystems, or continue to provide them with my services under contract. I had it all planned out. I'd serve my ten years, continue under contract, and save up enough money for a humanoid body. They're damned good these days. You can do everything but have babies, and I mean *everything*.

"Sounds like fun," Renn said mischievously.

"As I remember it was," Marla countered in the same spirit. "In any case, I had it all planned out. Then I learned Intersystems had stacked the deck. Every once in awhile they'd pull me in for a check-up, or a modification, and that cost them money, so they'd add six months or a year to my indenture."

"They planned to use you forever."

"Exactly. So, to make a long story short, I waited for one of the rare times when I was guarding some cash. About a million and a half in gold Imperials. All I needed was a quarter million, so that's all I took. I used robots to substitute an equal amount of weight, loaded my loot on a freight flier, wiped the robot's memory, and headed for a well known cybernetics clinic in Switzerland."

Renn gave a low whistle. "Smart. But how does a cyberdog move around without being noticed?"

Marla grinned. "Simple. I just hired an actor to accompany me. Man and dog, what could be more innocent?"

Renn laughed, and then touched the side of his head. The pain had started to return. "And then?"

Marla returned her gaze to the fire. "And then I got caught. During one of those modifications I mentioned, they'd installed a mini-beacon in my chest, and it was a simple matter to follow the beacon's signal to its source. I was arrested entering the clinic in Switzerland."

For awhile the sound was that of the crackling fire. Then Marla broke the silence. "So that's my story . . . what's yours Jonathan Renn? What's a nice guy like you doing in a place like this?"

Renn chuckled. "On hindsight, I'd say my crime was stupidity. When my father passed away . . . he left me a successful import business. For years he'd done pretty well by importing specialty items from the frontier planets, you know, exotic spices, herbs, perfumes, things like that. 'Keep it light and keep it small,' he always said, 'otherwise the freight will kill us.' And he was right. When I took over I decided to 'keep it light' and expand the business. At first I added a line of exotic freeze dried foods, then a line of off-world wines, and finally I began bringing in some pharmaceuticals, mostly for research purposes."

"By that time I had my own ship, a tidy little ex-navy scout, which I christened *Pegasus*. Like all successful business people, I had competitors, some nice, and some not so nice. Suffice it to say that having completed a business trip to the Rim, I returned to Terra one day, and suddenly found myself in deep trouble. I had a small shipment of pharmaceuticals aboard, some new anti-coagulants developed on Weller's World, but that was all. So imagine my surprise when a customs agent found a pound of Yirl hidden in my quarters, and placed me under arrest."

Everyone knew about Yirl, and Marla was no exception. Use was said to produce something akin to a prolonged orgasm, along with permanent nerve damage, and total addiction. Yirl was illegal by order of the emperor himself. Of course that didn't stop some people from selling the stuff, and others from using it, but Renn didn't seem like the type. "So you were framed."

Renn nodded. "It would appear so. I can't prove it from here, but I'm pretty sure it was a slimy little bastard named 'Shinto.' He was a competitor, and a crooked one at that, so framing me would be just his style. I know this sounds absurd, but somehow I'm going to find a way off this slime ball, and track Shinto down." He shrugged. "But at the moment it seems revenge will have to wait."

"Yes," Marla agreed, "I guess it will. I'm sorry Jonathan."

"Me too," he answered, running a hand over her soft fur. "Me too." And with that he rolled over next to her, rested his head on her side, and drifted off to sleep.

Chapter Three

Marla awoke to the sound of distant thunder, followed a few seconds later by a sudden deluge of warm rain. It came down in sheets, quickly extinguishing the fire, and matting her fur. In spite of the downpour, Renn remained where he was, curled up in a fetal position, soaked to the skin. She tried to gently nuzzle him awake. No reaction. Worried, she tried licking him with her long pink tongue. Still no reaction. Really worried now, she pawed at him and called his name. "Jonathan, it's Marla, wake up." He groaned a little, mumbled something she couldn't understand, and returned to his semi-comatose state. It didn't take a medical degree to see he was very, very ill. Probably an infection of some kind.

Marla sat back on her haunches and considered her options. She could stay, hoping he'd recover enough to travel, or go for help. While gathering fireweed she'd stumbled across a trail, and logic dictated that it led somewhere, quite possibly a settlement. Settlements and spaceports just naturally went together. Then too, Cyclops and his merry men had shown up without packs, which meant they'd come from somewhere close by. She could imagine them sitting in a saloon, hearing the shuttle pass overhead, and then heading for the LZ. Maybe it was part of their regular routine. In any case it seemed certain that some kind of town must be located nearby. The more she thought about it, the more she realized there was very little choice.

She nuzzled the side of his face again and said, "I'm

going for help Jonathan, you just stay here and rest, OK?" There was no answer.

Turning, she walked a dozen paces, stopped, and looked back. Renn hadn't moved. He looked pitiful lying there in the pounding rain. For a moment she just looked at him, and then she said, "I love you Jonathan." He made no response and she expected none. Turning away she activated all of her senses and loped towards the swampy trail.

Renn awoke when the little two-headed snake took a bite out of his calf. The two-headed snake wasn't especially partial to human flesh, but meat was meat, and one must take what's available. And Renn's plump white calf was available. While the snake's eating head took a tentative bite, its cognitive-sensory head maintained a sharp lookout. After all, there were plenty of larger predators who liked to nibble on two-headed snakes. It didn't occur to either head that dinner might suddenly wake up and attack them with a rock.

Having crushed the two-headed snake with a flurry of panicked blows, Renn looked around, and tried to remember where he was, and why. Then it came rushing back. The shuttle, Murphy, Cyclops and Marla. Marla! Where's Marla? He called her name, but heard only the rattle of rain on nearby leaves, and the dull rumble of distant thunder. Maybe she was away gathering fireweed . . . no . . . that didn't make much sense in the rain. Then he had it. Of course! He'd been such a fool! She'd left him for dead. And why not? She didn't owe him anything. The bitch! He felt a wave of self-pity roll over him and gloried in it. So he was going to die was he? Well, he'd show her a thing or two! Gathering all his energy he tried to stand, and almost made it, before crashing to the ground. He lay there panting for awhile allowing the rain to patter down against his face and trickle between his lips. Walking was out. And, if he remembered correctly, so was riding and flying. That left crawling. No problem, he knew how to do that. With a mighty effort, Renn rolled onto his stomach and crawled towards the other side of the LZ.

Marla ran with the same easy grace as a Terran wolf, a tireless lope, which conserves energy and eats miles. It felt good after weeks in a small cell. Her eyes probed ahead, constantly moving, searching for any sign of danger. Her ears monitored not only the surrounding area, but numerous radio frequencies as well, listening for signs of life. So far she'd neither seen nor heard anything unusual. Only the muddy trail hinted at a human presence.

The trail was quite wide. Wide enough for ground vehicles, and, indeed, it appeared some sort of tracked vehicles had used it quite recently. Delivering something to the LZ, or picking up supplies, it really didn't matter.

As time wore on, the trail became more and more swampy, slowing her progress. About three inches of muddy brown water covered the trail's surface, rippling here and there, as the driving rain summoned mud-dwelling life forms from their underground homes. They slithered off in every direction, eager to get out of her way, and go about the important business of eating and reproducing. Up ahead, the rain made an endless pattern of interlocking circles on the surface of the water. More than once she tripped in hidden pot holes, fell, and got up again. It was exhausting work, but she forced herself onwards, driven by the memory of Renn lying huddled in the rain.

To the right, her infrared vision picked up the warmth of two large bodies, skulking along beside the trail. Waiting to attack? She ignored them. Probably scavengers of some kind. Predators would have attacked by now.

Up ahead she saw the trail widen, and beyond, a blur of crudely constructed wooden buildings. They seemed unusually tall at first, but as Marla got closer, she saw they were built on five-foot pilings. The water apparently got pretty deep sometimes, which would explain the wooden boats were propped up against every available wall. It wasn't much of a town. There was a single street, with eight or nine buildings to a side, and a larger structure at the far end of town. It looked like a warehouse or something very similar.

Well, it didn't matter as long as they had a doctor. She chose the right side of the street, trotted up a short flight of worn stairs, and pattered along the wooden board walk. She wasn't looking forward to all the stupid comments and questions she'd have to deal with. "Look Martha . . . a talking dog! Oh Frank! Can we keep her? She's so cute! She'd make a swell pet." If only Renn were with her he could have deflected some of that stuff. It always helped to be with someone. Better to be taken for a dog than to explain things endlessly. She sighed, and read the signs as she walked along. "Let's see, some kind of a store, another store, a tannery, whoa, what have we here." The sign read, "Doctor Lester Fesker, M.D." And in smaller print, "I'm your only hope, so come in." She grinned. A doctor with a sense of humor.

Standing up on her hind legs Marla pushed against the door. It refused to give. For the millionth time she wished for hands, and swore under her breath. Using her right paw to scratch at the door, she also tried yelling "Open up in there," at the top of her lungs. One of the two strategies must have worked, because a few moments later she heard the thump of approaching feet, and a male voice called, "All right, all right, don't get excited, and if you're bleeding, be damned sure you don't get any on my new rug. It cost me six skins, and I won't have you bleeding on it."

Then the door was jerked open by a middle-aged black man. He had a two day growth of salt and pepper beard and wore a filthy smock. He looked right, left, and finally down. "A dog . . . we don't have dogs on Swamp."

"Well you do now," Marla said. "You're Doctor Fesker?"

The doctor nodded in amazement.

"Good, because I've got a patient who needs your help."

Renn tackled the trip to the other side of the LZ in stages. First he'd crawl ten to twenty feet, and then he'd pass out. Of the two, he liked passing out the best. Of course, crawling provided a sense of accomplishment, and, God knows, that's always welcome, but still, oblivion had a lot going for it, too. But somewhere along the line things got all out of whack. For some reason he couldn't crawl anymore. He had odd, disturbed dreams. He dreamt of strange faces that came and went, of warm blankets, and a bothersome jerking motion, that seemed to go on and on. Sleep tried to pull him down, but he fought it, certain there was something he should be doing. But try as he might, Renn couldn't remember what. So finally he decided what the hell, and let go. And as he fell through many layers of darkness he decided oblivion really was the best after all.

He awoke with considerable reluctance. At first he tried to ignore it, but the sound wouldn't go away, and before long he found himself waiting for it, anticipating the next time it would come, and dreading it. And then it came. Ping! Ping! And the cycle would start all over. What could it be? Reluctantly, he opened one eye, then the other. Overhead, raw planks sloped sharply upward towards the juncture of a peaked roof. Two or three little creatures took turns skittering across its surface. They looked like flat brown leaves. Leaves with wire thin legs, which they used to dash from one tiny meal to the next, occasionally pausing to say grace, or burp, he wasn't sure which. Ping! Ping!

Sitting up in bed he wondered where he was. The room was quite small, and except for his bed, quite bare. Ping! Ping! Aha! The sound water makes as it hits a nearly empty metal pan. Apparently the roof leaked. Mystery solved. He slumped back against the pillow. He really should get up and find out where he was. But the soft drumming of the rain, and the warmth of his bed sapped him of all energy. He decided to give himself just a few more minutes. Soon he was sound asleep.

Plop! Plop! Renn opened his eyes. Outside the rain still beat on the roof, and inside it still fell into the metal pan, which was nearly full. He noticed his bladder was full, too. He threw back the covers, swung his feet over the side of the bed, and stood. He felt a little light-headed for a moment and then recovered.

Just then the door burst open to admit an energetic black man. He wore a filthy smock, a day's worth of beard, and a big smile. He had a tube of burning vegetable matter clenched between his teeth, and a cloud of noxious smoke hung around his head like a gray halo. "So, sleeping beauty lives, another testament to my medical genius! Here, let me give you a hand."

With the other man's help, Renn made his way downstairs to a small bathroom, where he emptied his bladder into a metal toilet bowl. It had been liberated from the wreckage of a crashed shuttle. "I couldn't save the crew . . . but I did manage to salvage that," the black man said as he disappeared down a hall.

As instructed, Renn made his way to a comfortable sitting room, and sat down in front of a crackling fire. Moments later his host entered with a cup in his hand. "Here, tuck that inside you. Works better than most pharmaceuticals."

Renn took a sip, and found it to be a delicious soup. It had a creamy texture, tasty chunks of meat, and was piping hot. As the soup hit his stomach, a warm glow seemed to spread throughout his body. "Thanks," Renn said gratefully. "You should get a patent on that stuff."

Leaning back in his chair, the black man nodded smugly,

and emitted another cloud of noxious smoke. "True. Just one of the many commercial possibilities."

Renn put the soup down on a highly polished wood table, and stuck out his hand. "By the way . . . I'm Jonathan Renn."

"I know." The black man's grip was dry and firm. "I'm Doctor Fesker, though most people around here just call me 'Doc.'" He shook his head sadly. "I suppose it was inevitable, though a man of my education and superior intelligence deserves a little more respect."

"I agree, Doctor," Renn said solemnly, wondering what Fesker had done to end up on Swamp, and hoping it didn't involve professional negligence. "They are . . . I guess I should say 'we are,' lucky to have your services. Speaking of which, where am I, and how did I get here?"

The doctor waved his cylinder of burning vegetation in an expansive manner. "At the moment you are in the thriving metropolis of 'Payout,' so named because this is the closest settlement to the LZ, and LZ is where the shuttles land, and pay off the Hunter's Association."

"How poetic."

"Quite. And, as for how you came to grace my humble abode, that was at the work of your furry friend."

"Marla? She was here?"

"Of course," Doc Fesker said agreeably. "She came to my door, and informed me of your situation. Shortly thereafter I dispatched a couple of men to go get you. Apparently you'd crawled a few hundred yards in the wrong direction, so they had a little trouble finding you, but they managed, and subsequently brought you here." Fesker coughed, gave the tube of vegetation a critical glance, and continued. "You were damned lucky. Lucky you weren't killed and lucky you had a friend. A somewhat unusual friend, but a friend nonetheless. Friends are hard to come by on Swamp."

Renn flushed as he remembered what he'd thought about her, what he'd called her. He owed Marla an apology and a lot more. "Where is she? Where'd she go?"

Fesker shrugged, and disappeared behind a cloud of smoke. "I heard she went to work for a hunter named Skunk, but I really couldn't say for sure. Here on Swamp it's considered bad form to stick your nose into other people's business."

Renn felt disappointed, and abandoned somehow, but knew he shouldn't. He continued to ask questions, but either the doctor couldn't provide answers, or didn't choose to, which amounted to the same thing. So eventually Renn gave up, and took another tack. "So when can I be up and around?"

The doctor rubbed his unshaven chin and smiled. "How soon can you get dressed? You'll be shaky for a few days . . . but basically you're cured. Swamp is home to a plethora of nasty bugs, and when that slug creased you, half of them jumped in the open wound. Thanks to the efforts of the original survey team, however, we've got a pretty good array of drugs to work with, and you're responding nicely."

"Thank you doctor . . . I really appreciate all you've done." Renn glanced out a nearby window to see only darkness. "If it's all the same to you . . . I'll leave in the morning. I don't suppose there's any chance of recovering my gear?"

Fesker smiled. "None at all. Cyclops and his cronies regard the LZ as a fertile field which is theirs to harvest, and barring a hidden talent for physical violence, your chances of taking your gear back are just about zero."

"There's no law then?"

"None but that which we make for ourselves."

Renn nodded. "I figured it was something like that, which raises a problem. How will I pay you?"

The doctor waved his smoking wand in a negligent

manner. "Consider it my gift. Perhaps some day you will find some way to perform a small favor in return. Care for a cigar?" So saying, he proffered a box containing more green tubes like the one in his hand.

Renn wrinkled his nose in distaste. "No offense doctor, but those things hardly qualify as cigars. What is that horrible smelling weed anyway?"

Fesker held the smoldering roll of leaves between thumb and forefinger, and frowned. "You are somewhat tactless, sir. However I'm afraid you're right, this does leave something to be desired." He shook his head in disappointment as he placed the offending vegetation in the lid of an empty drug canister, and stubbed it out. "It is part of my ongoing search for a tobacco substitute. Unfortunately, the noble weed refuses to grow on Swamp, so I have dedicated myself to finding an acceptable substitute. Such a discovery would bring me personal succor, plus if it was good enough, commercial remuneration as well. My fellow citizens would pay well for a good smoke."

"But doctor," Renn objected, "what about the effects on their health? Surely you don't condone a habit which causes cancer?"

Fesker looked shocked. "Surely you jest! Of course I do! After all, cancer can be cured, and what good is a cure without a disease? Imagine, they buy a tobacco substitute from me, enjoy it, become cancerous, and I cure them! There's profit at both ends and happiness all around!"

Renn did his best to look agreeable, took another sip of his soup, and wondered if the doctor was serious or just putting him on. The two men continued to talk for some time, an activity which Fesker obviously enjoyed, and one which provided Renn with a lot of information about his new home. For example, he learned there were about a hundred thousand prisoners on Swamp, give or take a few thousand, because while some died every day, others were constantly arriving. There were three other major towns besides Payout, named Ditch, Black Head, and Clover. The latter was named for a person and not a plant. The planet's economy was centered on one thing, monster hunting. Monsters came in various shapes and sizes, some having more commercial value than others, and some being more difficult to kill. Basically, monsters fell into one of two commercial categories, which were referred to as "stinks" and "skins." "Stinks" it seemed, were hunted primarily for a small hormonal gland located near the third of their seven sub-brains, which when properly treated, yielded the main ingredient for some very exotic and expensive perfumes. Repeated attempts at synthesis had so far failed, making Swamp the only source of this valuable stuff.

Here Renn really perked up his ears, since this was not only valuable information, but it also had a bearing on his previous life. Having imported perfumes himself, he knew how protective the large companies were of both ingredients and sources, and wondered which famous brand was based on swamp-monster hormones.

Fesker went on to explain that while stink skins were OK, other monsters, the ones called "skins," were hunted for their valuable hides. Though not as valuable as stinks, skins were still quite profitable, and a lot easier to find. Properly tanned, their hides made a very distinctive leather which was not only waterproof, but damned near bulletproof as well. Yet in spite of its toughness monster hide remained supple and more importantly retained the capacity to match the color and texture of its surroundings. Skins, it seemed, had a chameleon-like ability to disappear into the background. And, for reasons no one had yet figured out, their hides retained that ability even after the death of the monster itself. As a result, monster skins were sought after for use in high-fashion clothing which constantly shifted color to match the wearer's surroundings, and light body armor, which was quite popular with both military officers and professional assassins.

In fact, the doctor said, the scientists who worked in Swamp's orbiting space station were trying to crack the biological mystery represented by an epidermis which continued to function after the death of its owner.

Here Renn was reminded of the leather clothing sported by Cyclops and his men, and how it had blended with the background. No wonder they hadn't stripped him of his environmental suit. They had something better.

As their conversation continued, Renn learned that while the economy centered around monster hunting, only a small proportion of the population were so engaged. The majority made a living by either supplying monster hunters with products and services, or robbing them after they'd been paid. This took two forms. There was the out-and-out theft of the sort practiced by people like Cyclops, and the more subtle kind, carried out by gamblers, prostitutes, and shopkeepers.

"So," the doctor added, throwing another piece of wood on the fire, "unless you have a special set of talents like mine . . ." Renn shook his head, "then your choices are clear. Shopkeeper is out because that requires capital which you do not have. That leaves a choice between hunting, stealing, or gambling, the call for your sexual services being somewhat limited. It happens that Swamp is blessed with more men than women. All things considered I would recommend the profession of gambler. It's nice clean work, only occasionally violent, and has considerable financial potential. After amassing a sufficient amount of capital, you could open a store, or engage in some other legitimate form of enterprise. Excuse me, I think there's someone at the door.

Privately, Renn couldn't picture himself as a gambler but kept his own counsel.

As Fesker headed for the door he warned the party outside of dire consequences should even one drop of their blood fall onto his brand new rug. He needn't have worried. The patient was more than a little drunk, and was suffering from a self-inflicted blaster wound. Like many blaster wounds this one was self-cauterizing and the rug was spared.

Retiring to his bed, Renn listened to the ping of water in the recently emptied metal pan, and wondered where Marla was, and if she was all right. Why would she go to the trouble of saving him, only to disappear without so much as a goodbye? It didn't make sense.

Eventually sleep came, and with it a dream. It centered around a beautiful brunette with a slim figure. She ran across a field of wild flowers with him close behind. No matter how hard he tried he couldn't catch her. Finally she tripped, and as she fell he caught her, eager to cover her lips with his. But as he pulled her into his arms, she seemed to wiggle, and suddenly became a dog. The dog smiled, and then laughed a barking laugh, which went on and on and on.

Chapter Four

As Renn left Doc Fesker's place, he felt a strange combination of fear and elation. The fear was easy enough to understand. For the first time in his life he had nothing more than the clothes on his back. The elation was harder to explain, but after a little reflection, he decided it came from the same source as the fear. His situation was frightening, but it was exciting too, and much to his own surprise he was almost looking forward to it.

So as he stepped out onto the boardwalk, he did so with a light spirit, and only a small rock riding in the pit of his stomach. Taking a moment to look around, he saw the town was organized along one main street, now invisible under a foot of water. And, judging from the rain, the water would get even deeper. All of which explained why the buildings were built on pilings. Most were one or two stories tall, and constructed of roughly-milled wood. Elevated boardwalks served to keep pedestrians up and out of the water. And there were plenty of them—people came and went all around him.

Most were a rough and ready lot, dressed in skins and carrying a variety of weapons. A few, however, wore finer attire, and had the look of shopkeepers, prostitutes, and gamblers. Nearly everyone managed to look right through him, except for the prostitutes, who met his eyes with bold smiles. Renn wasn't surprised. From his business trips out along the frontier he knew outsiders were always excluded. If he wanted a place here, he'd have to earn it.

Suddenly he heard a strange coughing sound. At first he didn't recognize it, but then it settled down into the steady roar of an internal combustion engine. Sure enough, a few seconds later a large flat-bottomed scow emerged from between two buildings, and cruised down the main street. In it, one man leaned on a long steering oar, while two more sat under a makeshift canopy. As the boat passed, the helmsman said something to the other two and laughed. Renn had the uncomfortable feeling they were talking about him. Nevertheless, he continued to watch, fascinated by the boat, and how it worked. The noise seemed to come from a metal box located towards the stern. From the sound, Renn guessed it was a large two-cylinder engine, and a crude one at that. He'd seen similar engines on a variety of frontier planets. They'd been outlawed on Terra for hundreds of years due to the pollution they caused. However, some worlds couldn't afford anything better, and if they happened to have large oil reserves, found gasoline engines irresistible. Though noisy and dirty they were also quite effective. As if to prove his point, the scow had already reached the other end of town, and disappeared from sight.

Interesting, Renn reflected as he started down the boardwalk. Gasoline engines. So Swamp had at least one oil well and a refinery. Plus a foundry and machine shop. The engine had to come from somewhere. All facts to add to his growing hoard.

"Well," he told himself, "enough sight-seeing. It's time to choose a suitable profession." He smiled at the thought. Apparently there weren't many choices. In spite of Doc Fesker's advice, Renn had no intention of becoming a gambler. He'd never enjoyed gambling, and besides, why wait for the money to come to you, when you could go to it? Yes, hunting was for him. On this planet the hunters were in control. Plus, they knew how to deal with Swamp on its own terms, and that appealed to him. His mind was made up. Somehow he'd become a hunter.

And beyond that, he had a second larger goal. Somehow

he'd get off Swamp, find Shinto, and clear his name. He didn't know how. But he'd do it or die trying. It felt good to have goals and a purpose, no matter how impossible they might seem. There was a spring in his step as he moved down the boardwalk.

The sign said "SALOON". He had no money, or whatever served as money, but perhaps he could get some information for free. Stepping inside, Renn found a large open room, which, though filled with a clutter of mismatched furniture, was almost empty of people. There was a man kneeling in front of the bar, a scattering of tools and wood chips all around him, two bored looking prostitutes sharing a corner table, and a gambler, who sat with his back against the wall, endlessly shuffling his cards. The customers would come in later. It was a bit early for serious drinking, even on Swamp.

The bar ran the length of one wall. It was actually a single tree trunk, which had been squared off and planed smooth. The wood was jade green all the way through, and had a fine texture with no sign of grain. A carved mural decorated a third of its length. It was beautifully done, and seemed to depict the history of the planet, starting with the first survey ship to touch down, then showing subsequent confrontations with hideous looking swamp creatures, and the construction of a town.

As Renn walked the length of the bar, he realized the man kneeling before it was actually the artist, hard at work, adding still more detail to his masterpiece. His back was turned, and he was down on hands and knees, using a small chisel to detail the foliage behind some kind of monster. He worked quickly, his left hand scooping out delicate scallops of green, while his right swept constantly back and forth over the mural's surface. His long greasy hair swung this way and that and he mumbled while he worked. Stopping to peek over the artist's shoulder, Renn was impressed. It was wonderful work. There was a restrained energy in the monster's corded muscle and sinewy grace, which threatened to spring off the wood and into the room. Remembering his decision to become a hunter, Renn sincerely hoped the monster was a product of the artist's imagination, and not a portrait of the real thing.

"You do wonderful work," Renn said.

"I'm glad to hear it," the artist answered without turning around. "Tell me, does the texture of the foliage seem consistent to you?"

Renn eyed the section in question. The foliage had been carved with an almost machine-like precision, so that it took nothing from the monster in the foreground, yet added depth. "It looks perfect."

"Excellent," the artist replied, getting to his feet. "That means it's time for a drink. Oh, garçon!"

"My name ain't 'garçon', booze brain," a wizened little man said, appearing from a back room. "What do you want now?"

"Some of your despicable swill would do nicely."

"Did you finish the section?"

"I did," the artist replied indignantly, "as my friend will attest." So saying the artist turned towards Renn.

With a sense of shock, Renn found himself staring into a whorl of ridged scar tissue. He could see no sign of the eyes which had once been there. A single black hole marked the man's remaining nostril, and when he spoke, it was through a lipless slit.

"Well, tell the man. Is the foliage complete or not?"

"It's complete," Renn managed to answer.

"All right then," the barkeep replied reluctantly, starting to turn away.

"And something for my friend," the artist said.

The barkeep stopped, and looked Renn up and down. He

smiled. "You the one who tried to kill Cyclops with his own gun?"

Renn nodded. Like in any small town news traveled fast.

The barkeep laughed. "Musta been something to see. Have a seat. This'll be your first and last free drink in the Payout Saloon."

As the barkeep poured two drinks, the artist stuck out a calloused hand. "This is an honor indeed. A man who not only has an eye for fine art, but the heart of a lion as well. My name is Maxwell."

"Jonathan Renn. What? No nickname?"

Maxwell chuckled. His laugh made a dry, rasping sound. "No, I am among the few spared that particular indignity. No one can bring themselves to call me 'scarface,' or something equally obvious. Would you be kind enough to bring the drinks?"

Renn said he would, accepted the drinks from the bartender, and followed Maxwell to a corner table. From the confident manner in which the artist moved through the maze of tables Renn knew he did it often.

"Now," Maxwell said, taking a seat, "to taste the fruit of my labors." Picking up his drink the artist took a careful sip. "Ahhhh, repulsive as always,"

Renn took a sip of his own drink. It was strong and had the faint taste of mint. At a guess, it consisted of about eighty percent alcohol. After burning a trail down his throat, the stuff hit his empty stomach like a sledgehammer. "Whew! Why drink this stuff if you don't like it?"

Maxwell's mouth formed a twisted smile. "Because I am an alcoholic, and disgusting though this tipple is, it packs a wallop. As soon as we finish our conversation I will return to work. In half an hour or so the garçon will grudgingly give me another drink. I will consume it, and the cycle will begin anew. If all goes well, the effects of this slop will be cumulative, and I will pass out at about ten or eleven tonight. Doing so is my only ambition.

"Well you're certainly the most organized alcoholic I've ever met," Renn said evenly.

"Thank you."

"The mural," Renn said, "imagination, or the real thing?"

Maxwell took another sip, careful not to spill a drop. "The real thing, friend Jonathan. Just as my eyes saw it."

"You were a hunter?"

Maxwell paused for a moment, and nodded slowly. "Aye, I was a hunter. One of the best. But that was before the battle, and before this." A hand went up to touch the scar tissue which covered Maxwell's face.

"Battle?"

"Aye. It was a stupid thing to do, but a few years ago, many of us banded together to ambush a shuttle. We hoped to capture it, and then use it to get aboard the supply ship." He shrugged. "Needless to say, we didn't succeed. The lucky ones died. I survived."

"I'm sorry." Renn thought of his own hopes to get off Swamp. All right. The shuttle was out . . . but he'd find another way.

Maxwell drained his glass and set it gently on the table. "Thank you, friend Jonathan. I sense your sorrow holds no pity . . . and for that I thank you doubly. But enough of my troubles. Unless I miss my guess, you have problems of your own."

"Not really," Renn replied. "I'm completely broke . . . but otherwise fine. You wouldn't know where I could get a job, would you?"

"No special skills?"

"No, but I'd like to become a hunter."

Maxwell nodded sagely. "Are you going to finish that drink, friend Jonathan? If not I would happily dispose of it for you."

Renn pushed his glass across. "Please, help yourself."

Maxwell did, draining the glass to the very last drop, and licking thin lips. "Thank you. Now if you really wish to become a hunter, and have no resources, there is only one solution. Did you notice the large building at the north end of town?"

"Yes."

"Well, that is the Hunter's Association warehouse. That is where they sell their skins. It is also where they pick up indentured assistants."

"Indentured? As in near slavery?"

Maxwell laughed his dry laugh. "Aye. But it is not as bad as it sounds. In return for a one-year indenture, most hunters provide a full set of gear, food and lodging, and a first-class course in monster hunting. If you really wish to become a hunter, it would be the best way to learn, even if you had funds."

"It sounds like the way to go," Renn replied as he got to his feet. "I'll check it out. Thanks."

Maxwell stood and extended his hand. As Renn shook it, the artist said, "It was my pleasure, friend Jonathan. You meant what you said? About the mural?"

"It's beautiful, Maxwell," Renn answered sincerely. "The best I've ever seen."

Maxwell nodded. "Good. Kill lots of monsters, and after you do, remember to buy me a drink." Then, with head up, and back straight, the artist returned to his work.

Outside it was raining harder than ever. Although most of the buildings had extended eaves, which covered the boardwalks, there were gaps and numerous leaks. While his suit kept him dry, Renn's hair was soaked by the time he made it to the other end of town, and crossed the plank bridge which connected the boardwalk to the warehouse.

The first thing he noticed as he stepped into the warehouse was the smell. It wasn't unpleasant—just strange. An acidic mustiness filled the air. A chemical smell. Something to do with monster skins, perhaps.

He looked around but there was no one in sight. Although it was dim, he could make out the angular shapes of two large crawlers parked towards the rear of the building, and in front of them, rows of pallets, some empty, and some piled high with skins. Following the sound of distant voices, he wound his way between the piles of skins and stepped into an open area. Three men and a woman sat around a rickety wooden table playing rockets and stars. Beyond them were rows of backless benches, empty now, but clearly used for meetings. A single light dangled over their heads fixing them in a cone of yellow light. At the sound of his footsteps they turned as a group. All were dressed in skins, and all wore sidearms. The woman spoke first. She had piercing blue eyes, high cheekbones, and wore her hair in a crew cut. "I'm about to clean these jokers out, so keep it short."

"That'll be the day," one of the men replied, eyes twinkling. "We cheat better than she does." He was short, barrel chested, and unless Renn missed his guess, strong as an ox. He had an open face and a friendly smile.

"I'm looking for work. I'm willing to accept indenture."

The woman looked him up and down. "Kinda chubby for monster hunting, aren't ya?"

Renn found himself blushing in embarrassment.

"Who sent ya?" The question came from another one of the men. He had one arm and a belligerent thrust to his chin.

"A man named Maxwell."

The first man nodded. "All right then. We'll see what we can do. As usual, there's a good many hunters who need an assistant. Deal me out . . . and I'll show the lad around."

"Sure, Slim," the woman said, pushing a pile of metal stars his way. "The minute you start losing it's 'deal me out.' "

"I'll tell you what, lass," Slim said mischievously, "if you'll spend the night with me, I'll give you all that's on the table."

"It'll take a lot more than that to get me in bed with you," she replied with a snort. "Like a brigade of Imperial marines."

"Cut the crap and deal," the belligerent man said, glowering from under bushy brows. The third man, almost invisible behind the smoke from his huge pipe, nodded in agreement.

Slim shook his head in mock sorrow, scooped up his winnings, and dumped them into a pocket of his monster hide jacket. Renn saw it shift to match the dark wood on the wall behind him. Turning, Slim held out his hand. "The name's Slim."

"Jonathan Renn. Pleased to meet you."

"Well, Jon my lad, follow me back to my office and we'll fix you up."

Renn followed him back to a corner office, which boasted a makeshift desk, a host of odds and ends, and a sheet metal stove. A wonderful warmth suffused the room. As Slim opened a crudely made door, and threw in another chunk of wood, Renn held out his hands and enjoyed the heat.

Turning to his desk, Slim sorted through the tools, weapons, maps, clothes and other junk which covered its surface. Finally he uttered a grunt of satisfaction, and pulled out a keyboard. "She ain't fancy . . . but she gets the job done," he said, brushing aside some more debris to reveal a battered screen and console.

"What do you use for power?" Renn asked, somewhat surprised.

"Got a generator out back," Slim replied, his blunt fingers already tapping away at the keyboard. "Maybe we're nothing more than a pimple on the empire's backside, but we've got our rules. Rules on buying, selling and making rules. So many we can't remember 'em all unless we write them down. And that's where the computer comes in." Slim sighed. "It gets worse all the time. Well, let's start with your full name."

Renn's name was only the beginning. By the time Slim declared himself through, his battered computer had consumed information about Renn's parents, his education, his profession on Terra, his medical history, and a good deal more. Everything in fact which Renn knew about himself, with one notable exception. There hadn't been one single question about his criminal record. Why?

He was still wondering about that a half hour later, when, armed with some durasteel coins advanced by Slim, he entered the town's only restaurant and ordered a sandwich. It came with a bowl of hot vegetable soup and a cup of imitation coffee. It tasted wonderful.

As he ate, Renn considered what he'd learned so far. Without conscious thought he lapsed into the kind of business analysis which always accompanied expansion into a new market. First, a complex economic system was evolving on Swamp. The population had already moved out of the hunting and gathering stage, and into something more specialized. A small number of people hunted, while a larger number performed tasks which directly, or indirectly, supported hunting. Included were activities like refining oil, building engines, shopkeeping, and prostitution. All were part of a growing service economy. Technology in the form of the gasoline engine was being used to counteract a chronic labor shortage, and as a result of all these factors, the wealthier members of society had begun to enjoy a small surplus—like Doc Fesker's precious rug. And, in order to keep their increasingly complex economy running, the locals had been forced to create some rudimentary civil law, plus a system of records to back it up. Given that, could a criminal justice system be far behind? Due to the fact that all the current citizens were criminals, they might resist such an idea at first. However, that would change over time. Eventually they'd tire of people like Cyclops and clamor for law and order. All this, Renn realized, explained why Slim hadn't inquired about his criminal record. Either consciously or unconsciously, the citizens of Swamp were starting a brand new society. A record was assumed, but not considered important. In fifty or a hundred years, society would probably be just like that found on most frontier planets. The majority of the people would be good law-abiding citizens, hardy folk, who complained about the small number of criminals in their midst, and built new prisons to house them. He smiled at the thought. Self-reforming prison planets! Had the emperor foreseen such a possibility? Or was it entirely fortuitous? There was no way to tell.

Renn killed the rest of the day wandering in and out of stores, analyzing the goods he saw in them, and watching the citizens of Swamp go about their daily chores. There were a lot of hunters in town. Apparently the onset of the rainy season signaled the end of one hunting cycle and the start of another. As a result, many hunters came in to sell their skins and stinks, and buy supplies. As he moved among them, Renn kept an eye peeled for Marla. He didn't see her, or any other dogs for that matter. Damn it . . . where was she anyway? He'd even asked Slim, hoping the answer might be in his computer. But the hunter had simply smiled, saying the records were confidential. Well, she had to be somewhere, and he'd keep looking until he found her.

As he drifted around town, Renn kept an eye out for Cyclops and his men too. Under the impression that they'd cancelled his ticket, they might resent his sudden resurrection, and seek ways to reverse it. And much as Renn wanted to even the score, he knew he wasn't ready yet. He needed weapons and the ability to use them. Revenge would have to wait. Fortunately, he didn't see them, and the afternoon passed without incident.

At about six o'clock he joined the steady dribble of hunters entering the warehouse. As they flowed around him, Renn paid close attention to their clothes, weapons, and style. After all they were what he planned to become.

As the hunters drifted into the open area, they gradually filled the rows of bench seats. For a while profanity, crude jokes, and loud conversation filled the air. Then Slim mounted an empty ration case, whistled, and stomped one foot for order. "All right, quiet down. This meeting of the Hunter's Association is hereby called to order. All right, under old business we got this matter of grading. Some of you clowns have been softening class-three skins with chemicals and passing them off as class two's. It ain't gonna fly anymore. Starting next cycle, the Impies say they're gonna pull a random check on every load. They'll be checking for chemical treatment, mechanical stretching, everything in the book. So it was nice while it lasted, but the party's over. Don't make me pull your trading rights for a month. All right, new business. . . ."

There was a great deal of new business, including everything from territorial squabbles between hunters, to the question of which refreshments should be served at the Hunter's Ball four months hence. After a while Renn lost interest and began day-dreaming. He was right in the middle of a wonderful fantasy involving a large bed, and the rather attractive brunette seated to his right, when someone called his name.

"I assure you Citizen Renn is normally more responsive," Slim said to general laughter. "Are you with us now lad?"

Flushing with embarrassment, Renn nodded.

"Well, good. Perhaps you'd be kind enough to stand and let everyone have a peek at you."

Renn stood, doing his best to ignore all the comments, rude and otherwise. "He's a bit over-fed ain't he?" "Is he the one what almost cancelled the Clops?" "No . . . I think you're wrong . . . you just gotta train 'em right that's all." ". . . And the second you train one, some monster takes his head off and it's all wasted."

"I'll take him. Standard one year contract . . . plus one percent of everything over ten thousand trading units." The voice had a deep booming quality that rolled over the background noise. Turning towards the sound, Renn saw a man with white hair, a goatee, and a gigantic beer belly.

"We have an offer from the Boater," Slim intoned evenly. "what say you Citizen Renn? Do you accept?"

Renn was a little unsure of what was going on, but he got the impression his services were up for auction, and apparently he had veto power. Before he could answer, another voice cut through the conversation. "Unlike the parsimonious old skinflint with the protruding abdomen, I offer a standard year's contract, plus two percent of everything over ten thousand units." An appreciative chuckle swept through the audience, interspersed with a few cat calls and whistles.

Turning to his left, Renn saw this bidder was a woman, although her voice was deep enough to be a man's. However, her figure left no doubt as to her sex, and Renn perked up. Six months in the swamps with her might be very entertaining indeed.

Slim nodded, clearly enjoying the competition along with the rest of the audience. Renn got the impression the process was considered more entertainment than business. "We have another bid Citizen Renn . . . do you wish to consider it?"

Once again Renn's answer was preempted. "If my opponent's brain were half as big as her chest, she'd perceive that this pathetic specimen is unworthy of one percent, much less two. However, I raise my offer to five, hoping to spare this poor wretch her incompetence, thus saving his life." As Boater finished his speech, he used both hands to shift his enormous gut into a more comfortable position, and glared his defiance.

"Well, Reload," Slim asked, "do you want to make a counter offer?"

Reload dismissed the possibility with the flick of a wrist. "I think not. Stupid though he is, my opponent is correct about the worthlessness of this rather corpulent candidate, and if he desires to pay five percent so be it. My offer stands at two." The audience reacted to Reload's statement with loud applause and foot stomping.

By this time Renn was more than a little angry with both of his potential employers. He realized there was a certain amount of ritual involved here, but was growing increasingly sensitive about his weight, and didn't appreciate the title "corpulent candidate." He reacted therefore more out of anger than logic, choosing to reject the most recent insult.

"I'll take the five percent offered by Boater."

Reload took her seat, while Boater bowed to the audience, and accepted their applause. A few minutes later the meeting broke up, Renn thumbprinted a standard one-year contract complete with a five-percent clause, and became the temporary property of Boater Smith, one-time crime lord, now monster hunter. Then, as Boater and Slim shook hands, Renn glimpsed a tall woman with a streak of white running through her jet black hair, leaving the warehouse. And walking by her side was a huge dog. "Marla!"

Renn leaped over two benches in succession and ran for the door. Hunters swore as he pushed between them and struggled to get through the crowd. Finally he broke free and ran across the bridge and onto the boardwalk. He stopped and looked in every direction. There were people all over the place, but the tall woman and the dog were nowhere in sight.

──── Chapter Five ────

Boater Smith woke Renn bright and early the next morning. It was just a taste of the weeks and months yet to come. "Get off your butt Jonnie my lad . . . there's work to do."

And there *was* work to do. Lots of it. They'd slept aboard Smith's boat. It was both his pride and joy and the source of his nickname. Boater called the boat *"Fred,"* because women were nothing but trouble, and he'd be damned if he'd use a female name on something as important as his boat. And Boater insisted that *Fred* be cleaned "fore and aft" first thing every morning, a task for which he thought Renn especially suited. "After all," Boater said, tugging his goatee, and squinting at Renn through tiny bloodshot eyes, "you ain't good for nothing else." And with that Renn's employer adjusted his paunch, and started breakfast, a job he refused to entrust to someone other than himself.

As Renn moved the length of the craft, scrubbing and cleaning, he quickly came to appreciate the boat's design. It was constructed of wood, was flat bottomed, to handle shallow water no doubt, and about thirty feet long. Later he'd learn swamp boats never ran much more than thirty feet. Longer boats couldn't maneuver in the smaller channels with their tight turns.

The first ten feet of *Fred's* length were given over to an open cockpit. It was about ten feet wide, and lined with thin sheets of durasteel, which were joined together by some neatly executed welding. The bottom of the cockpit featured a built-in tilt from bow to stern. As Renn hosed it out, the water ran downhill, collecting momentarily at the bottom, before disappearing into drainage tubes which carried it over the side. It reminded him of a huge metal sink. And he suddenly realized that's exactly what it was. A sink for cleaning and skinning swamp monsters.

The deckhouse was just aft of the metal-lined cockpit. Here Boater had opted for comfort, making the structure well over six feet tall, and fitting it out with two bunks which served as seats during the day, a clever little galley, and even a small head, complete with flushing toilet.

In an effort to be friendly, Renn commented on the head as he made the bunks. "I'm too damned old to go any other way," Boater said grumpily, as he pushed some sizzling meat around the bottom of his frying pan. "At my age it ain't dignified to hang your rear over the side."

"Plus it might scare the hell out of some poor swamp monster," Renn thought silently.

The stern featured another open cockpit. It was surrounded by weather-sealed metal storage units which contained an incredible variety of gear, all neatly stowed and well maintained. There was rope, heavy tackle, floats, shoulder weapons, ammunition, explosives, tools, spare parts, and lots more. Monster hunting clearly called for a large capital investment, plus a lot of expertise. No wonder Maxwell suggested he indenture himself. There wasn't any other way to learn, and while Boater Smith was no prize, he did seem to know what he was doing. Still, a more congenial tutor would've been nice. Reload's figure came to mind and he smiled. Another one of his brilliant decisions.

Boater had moored *Fred* under the Hunter's Association warehouse, and although the structure sheltered them from much of the rain, some still managed to get through. It felt good to step into the cozy cabin and close the door behind him. The wonderful smell of real Terran coffee filled the small space and caused Renn's stomach to growl in response. Boater had placed breakfast on a fold-down table and it looked good. There was lots of fried meat, Renn didn't ask what kind, and fresh rolls made from imported flour. Maybe Boater's company left something to be desired but he sure knew how to cook.

As he lowered himself into his seat, Boater fixed Renn with a malignant glare. "I pray before each meal, so shut up." Without waiting for Renn's reaction, Boater dropped his head, and muttered the ancient words his mother had taught him seventy years before. When he was finished Boater looked up, glaring. "So what the hell are you looking at? Haven't you ever seen someone pray? No, of course not. Ignorant heathern." Boater continued to mumble while he served breakfast with a generous hand.

For a long time neither man spoke, Boater because he was too engrossed in his food, and Renn because it hardly seemed worthwhile. No matter what he said Boater seemed to take offense. Still, they'd soon be stuck with each other, so maybe it was worth one more try. He waited until the other man was sipping a final cup of coffee, and then said, "That was an excellent breakfast, Boater. You're one hell of a cook."

Renn saw the other man's features soften for a fraction of a second, and then drop back into the familiar harsh lines. There was a long pause while Boater swallowed his coffee. Then came a muffled, "Umpf. Glad you liked it, Jonnie lad."

A full minute passed before Boater spoke again, and when he did, his face registered something approaching genuine pain. "I watched your work this morning and it could've been worse." Then, relieved to have the compliment behind him, Boater heaved himself to his feet and glared down at Renn. "Well, come on, get off your butt, we've got supplies to buy. Another couple of days and the rain'll stop. Then all the water drains into the swamps. Could leave *Fred* with his ass in the air. Can't have that."

Renn struggled to hide a smile, and did his best to nod gravely. The man was incorrigible, but human. At least it seemed that way at the moment. By dinner time that evening he wasn't so sure. The process of buying supplies was a nightmare. Or perhaps a daymare. In any case, a shopping trip with Boater was an incredible experience. It started with Boater moving down the middle of the wooden board walk, his paunch thrust out before him like the prow of a mighty ship, dividing the other pedestrians right and left. As he moved forward Boater's beady little eyes were firmly fixed on his next objective, and woe be to the animate or inanimate object which barred his path. And once that objective was attained things got even worse.

Boater didn't enter stores, he exploded into them, scattering clerks and shoppers alike in every direction. Then, sweeping the unfortunate establishment with a steely gaze, he would demand to see the proprietor. Once that unlucky individual stood quaking before him, Boater would look him up and down in the manner of a sergeant-major inspecting an errant private, and shake his head sadly. "So you're the one responsible for this collection of over-priced junk."

Renn soon learned this was the way Boater always opened negotiations. And it usually worked. Even shopowners who'd dealt with Boater before still seemed intimidated by his imperious gaze and abrasive manner. And so it went in store after store, while Renn made constant trips back to *Fred,* loaded with every conceivable kind of supply. Included were various kinds of equipment, a goodly quantity of food, ammunition, and, Renn noticed with amusement, no small amount of booze.

The final stop of the day, however, was dedicated to Renn himself. Bursting into a store bearing the sign,

PERSONALS, Boater rounded up a depressed looking shop owner, pointed a quivering finger at Renn, and proclaimed, "Outfit that man." Renn knew that under the terms of his indenture, Boater was obliged to provide him with a "full outfit," but was free to define "full outfit" any way he chose. And given Boater's parsimonious ways Renn feared it might be on the skimpy side. But, in fact, Boater seemed to take an absolute delight in making sure his assistant was fully equipped.

By the time he emerged a couple of hours later, Renn owned three sets of hunting skins, one set of fancier dress skins, two pairs of boots, and everything he needed to go with them. He had a set on and they felt good. Hurrying to keep up with Boater, Renn said, "Thanks Boater."

Without looking back, Boater said, "Umpf. You may look like a hunter, but you still don't know your ass from a hole in the ground."

Renn shook his head in disgust and followed along behind.

A few minutes later Boater led the way into a store full of weapons. The proprietor had a CLOSED sign in one hand, and was just about to turn them away when he saw Boater's expression. His demeanor suddenly changed. "Yes sir? How may I help you?"

"My assistant needs some personal weapons." What ensued was an interesting mixture of bargaining and ballistics. The owner would suggest possibilities, Boater would either shake his head in disagreement, or tug on his goatee thoughtfully while he haggled over the price.

When it was over, and the shopowner was still scurrying around after ammunition and various accessories, Boater pointed to Renn's new arsenal, and said, "Meet the only true friends you'll ever have on this planet, lad. You take care of them, and they'll take care of you. From now on you'll wear at least one of them at all times."

Renn looked at the weapons spread out before him. It was quite a collection. First there was a heavy duty .75 caliber semi-automatic pistol. It could fire explosive, or armor-piercing ammunition, and would provide back-up for his brand new blast rifle. Then there was the light hand blaster for personal protection, an ugly little two-shot hide-out gun, a force blade for skinning, two throwing knives, and a hide-out blade disguised as a belt buckle. "I don't know, Boater, I appreciate the investment, but aren't we overdoing things a bit? I notice you don't wear any weapons."

There was a sudden blur of motion and Renn found himself looking down the bore of an ugly little handgun. "Wrong, lad. Take a moment to think. Minutes after you landed, the Clops and his men damned near killed you. Then, soon as they left, the planet sent things to eat you, and water to drown you. So here's your first lesson. Everyone and everything on this planet is dangerous. Only the strong survive here. Forget that for one second and you'll wind up dead." There was another blur of motion and the gun disappeared.

Renn gulped, and nodded his understanding. With Boater's advice, and the shop owner's help, Renn put on his full arsenal. The hand blaster went into a shoulder holster concealed under his short jacket, the .75 recoilless hung low on his right thigh, the little hide-out gun went into his left boot top, and he had knives all over the place. He felt self-conscious, and more than a little dangerous, in spite of the fact that his weapons were still unloaded.

Boater looked him up and down as if judging a side of beef. "You *look* like a hunter. Unfortunately you don't think like one. Ah well, one thing at a time."

It was almost dark by the time Renn and Boater emerged from the store and walked towards the warehouse. The light was dim, and she was on the other side of the street, but thanks to her enchanced vision, Marla recognized Renn right away. She lunged forward but the heavy chain brought her up short. The woman called "Skunk" had secured it to the railing with a strong lock. Marla wanted to say something, to call Renn's name, but she couldn't. Skunk had also wrapped three feet of durasteel wire around her muzzle. She said dogs shouldn't talk. And try as she might, Marla had been unable to break the wire. Nevertheless she strained at her chin and whined deep in her throat. If only Renn would look her way, he'd free her, and she'd rip Skunk's throat out. But the two men continued on their way. Marla swore silently as she watched them out of sight. Once they were gone, she sighed internally, and lay down to wait. In three or four hours Skunk would emerge from the saloon, throw up over the rail, jerk Marla's chain, and drag her off to their filthy quarters in a shack at the edge of town. It was going to be a long unpleasant year.

Bright and early the next morning Boater filled *Fred's* tank with gas, complained bitterly about the price, and reluctantly paid the bored looking man who ran the Association's fuel barge. But he smiled when *Fred's* engine roared into life. "Good boy," he said, patting the engine cover and nodding his approval.

As Renn cast off the last mooring line, and pushed *Fred* away from the nearby pilings, he noticed the rain had stopped. According to Boater it rained on and off all the time, with six major rainy periods spread throughout the year.

As they slid down Payout's main street, Boater leaned on his steering oar, and waved regally to the few early risers. Most waved back and shouted a cheerful greeting, although Renn saw at least one rude gesture, and got the feeling Boater was not universally loved. *Surprise, surprise*, he thought with a grin.

"Stop grinning like an idiot, and pay attention," Boater said as they neared the far end of town. "From now on you'll use what little intelligence you have to memorize our route. Lesson number two. The swamp constantly changes. Old channels disappear and new ones open up. So even with the latest satellite maps it's easy to get lost. Suppose your incompetence gets me killed? How the hell are you gonna find your way back here to spend all my hard earned credits? Aha! That got your attention, didn't it, Jonnie lad? Well good. It might save your worthless life."

Once out of town, Boater turned *Fred* into a broad channel many miles wide. In between rainy seasons it was a river, but at the moment its regular banks had disappeared beneath a flood of muddy rainwater. Great rafts of floating debris rode the current. Boater carefully steered around most of these, occasionally cutting through others, somehow able to distinguish between those which were solid, and those which weren't. From time to time a fin or tentacle would break the river's surface offering ominous hints of a world below.

As *Fred* putt-putted along, Renn did his best to scan his surroundings, compare them to the satellite map Boater had spread out before him, and simultaneously field strip the .75 recoilless. Boater insisted he learn how to strip, clean and load all his weapons blindfolded. As Renn fumbled the barrel into the receiver mechanism, he decided the blindfold part would have to wait for awhile.

Lunch came and went, as did the rain, and gradually the .75 went together with less and less effort. In fact Renn was enjoying himself. A good lunch, a period of warm sun, and the exotic scenery had all combined to make him comfortable and a little drowsy. Leaning back against the cabin he was soon asleep. So he didn't notice when the huge shadow fell across him, and the lifter dropped out of the sky.

The lifter's huge wings pushed a wall of humid air into

his face as it landed beside him, and bent a long curving neck towards his face. He awoke as the lifter's beak-like mouth opened in a squawk of victory, and its fetid breath washed over him. Without conscious thought, Renn brought the .75 up and pulled the trigger. The explosive bullet entered the lifter's narrow chest and blew up somewhere inside. The creature shuddered from hydrostatic shock but remained upright. Renn pulled the trigger again. Another explosive bullet followed the first and this one did the job, severing two major vessels, showering him with greenish blood. The big bird gave one last squawk and collapsed.

Swearing a blue streak, Renn managed to wriggle out from under the bird's corpse. Where the hell was Boater? Getting to his feet he looked back towards the stern, and to his shock, saw Boater leaning on the steering oar, a big grin on his face.

Seeing Renn's expression, the older man shook his head in amusement, and yelled over the noise of the engine. "Lesson number three, lad. Don't sleep in the open, don't sleep deep, and don't sleep when you should be working."

"Damn you Boater . . . you let it attack me!"

Boater shrugged. "Try to look at the bright side Jonnie. Lifters are good skins. There's a prime patch of leather under each wing. So you learned something, and we picked up a few credits to boot. Not a bad deal, huh?"

"Not bad? Not bad?" Renn spit the words out one at a time. "Hell, you used me for bait!"

"And fine bait you were lad," Boater agreed smugly. "By the way, always fire two rounds, not just one. Like you just found out, most of the critters around here take a lot of killing. So if one's good, two's better."

Boater went forward and ordered Renn to steer. Grunting with the effort, he dragged the lifter into the center of the metal-lined cockpit, and went to work. It didn't take long. His force blade hummed, incisions appeared, blood gushed, and huge gobbets of meat went over the side. Renn noticed these were eagerly pulled under the water by things unseen. He made a note to give up swimming.

Soon only the lifter's wings were left, and Boater skillfully stripped those of the soft underskin, throwing the rest into the channel. The wings floated on the surface of the water for awhile, and then, when Renn looked away for a moment, suddenly disappeared.

Renn refused to speak with Boater for the rest of the day. But he paid close attention to their route, and worked unceasingly with his weapons, constantly scanning his surroundings for danger. Next time he'd be ready.

When evening came Boater nosed *Fred* up to a large tree isolated some distance from shore. Moments later Renn passed a mooring line around its smooth trunk and made it secure. Boater cut the engine and allowed the current to push *Fred* down to the end of the mooring line.

Silence fell around them like a heavy curtain. Tentatively at first, and then with increasing eagerness, the night sounds gradually crept in. Before long a chorus of grunts, screeches, and howls combined to hint at events unseen. Hidden by the dark embrace of the swamp, things gave birth, hunted for food, and died. Violent death was the rule, not the exception. In the swamp no quarter was given or expected. Renn's fingers unconsciously strayed to the butt of the .75. Boater saw and smiled. The boy was learning.

By morning Renn was speaking to Boater once again, though he was still angry, resentful. As a result he took pleasure in finding little ways to annoy the older man, like taking the last biscuit out from under his employer's descending fork, and snatching the last piece of meat. But Boater refused to rise to the bait. Instead he belched loudly and retired to the stern cockpit with his coffee.

Renn did the dishes and emerged from the cabin expecting to see Boater casting off. Instead the older man was still seated sipping the last of his coffee. "Finally. I swear, you're the slowest dish washer I've ever had."

"Oh yeah? How many have you had?"

Boater tugged on his goatee thoughtfully. "Can't quite remember . . . but it seems like ten or fifteen by now."

Suddenly suspicious Renn asked, "Why me, then? What happened to your last assistant anyway?" As soon as the words were out of his mouth Renn knew he'd been set up.

Boater's face broke into a wide smile. "Why, a stink got him. Silly bastard missed his shot." Boater shook his head sadly. "Too bad. I kind of liked him . . . though he snored something awful."

"And?" Renn asked, his voice heavy with sarcasm.

"And, the same thing could happen to you, shit-for-brains," Boater said amicably.

"I hit the lifter didn't I?"

Boater raised one eyebrow. "Why yes you did, Jonnie lad. From about three feet away. Now let's see you hit that snag over there." He pointed to the right. "Take your time. If you hit it first shot . . . I'll take over all your chores today."

Renn looked at the dead tree. It was about three feet in diameter and maybe fifty yards off. Pulling the .75, Renn took careful aim. He felt *Fred* move gently up and down beneath his feet. No problem, he'd compensate for that. He felt the light breeze against his left cheek. All right . . . he'd allow a hair for windage. He took a deep breath, and squeezed the trigger twice, just as Boater's plastic cup hit him in the face. Both shots went wide.

Whirling, Renn formed the words "You tricked me" in his mind, but bit them off. Boater had just made another point. Turning back towards the snag, Renn pointed the .75 as if pointing a finger, and squeezed the trigger fourteen times. The first two hit the water at the base of the snag, and the rest walked their way up its length, knocking huge chunks out of the rotten wood as they exploded. As the last slug left the gun Renn thumbed the magazine release, allowing the empty to land at his feet, and slammed a fresh one into the butt. Then he turned back towards Boater. To his surprise the old man was smiling.

"Not bad Jonnie, not bad. From now on target practice every morning after breakfast."

As the day progressed, Renn noticed a change in Boater's behavior. For one thing, he spent a lot of time looking back over his shoulder, and for another, he kept pulling into little side channels, where he'd shut off the engine and wait. Renn wanted to ask Boater what was going on but didn't want one of the old man's sarcastic replies. He managed to resist questioning him for most of the day but finally his curiosity got the better of him, and he caved in. As Boater pulled into a small cove and cut the engine, Renn said, "All right, Boater, what the hell's going on? You've been looking backwards and taking breaks all day. I thought you were in a hurry."

Boater shook his head in pretended amazement. "Well, I'll be damned. He *was* paying attention. So here comes lesson number four. We're getting close to my lodge. A hunter's lodge is where he lives between trips into the deep swamp. It's where he stores his supplies, skins, and stink. Knowing that, the Clops, and others like him, try to follow hunters to their lodges. Once they know the location they go away. Meanwhile the hunter works his ass off for the better part of a year, piles up skins and stink, and dreams of the day he'll load up for Payout. Then, just when he's about to head in, they kill him and clean out his lodge."

Both men were silent for a moment. Then Renn spoke. "So you've been watching to see if we were followed. Were we?"

Boater shrugged. "I don't think so. But you can never be completely sure. No matter how careful you are, if someone wants you bad enough, they'll find you in the long run. Or just stumble over you by accident. Either way it adds up to the same thing."

Boater looked suddenly weak and vulnerable in Renn's eyes, and with a sudden flash of insight, he knew that deep down the gruff old hunter was scared. Scared that one day they'd come and take the little bit he had. Age brought no privileges on Swamp. No retirement homes, no government living allowance, no sympathetic relatives. Only the merciless swamp in which living to old age was the exception, and violent death the rule. As quickly as the moment came it was gone, as Boater heaved himself to his feet, and growled. "Well come on . . . if we get a move on we can reach my lodge by nightfall."

And reach it they did. A few hours later Boater sent Renn into the bow with a long pole, and instructions to fend off obstructions. Then he pushed the steering oar to the starboard, and *Fred* made a hard turn to port. With the engine just barely turning over, the boat slid silently into a narrow side channel.

From Renn's vantage point, it looked like another dead end, similar to countless others they'd passed along the way, but moments later the channel opened to the right and became a small bay. A sturdy-looking dock dominated the bay, and beyond that, he saw a small lodge made of local timber. It blended into the surrounding jungle and almost disappeared. That, plus the nondescript channel, would make Boater's hideaway almost impossible to find. Which is the whole idea, Renn thought, as he used the pole to fend off a submerged log. A lot of thought and work had gone into Boater's hideaway. The threat from raiders must be very real indeed.

Fred fit the dock as if it had been made just for him, which it had, and was soon secured. As they followed a short path up towards the lodge, Renn noticed Boater was carrying a short, ugly-looking energy weapon, and pausing frequently to look around. Then he'd grunt his satisfaction and move on. In coming days Renn would also learn to look for the tiny signs which would signal a foreign presence. The flat rock in the middle of the path with two pebbles on it, the almost invisible thread across the steps, the piece of wood which should lay just so, and many more.

Finding all as it should be, Boater unlocked the door to his lodge and led Renn inside. Moments later lanterns filled the cabin with a yellow glow. Though not fancy, the lodge did have a warm homey feel, and Boater was visibly proud of it.

There was one big room, which served as both kitchen, dining room, and living room, plus a separate bedroom for Boater, and a curtained-off corner for Renn. A back door led out to a substantial wood pile, an outhouse, and a tiny dock at which a small flat-bottomed skiff was moored.

In answer to Renn's questioning look, Boater said, "That's lesson number five, lad. Always leave yourself a back way out, and if they have you outnumbered, have the good sense to use it. It's better to lose your lodge than your ass. That there's a different channel than the one we came in on, and there's enough stuff hidden under the seats of that skiff to get us all the way to Payout if need be."

Renn remained for a moment after Boater had stumped back into the cabin. As darkness fell the night sounds no longer frightened him. He was used to them now. As he went inside Renn decided it was a good omen. For the moment this would be home.

While Renn unloaded *Fred*, Boater prepared an excellent dinner, and they ate in companionable silence. Later, after the dishes were done, they sat before a roaring fire and told each other stories. It seemed Boater had been something of a minor crime lord on one of the inner planets. He declined to say on which one, but some of his adventures were absolutely hilarious, so that by the time Renn crawled into bed he was happier than he'd been in a long time.

Within minutes he'd drifted off to sleep and started to dream. He found himself walking the surface of a dark planet. A place where flowers blossomed only at night, shivered in the pale light of three moons, and hid within their leaves during the short day. Around him dogs pranced through the twilight on hind legs and spoke of many things. One in particular caught his attention, and without choosing to do so, he found himself following her towards the top of a softly rounded hill. As she reached the summit, the moonlight fell on her like a soft cloak of white, she seemed to shimmer within its glow, and was suddenly transformed. She was a dog no longer. Suddenly she was tall and slim with long brown hair cascading down around a perfect heart shaped face. She smiled and laughed from the pure joy of being alive. He rushed forward, and just as she entered the circle of his arms, she disappeared. And all around him the dogs danced and laughed while he stood in the moonlight and cried.

──── Chapter Six ────

The next few months of Renn's life were like a visit to hell. A green hell, in which he must kill, or be killed. All of his activities centered around that one grim reality. Each day started the same way, breakfast, then target practice. Boater was always there, sipping a final cup of coffee, grunting his approval, or shaking his head in disgust. He started with stationary targets, booze containers thoughtfully emptied by Boater the night before, and gradually progressed to moving targets, which were placed further away each day. As time passed Renn's proficiency improved. He worked with each weapon until it was a part of him, an extension of his will. Then Boater invented games to further hone Renn's skill. His favorite involved creating a target range out behind the lodge. Once the targets were in place, Boater would call for certain weapons. "The pond, lad, use the .75, first the right hand, then the left."

Renn's right hand dived for the big .75, bringing it up into a two handed grip. There were eight chunks of wood floating beyond the skiff. Renn squeezed his shots off in groups of two, working from left to right, blowing the chunks of wood into splinters, until only two slugs were left. Shifting the weapon to his left hand, he squeezed the trigger twice, watching as both targets ceased to exist. Then he released the empty magazine and slammed a fresh one home.

"Bravo Jonnie! Now your blast rifle. Take the monsters."

Renn knew Boater was referring to the large pieces of plastic secured to the trees on the far side of the channel. A light breeze was tossing and turning them this way and that. Renn reached back, pulled the blast rifle from the scabbard on his back, and brought it to his shoulder. A quick squint through the open sights, a double tap on the firing stud, and two beams of blue light screamed across the water to punch holes through the first target. A quick shift to the right, and the second sheet of plastic met a similar fate.

"Blast rifle malfunction! Quick behind you!"

Renn released the blast rifle as he spun around and saw the glint of Boater's coffee cup spinning high over his head. He could have hit it with the .75, but chose the hand blaster instead, knowing he needed the practice. He fired without aiming, feeling the almost magical connection between weapon and target which flows from muscle memory, experience, and intuition. The coffee cup disappeared in a flash of blue light.

"To your left . . . the stump . . . throwing knife!"

Renn flexed the muscles in his left forearm just so, triggering the spring loaded sheath, which delivered a double-edged throwing knife into his right hand. In one smooth motion his hand went back and then forward. The perfectly balanced blade flipped end over end twelve times, thudded into the stump, and vibrated like a tuning fork.

And so it went, until even Boater expressed grudging satisfaction. "Umpf. You're death on stumps lad . . . but monsters fight back We'll see how you do against them."

But it was a long time before Renn took on any monsters. There was a great deal to learn first. Boater's lessons began with swamp ecology. Renn soon discovered his employer had memorized every word of the original survey team's bio scans, had added his own experiences and observations to that considerable body of knowledge, and was determined that his assistant do likewise.

First Renn learned about stinks. From the shots in Boater's little hand-held holo tank, Renn decided they looked like large rubber balls. Adult specimens grew to be twenty or thirty feet in diameter. Boater explained that their external appearance stemmed from the large air bladder which surrounded their internal organs. The air bladder allowed them to roll across large bodies of water, and to use rivers the same way ground cars use highways. They could move freely wherever there was water, including marshy areas, but couldn't move through dense undergrowth. By expelling air through the vents spaced across the surface of their bodies, stinks could control both the direction and speed of their movements. Boater said he'd also seen them take advantage of the wind, allowing themselves to be blown across larger lakes, content to go wherever the wind took them.

"Still," Renn said lightly, "one shot and they must pop like balloons."

"That would be nice," Boater agreed dryly. "Unfortunately mother nature wasn't that kind. Instead of just one chamber, their air bladders contain millions of little air tight compartments. You could shoot 'em all day long and they'd still float. No, you've got to hit something vital, preferably the fifth subbrain which provides their motor control."

"And how the hell do you manage that?" Renn asked, trying to figure out how someone could hit a single organ within such a large body.

"Very carefully," Boater replied with a grin. "Now let's take a look at their diet."

Though quite large, stinks were vegetarians, existing on a diet consisting of three main plants. One by one Boater showed Renn each plant, described its life cycle, and forced him to eat portions of the two that were nontoxic. All three plants lived in marshy areas, where the stinks could roll up to them, extrude up to four tubular feeding organs, and inhale a few hundred pounds of the dripping stuff. Boater couldn't prove it, but felt sure the stinks played some role in the reproductive cycle of at least one of the plants, similar to the relationship between bees and some Terran plants.

"So they're hard to sink, eat a lot, and cross-pollinate plants," Renn said. "They still sound like easy pickings."

Boater took the holo unit, ran the recording ahead, and handed it back. "Take a look at that, lad."

Renn held the unit up and gave it a gentle squeeze. Obediently it played back. What he saw was a large stink rolling up a narrow channel of water towards the camera. In its path was a small inflatable boat. A woman was paddling with short desperate strokes, trying to outrun the stink, and steadily losing ground. She looked back over her shoulder, and then back towards the camera, and Renn could see the horror on her face. "Go to either side!" Renn urged. "It can't follow you into the undergrowth." But of course she didn't. As the stink came up behind her, it extruded thousands of needle sharp spines and rolled right over her. Renn winced as she threw up her hands and the spines came out through her chest, tipped with red. Then she was gone, rolled under by the advancing monster, reappearing moments later as the stink's forward motion brought her up and over the top. She was crucified on a hundred spines, her eyes bulging, her mouth open in a silent scream. Then the viewer went black as the stink rolled over the holo cam and destroyed it.

"My God, Boater, that was horrible!" Renn said, as he handed over the viewer. "Why didn't the camera operator do something to help her?"

Boater accepted the viewer with a philosophical shrug. "There wasn't any camera operator. She was a xeno biologist attached to the first survey team. The camera was running on automatic. Now let's take a look at some skins."

Skins, it turned out, came in a number of shapes and sizes. And although Boater assured him they were all related, Renn found it hard to believe since they looked so dissimilar. One type appeared quite snake-like, having a long sinuous body, and an evil-looking bulbous head. Unlike Terran snakes, however, it came equipped with ugly-looking suckers, which helped it climb trees, and also served as tiny mouths. Another looked like a Terran kangaroo, about the same size, with a long tail and large hind legs. Except it had a mouth full of needle sharp teeth, walked rather than jumped, and didn't really have a tail. The tail was actually another skin, linked with the roo monster through symbiosis, and quite dangerous itself. And there were others, too, even airborne variations—like the lifter which had attacked Renn earlier.

Different though these creatures were, Renn eventually began to see the similarities. They all shared the chameleon-like ability to match their surroundings, and they were all carnivorous, oviparous land dwellers. As with the stinks, Boater insisted next that Renn understand the food chain which supported them.

His lessons began with a microscopic examination of swamp water. Boater's microscope was a primitive instrument, far from powerful, and relied on reflected light. Still, it was more than adequate for the task at hand. Carefully preparing a slide with a drop of swamp water, Boater looked through the eyepiece, made a fine adjustment, and grunted his satisfaction. "There they are . . . the little critters who make skins possible."

Looking through the scope, Renn saw the water was teeming with small almost transparent creatures. They seemed to come in three or four basic shapes and sizes. They wiggled this way and that, bumping into each other, busily filtering the water for nutrients.

It was their role to nourish small marine creatures, which provided sustenance to larger marine creatures, which were eaten by airborne and land dwelling lifeforms, who in turn were consumed by the skins. "So," Boater concluded, "those little mites are a hunter's best friend. If you hurt 'em you hurt yourself."

And the lessons continued. Boater gradually introduced Renn to the swamp itself. Through the older man's eyes, Renn learned to see both its beauty and ugliness. He learned that while it could kill, it could also nourish and protect. And he learned the skills which would enable him to survive there.

In spite of the older man's considerable bulk, Boater could glide through the swamp like a ghost. He showed Renn how to move so that the thick carpet of dead vegetation would muffle his foot steps, how to pause every few yards to look and listen, how to fade into the background, allowing his monster skin clothing to conceal him.

Gradually Renn learned how to tell firm ground from weak, good plants from bad, and harmless life forms from those which could kill. His fat melted away to reveal hard flat muscle, his movements became smoother, and more coordinated. He learned to trust nothing but himself, to kill without compunction, to place survival before all else. Gradually, without fully realizing it, he started to welcome his time in the swamp and even seek it out. Seeing this, Boater decided his pupil was ready for one final test. He delivered the news over breakfast the next morning. As usual he was sitting down while Renn was up and doing the dishes.

"Well, Jonnie we've wasted enough time and ammunition on your training. It's time to get some work out of you."

Renn didn't bother to point out that he already had done most of the work. He knew from experience the irony would be lost on Boater. "Good," Renn replied. "It's about time. When do we go after some monsters?"

"Soon," Boater promised. "But first I have a little errand for you. I've got an emergency cache about twenty miles from here. It hasn't been checked out for a year or more. Who knows? By now it could've been flooded out, or looted. Anyway here's a map. Take the skiff, some supplies, and see if everything's still there."

Renn dried his hands on a rag and accepted the map. There was something about the expression in Boater's beady little eyes he didn't like, but he wasn't quite sure what it was, so he just nodded and tucked the map into an inside pocket. No matter what his employer might be cooking up, the idea of getting out on his own for a few days sounded very good indeed. "Fine, Boater. I'll get ready."

A few hours later Renn poled the loaded skiff away from the dock, as Boater stood on the shore, and smiled. He even waved goodbye. Renn was very suspicious as he waved in return. Boater smiling? Boater never smiled unless he was getting the best of somebody. But how did that apply here? The question continued to plague him as he entered the main channel, took a compass bearing, and headed north.

Much to his own surprise Renn felt quite comfortable as the skiff slipped silently through the swamp. It was a warm, humid day. Dappled sunlight found its way down through the lush green foliage to splash the skiff with light. Colorful insects, some the size of small birds, flitted from one tree to another, their wings humming. Somewhere a lifter croaked its victory cry. And every now and then, a light breeze stirred the branches overhead, causing them to rustle gently. In fact there were noises all around him, but he knew what made each of them, and knowing made all the difference. He wasn't afraid. Well, not much anyway. Besides he had his weapons. They were part of him now. The blast rifle in its back scabbard, the .75 on his hip, the hand blaster in its shoulder holster. Thanks to them he could take on whatever the swamp had to offer, stinks and skins included.

A short time later Renn steered the skiff over to the bank,

brushed aside some branches, and pushed his way into a small, tight channel. As the branches fell into place behind him, he became invisible from the main channel. Then, by rearranging his supplies a little, Renn created a comfortable place to lay down. Shrugging off the rifle and scabbard, he made sure the weapon was close to hand, and stretched out. Placing his hands behind his head, he looked up through the branches towards the distant sun, and smiled. This sure beat hell out of running and fetching for Boater. He closed his eyes but didn't go to sleep.

Time passed, and then, right in a middle of a rather pleasant daydream, he heard it, the gentle putt-putt of *Fred's* engine. Sitting up he peered through the branches. The noise got gradually louder until *Fred's* familiar shape slid into view, Boater and all. So the old bastard was up to something after all! Renn grinned. Well, all right, whatever the game was, two could play as well as one.

Renn waited until Boater had disappeared from sight, eased the skiff out into the main channel, and followed. Normally it would be impossible to keep up, but Boater was barely moving, apparently afraid he'd overrun Renn, so Renn managed to tag along behind.

And so it went for the rest of the day, Boater putt-putting along, with Renn bringing up the rear. Boater paused twice, to fix something to eat, Renn decided, and both times he almost blew it. But luck was with him on both occasions and he managed to pull back without being seen. After the second such occurrence, Renn made it a habit to peer around curves first, and that solved the problem. When night fell, Boater pulled into a side channel, fixed himself an elaborate dinner, and retired early. Renn knew this, because he was watching from the undergrowth as it happened. Crouched there in the darkness, he had mixed emotions. He was proud of his ability to watch Boater undetected, ashamed of doing so, and scared that it was so easy. The old man looked so vulnerable as he moved around inside his cabin, humming a Terran tune, and cooking his dinner. For the second time Renn realized his employer wasn't young any more. Suddenly he felt like a child, who, used to seeing his parents as all powerful, is suddenly confronted with obvious weakness. Careful not to make any noise, Renn stood, and faded back into the night. As he left, Boater looked up and smiled into the darkness.

The next morning Renn awoke early, cooked a simple meal on a chemical stove, and followed when Boater headed up channel. The second day passed much like the first. Good weather, easy progress, and occasional stops while Boater prepared a snack. Renn used these breaks to consult the map Boater had given him, saw they were sticking to the original route, and should arrive by mid-afternoon. But why the charade? What was the old geezer up to anyway? Was he following along in case Renn got into trouble, or was there some other reason? Renn heard *Fred*'s motor start up. He shrugged. Only one way to find out. Tucking the map back into his inner pocket, he picked up his pole, and pushed away from the bank.

Three hours later they reached the destination Boater had marked on the map. Peeking through some thick vegetation, Renn saw a large lake, with an island towards the middle of it. Even without a look at the map Renn knew that Boater's squiggly line ended at the island. What the hell? He watched as Boater steered *Fred* towards the island. Just when it appeared certain that he'd run *Fred* aground, the boat suddenly disappeared.

Renn pushed off and headed for the spot where *Fred* had vanished. As he got closer Renn decided the island had a spooky feeling. He couldn't put his finger on the reason, but he knew it was different somehow, and didn't like it.

The vegetation grew thick and heavy along the shoreline, and even though he knew approximately where the channel was, it was still hard to find. In fact if it weren't for the freshly broken branches he would've gone right by it. They practically screamed at Renn to follow. Why? Did Boater know he was following along behind, instead of leading the way? But how could he? Troubled, Renn forced his way through the foliage and into the narrow channel.

As he poled along, his earlier feelings became even stronger: spookiness, mixed with something else, danger of some kind. He unconsciously reached back to touch the stock of his blast rifle, his eyes scanning right and left, his ears attuned to the slightest sound. Everything was quiet. Too quiet. Gone was the humming of insect wings, the distant call of swamp birds, the rustle of small animals. Probably just *Fred's* recent passage he told himself.

Then he noticed it. Pushing over to the side of the channel, he grabbed a machete, and used it to scrape away the thick layer of vegetation that slanted down to the water. It couldn't be! Running his hand over the smooth surface thus exposed, Renn knew he was touching an artificial surface, something like duracrete, only different, more finely textured. The symmetry of the channel had given it away. The damned thing was as uniform as an Imperial expressway!

Except no Imperial engineer had constructed this. Before its designation as a prison planet, Swamp had been an undeveloped frontier world. Everyone knew that. And Swamp didn't have any indigenous sentient life forms. Suddenly Renn realized what that meant. Swamp was an artifact world!

He knew there were others of course, many had been discovered during the early days of space exploration. In most cases they weren't much to look at, empty ruins mostly, worn down by the effects of weather and the passage of time. Commonalities in architecture, and other archeological similarities, made it certain that all the ruins were the remnants of a single galactic culture. But what of the Builders? Where had they gone? Artifact planets were always devoid of intelligent life, except where native life forms had evolved into sentience, long after the Builders had departed. Whatever the answer, the Builders had once lived here, and Boater had known about it for some time.

The feeling of danger persisted as Renn poled his way up the channel. A few moments later he saw *Fred*'s homely shape and pulled up alongside.

"Boater? Hey Boater, what the hell is this all about?" No answer. Climbing over the side Renn checked the cabin. Nothing. Boater had evidently gone ashore.

Stepping up onto the bank Renn saw a narrow path which led off into the jungle. A game trail from the looks of it. Something was using it on a regular basis, and unless the Builders were still hanging around, game was the most likely answer.

Pulling the rifle from its scabbard, Renn started up the path. Around him there was only the brooding silence and humid stench of the jungle. Not knowing what to expect, he tried to look for everything. Ambush sites, trip wires across the path, tree monsters, anything that might attack from above or either side. Then something reached up through the surface of the path and pulled him under.

Renn had a brief glimpse of his attacker as he fell, an eyeless head, searching white tentacles, and a vast slug-like body. No doubt the thing regarded the trail as its own personal buffet, reaching up occasionally to pluck whatever tasty morsels happened by. Except this morsel didn't want to be plucked.

Renn landed on his back, but the thick layer of humus carpeting the tunnel's floor cushioned his fall, allowing him to aim and fire. Bolts of coherent energy punched through the soft-skinned creature to splash against the wall. A high-pitched scream filled the tunnel, and the thing split open like rotten fruit, spilling half a ton of its blue-black guts into the small space.

Renn scrabbled at the side of the tunnel trying to get up and away from the rising tide of stinking viscera. But his searching fingers found nothing but the smooth featureless walls left by the Builders thousands of years before. Overhead he saw the green of the jungle, and beyond that, patches of blue sky. He jumped. It was hopeless.

To his right he heard a distant gibbering noise, then another, and another, blending into a single chorus from hell. The dead monster was attracting guests for dinner. Looking left Renn verified that the huge, slug-like body had completely blocked the tunnel. He couldn't go up, and he couldn't go left, so he turned to the right and prepared to face whatever was coming.

"All right," Renn thought grimly, "come and get it." Sloshing through the monster's putrid guts he flicked on the rifle's laser sight. It threw a disc of red light up the tunnel. It wasn't much, but it would help. Seconds later they appeared, dark shadowy figures moving forward with short jerky movements. From what he could see they had elongated bodies, three or four pairs of short stubby legs, and lots of teeth. Each time the red disc touched one of the things, he pressed the firing stud, and a pulse of blue light raced up the tunnel to destroy it. Soon their death screams and gibbering mixed together to create a horrible cacophony. But for each one he killed two more soon arrived.

He was like a machine now, aiming, firing, aiming, firing, in an endless sequence of death. Until finally he pressed the firing stud and nothing happened. Empty. Shifting the rifle to his left hand he pulled the .75. It boomed and roared, creating a thunder of sound that bounced around the tunnel walls and echoed off into the distance. Renn kept firing—and suddenly the tunnel things turned and ran away. At first Renn couldn't understand

why. Then he had it. Noise. They didn't like the noise of the
.75. The whine of the blast rifle didn't bother them, but they
couldn't stand the roar of the .75. Being tunnel dwellers
they had poor eyesight, an excellent sense of smell, and
acute hearing. "Not any more," he thought happily, squeezing off two more rounds for good luck.

As the last echo died away, and Renn slammed a fresh
magazine into the butt of the .75, a shaft of sunlight hit the
tunnel floor fifty feet ahead, followed by a makeshift
wooden ladder. Moments later Boater's boots appeared,
soon followed by the rest of his rotund form. There was a
blast rifle across his back and a spotlight in his hand. "Hello
Jonnie, just thought I'd drop in and give you a hand. Looks
like you don't need it, though."

Renn felt an upwelling of anger so intense it left him
speechless. He was still trying to form words as Boater toed
a corpse and shook his head. "Been meaning to clean out
these tunnels for the last couple of years . . . but just
never seemed to get around to it. No, that's not quite true
lad, the truth is, I'm a bit past this kind of thing. That's why
I thought you'd enjoy a go."

"Enjoy? Enjoy? Why you lying, cheating, miserable old
bastard, I damned near got killed! You mean to tell me you
knew about this, knew I was following you, and let it
happen? I should kill you right here!"

Boater nodded in agreement. "That's right lad. You
probably should, and certainly could, and that's the whole
point."

Knowing he was being sucked in, but somehow unable to
help himself, Renn asked, "What's the whole point?"

Boater grinned. "Take a look at yourself. You smell like
the bottom of a one-holer, you look like hell, but outside of
that there's not a scratch on you."

Renn ran a mental inventory. The other man was right.
There wasn't a scratch on him. "So?"

"So," Boater replied, "congratulations. Your training is over."

Renn looked at him for a moment, and said. "You're a complete and total bastard, Boater."

The older man smiled. "You're right about that lad, you're right about that. Come on . . . I'll buy you a drink."

Boater took him on a tour of the ruins, explaining that he'd discovered them by accident years before, and used them as an occasional base ever since. He really did have a cache of supplies there, not to mention a shelter, complete with some rough and ready homemade furniture.

So as the sun went down, they sat in the great hall of a long vanished race, and drank to each other's health. And as the hours fled away, and they told stories into the night, things were somehow different between them. By unspoken agreement the relationship of teacher and student was gone, replaced by something which if not friendship, was at least a meeting of equals.

And that relationship endured. Weeks and months passed. Boater insisted that Renn never tell anyone about the ruins, saying there was nothing to be gained by letting others know, and pointing out that the old buildings seemed to attract monsters. Renn wasn't so sure the ruins should be dismissed so lightly, but was happy to humor his friend, and knew Boater was right about the monsters. There were lots of them on the island, and that meant good hunting.

Plentiful though they were, after a few weeks of hunting, the monsters started to grow scarce and they moved on. Relying on Boater's past experience, they traveled from one place to another, pausing at his favorite camping spots, and hunting along the way. And for the most part things went very well. In fact, Boater said it was the best season for skins he'd ever had, and credited Renn with bringing him good luck.

But there was still something missing. Where the hell were the stinks? Boater swore they should have seen five or six by now, and spent a lot of time mumbling about too many hunters, and how there used be a stink hiding behind every tree. In fact, Boater was ranting and raving on that very subject one morning when he rounded a curve a hair too fast and ran right into a full-grown stink.

The poor beast was right in the middle of breakfast, with three of its tubular feeding organs busily sucking up succulent swamp weed, when *Fred* rammed him, bounced back a good two feet, and then shot forward again as Boater struggled to engage reverse.

That was the first and last time Renn ever saw Boater lose control. Instead of placing the engine in reverse, Boater accidentally killed it, and as they drifted slowly down channel, his face turned beet red with anger and frustration.

Meanwhile the stink extracted its feeding organs, extruded thousands of needle sharp spines, and prepared itself to roll over the strange apparition which had just interrupted its meal.

"Shoot lad! Kill the sonovabitch or we're done for!"

Renn didn't even hear. The entirety of his being was concentrated on the stink. It was huge. It filled the sights of his blast rifle. He couldn't miss. But Boater's past words were suddenly ringing in his ears. "You could shoot 'em all day long and they'd still float. No, you've got to hit something vital, preferably the fifth subbrain which provides their motor control."

Terrific, Renn thought, *but easier said than done*. The monster was moving now, and in a few short seconds it would be up to speed, and would cross the short span of water separating them in about two seconds. Forcing himself to stay perfectly still, while his whole being screamed at him to run, to get away, Renn summoned up a memory of the crude anatomical drawing Boater had made one evening. It showed each of the monster's five sub-brains, and their location within a stink's ball-shaped body. The fifth was a little off-center left, below the third, a tiny bit larger than the other four. Carefully superimposing that image, over the huge thing which was now speeding towards him, Renn squeezed the trigger.

As the lance of blue energy impaled the oncoming monster, he gently moved it up and down, back and forth, hoping to find the fifth subbrain and slice through it. Because the stink was rolling forward, the beam cut downwards in layers, etching a continuous black line into the surface of the creature's body. The line looked like a black snake as it crawled upwards, smoking as it burned through living tissue, turning moisture into steam. Then the line disappeared over the top, reappearing seconds later, like a snake biting its own tail. But with each revolution, the beam cut a little deeper, until it finally found and cooked its target. By then, the monster was almost touching *Fred*'s bow, but suddenly it lost all motor control, stopped, shuddered, and partially collapsed.

Both men were silent for a moment as they thought about how close the monster had come, and how lucky they'd been. Boater was the first to speak. "Well, lad, I hope next time you'll be a little bit more careful. Something to think about as you carve this critter up."

Time passed, and while they didn't encounter any more stinks, the skins continued to pile up, until there were too many to carry in one trip. So they put the first load aboard *Fred* and headed for the lodge. After an uneventful trip they found the lodge just as they'd left it months before.

After unloading, and resting for a couple of days, Renn volunteered to make the second trip alone. Boater agreed, promising to have the first load of skins ready for sale by the time Renn returned.

As Renn pulled away from the dock they both clowned around and showered each other with friendly insults. Boater was still acting out the episode in which a sizable but harmless insect had fallen inside Renn's shirt, and caused him to stage an impromptu dance, when Renn rounded a curve and disappeared from sight.

It took six days to make the round trip, and Renn was still miles away when he saw the smoke, and felt a growing sickness in the pit of his stomach. Boater never built a fire during the day. "Smoke is like a big gray finger, lad, pointing straight down at your location, so don't build a fire unless you want company."

Opening up the throttle, he ignored any attempt at subtlety or swamp craft, knowing it was already too late for that. Instead he charged down the intervening channels like an enraged beast, scattering wild life in every direction, and swearing steadily. Steering with one hand, he checked his weapons with the other, and prayed it wasn't too late, even though some primitive part of him knew it was, and had already begun to mourn.

So he was looking for something to kill when he roared up the channel and into the pond. An opportunity to avenge himself for what he knew was waiting. He cut the engine at the last second and allowed *Fred* to coast towards the dock. There was no one in sight. The attack was days old.

"Boater! Boater it's Jonnie!" His voice sounded small in the vastness of the swamp. There was no answer.

As the boat hit the dock with a gentle bump, Renn leaped ashore and whipped one of *Fred*'s mooring lines around a piling.

His rifle was in his hands as he started up the path, and every nerve was on edge. Every single one of Boater's warning devices had been tripped. Up ahead the lodge had been reduced to smoking ashes. Boater had apparently put up a pretty good fight. There were bullet holes and blaster burns everywhere, and a large patch of red sticky stuff on the path which could only be human blood. Good. Renn hoped the bastard bled to death. Maybe his friends had carried the body off. Meanwhile there was no sign of Boater. Where was he?

Renn circled the lodge and found the answer to his question. Two long poles had been sunk into the ground to form a large X. Boater had been nailed to it. He was dead and had been for a long time. They'd stripped him naked, so Renn could see the long spikes which they'd driven through his arms and legs, and the countless brandings which covered his body. The metal had been heated in a fire they'd built at his feet. His legs now ended in blackened stumps.

"Why?" Renn asked. "Why didn't you take the skiff and run?" But deep down he knew why. The lodge was Boater's home. Everything he had was here. Moreover he was a stubborn old bastard, too old to start over.

From all the booze and food containers littering the ground, it was clear they'd thrown a party, and used Boater as the entertainment. He'd taken a long time to die.

A green bird landed on the back of Boater's slumped head, and began to peck at the top of his skull, hoping to reach his brains. When the .75 caliber slug hit the bird it exploded into a thousand scaly fragments. Killing the bird helped, but it didn't begin to quell Renn's anger, or satisfy his growing need for revenge. But that would have to wait. First there was a burial to perform. Putting down his rifle, Renn approached the cross.

As he got closer, Renn noticed something strange. While both of Boater's arms were nailed to the timbers, his right hand was balled into a fist, with his index finger pointing towards the sky. Bending closer, Renn saw the finger was actually pointing towards some sort of design on the wood just under his fingertip, a crude oval, with a circle drawn inside it. An eye! Boater had used his own blood to draw an eye! Cyclops! Cyclops and his men had done it! Renn nodded grimly, and murmured, "I hear you old friend, I hear you."

Renn buried Boater on a slight rise, up beyond the ruins of his lodge. As he worked, the first warm drops of rain hit his skin. The fifth rainy season was just about to start. One more and it would be a year since he and Marla had been dumped onto the surface of the LZ. He wondered where she was, and what she was doing, hoping things had gone well for her. If only—but what the hell, she hadn't, and that was that.

It was hard work, but two hours later the job was done. Over the grave Renn carefully placed a wooden cross like the one the old man had worn around his neck. And, as he said goodbye, his tears mixed with the warm rain, and he found it difficult to speak. "Goodbye, Boater. I'm sorry it ended like this, you deserved much, much better. But they made a mistake, Boater. They left me alive. And thanks to you, I'm a hunter now. So I'll find them, Boater. And when I do I'll kill them."

PART TWO

Hunter

—— Chapter Seven ——

As he combed the ruins of the lodge Renn's anger burned with a flame that provided no warmth. He turned up some salvageable equipment, plus quite a bit of useful information. For example, by examining footprints and garbage the killers had left behind, Renn deduced that five men participated in Boater's murder. It didn't take a genius to figure out who they were, Cyclops, Blaster, Knife, Trap, and Scuz.

A walk along the bank revealed that two boats, both smaller than *Fred*, had been run aground and pulled up onto the mud. Both had left distinctive marks. One had a sharp keel which left a four-inch wide groove in the mud, while the other had a pointed bow, which made a triangular indentation in the soft bank.

Renn also found ample evidence that one of the five men was badly wounded. First there was the blood stain he'd found earlier, plus numerous blood-soaked bandages he'd found laying around in the garbage. From the size and shape of the bandages, he deduced a leg or upper-arm wound, possibly involving a major vein or artery. Nothing less would account for the volume of blood the wounded man had lost.

So, as Renn took one last look at the smoking ruins, and the newly dug grave beyond, he sent Boater one last thought. "Rest easy old friend. They won't get far."

Renn checked his map as he guided *Fred* out into the main channel. With loot to sell, and a wounded man to care for, Cyclops and his gang would head straight for town.

Both their boats were a lot smaller than *Fred*, and Renn was pretty sure that only one was equipped with an engine, which meant the second was not only loaded with stolen skins, but was probably under tow as well. That might slow them just enough. He grinned at the thought as he opened *Fred*'s throttle, and plowed up-channel.

As the hours passed, the sound of *Fred*'s engine became an endless drone in Renn's ears, and his legs ached from standing. His eyes burned from scanning the monotonous green of the jungle and his nerves were stretched wire tight. Each side channel and clump of vegetation seemed to pose a threat. What if Cyclops had prepared an ambush? He'd asked himself that same question countless times, and each time he'd given himself the same answer. If there's an ambush ahead, then I'm dead meat. But if I slow down and get cautious, I'll never catch them. Besides, chances are they don't know about me, or if they do, figure I don't count. They've got a full load of skins to sell, plus a wounded man to care for, so there's damned little chance of an ambush.

Renn liked that answer, and always felt better after listening to it. But before long the feeling of well-being it brought began to fade away, doubts crept back in, and the whole cycle started over.

He slowed down as dusk approached, cutting the engine every now and then to listen and watch the horizon for signs of smoke. On Swamp nobody did any serious traveling at night. It was too easy to get lost in the maze of channels and bays. So Cyclops and his men would camp for the night. Renn knew there wasn't much chance he'd catch up to them on the first night out. Besides, he needed a safe moorage for himself, and knew he wouldn't find one going full out.

Even so, Renn almost missed the thin smear of black against the lavender sky. Smoke! Cutting the engine he allowed *Fred* to coast into shore. Quickly wrapping the bow line around the nearest tree, Renn checked his blast rifle, ran a hand over his other weapons, and slipped into the jungle.

He moved without conscious thought. Six swift steps from one piece of cover to the next, pause, listen, smell, look, and repeat. A game trail ran in the general direction of the smoke. Stay away from it. Trails attract trip wires, traps, and ambushes. Watch your back trail, watch the trees above, watch for things which shouldn't be there. An empty booze container! One of Boater's! Slow now . . . there's a clearing just ahead . . . damn the fading light. Circle left. Still another booze bottle. An unobstructed view of the clearing. Empty. Last night's camp.

Checking along the river, Renn quickly found the telltale groove left by the first boat's keel, and saw where the other boat's pointed bow had cut into the soft mud of the bank. They were gone but he'd cut their lead. Stepping into the clearing, he used a small flashlight to check their garbage. A booze bottle, some empty meal paks, and yes, some bloody bandages. So the wounded man was still alive, and still slowing them down. Good. He carefully smothered the fire lest the sight or smell of smoke attract more visitors, took one last look around, and faded into the jungle.

After making his way back to the boat, Renn prepared a simple meal in *Fred*'s blacked out cabin, and got ready for bed. Then, just prior to retiring, he scattered a thin layer of gravel over all the decks. If someone tried to board during the night the crunching sound would wake him. Another one of Boater's little tricks. Then he ducked below, checked his hand blaster, and stretched out on his bunk. It felt heavenly. Seconds later, Renn was asleep.

The night passed without incident and Renn was up bright and early the next morning. He ate a cold breakfast, swept up the gravel, and dumped it into the bucket reserved for that purpose. Then he started the engine and got under way.

The second day passed much like the first. An endless ordeal of physical strain, unrelieved monotony, and cyclical fear. Twice he spotted places where his prey had stopped for a meal, and twice he pulled in to investigate. There was always a lot of garbage laying around. This surprised him at first, since it made them so easy to follow, but apparently Cyclops and his companions were so used to hunting, they couldn't conceive of being hunted themselves. Renn smiled. So much the better.

The second time he stopped Renn was able to add one more piece of information to his growing list. As usual there were bandages among the other garbage, and as usual they were bloody, but this time there was something new, a discoloration, and a very bad smell to go with it. A smell like pus. And pus means infection. The wounded man was getting worse.

As Renn jumped back aboard *Fred*, he began to worry. What if Cyclops left the wounded man behind? The possibility that Cyclops was the wounded man never even occurred to him. Renn somehow knew the one-eyed man was untouched. So, what if Cyclops left the wounded man behind to make better time, and reached Payout first? It would blow his plan out of the water. Five to one odds were bad enough in the swamp, but to face them in town, where the fire probably had friends and allies, well, that seemed suicidal. So everything depended on at least thinning them out a bit before they reached town. With a renewed sense of urgency Renn cast off and restarted the engine.

Hours passed, and once again the light had begun to fade when he saw the column of smoke. From its dark color Renn knew the fire was still burning. Once again he cut the engine and allowed *Fred* to coast into the bank. With a tight feeling in his gut he tied the boat up and slipped into the dense undergrowth. Using every bit of bush craft he knew, Renn slowly closed on the smoke, every nerve, every fiber of his body tense with a heady mixture of fear, anticipation, and adrenaline. Sweaty hands gripped the blast rifle, air passed in and out of a dry throat, and tight nerves screamed for release.

There was a sudden clatter of sound as someone opened up with an auto slug thrower. Renn dived forward as a hail of lead ripped through the foliage around him. Rolling behind a fallen log, Renn came up on his elbows. He searched for a target and saw none. Just as suddenly as it started the firing stopped, and a hoarse voice called out, "That'll show you bastards. I know you're out there. I seen you creepin' all around. You want the Blaster? Well you just come and get him." The sentence was punctuated with another barrage of automatic fire, this time off to Renn's right.

Renn peered over the log but couldn't see a thing. What the hell was going on? Who was Blaster talking to? And where were his friends? On the theory that if he couldn't see Blaster, then Blaster couldn't see him, Renn ripped a large leaf off a nearby plant and waved it in the air. Nothing happened. Thus encouraged, he elbowed his way ahead, timing Blaster's fire, moving during the short intervals in between.

A short time later, he was peering through the crotch of a large tree at a very strange sight. A fire had been built in the center of a small clearing. Blaster sat in front of it, his back propped up against one of Boater's equipment bags, jamming a new magazine into his auto slug thrower. His right leg was thrust stiffly out before him, and there was a dirty looking bandage wrapped around his thigh. Renn remembered his red hair and tatooed face from the confrontation at the LZ. Not far away was a second figure, this one curled up in the fetal position, apparently asleep. So Blaster was the wounded man. But if so, who was the other guy, and why was he just laying there? And how could he sleep with all that noise? Just then Blaster yelled something unintelligible towards the sky, and ripped off another twenty rounds straight up.

Renn ducked behind the tree to think things over. Blaster was delirious. As he'd feared, Cyclops had left him behind in order to travel lighter and faster. So much for nailing all of them in the Swamp. Still one, and maybe two, was a lot better than none.

Renn poked his head up, and saw that Blaster's attention was on the other side of the clearing. Resting the barrel of his blast rifle in the crotch of the tree, Renn took careful aim, and squeezed the trigger. Due to the angle, the energy beam sliced through Blaster's left arm near the elbow, and his right arm at the wrist. His hands still gripped the slug thrower as it fell into his lap. Blaster stared at the mess in his lap for a full second before he started to scream.

Holding his blast rifle at the ready, Renn stood, and strolled into the clearing. Blaster had pulled his stumps against his chest and sobbed as he rocked back and forth.

To Renn's surprise the second man hadn't budged an inch. He was still curled up in the fetal position. Wary of a trap Renn approached from behind. Then he placed the barrel of his rifle in the man's ear, and said, "Good morning sweet cakes . . . time to get up."

Nothing. Walking around to the other side, Renn placed a boot against the man's chest, and pushed. It was like turning a rock over and looking underneath. The man had an empty booze bottle clutched to his chest. His clothes were filthy. Hair crawled all over his face, spit drooled from the corner of his mouth, and he stank. Scuz. Lost in an alcoholic stupor and living up to his name. Renn eyed the handgun Scuz wore in a cross-draw holster, and decided to leave it alone. Removing his foot Renn allowed Scuz to fall face down in the dirt.

Keeping a careful eye on Scuz, Renn walked over, and sat down next to Blaster. The red-haired man was still staring down at his lap and moaning. "Gee, Blaster . . . that looks real painful . . . I sure hope it is."

For a moment Blaster made no response. Then slowly, almost imperceptibly, his head came up and Renn found himself looking into bewildered bloodshot eyes. The moaning stopped, and when Blaster spoke, it was with the mystified voice of a child, punished for something he couldn't understand. "You hurt me . . . you shot my hands off."

"True," Renn agreed.

"But why? I never did nothin' to you. I don't even know you."

Blaster didn't recognize him. Not too surprising considering how much he'd changed since that day at the LZ. Renn smiled. "I'm afraid you're wrong about that, Blaster. The day I landed, you and the rest of your gang stole my gear, and left me for dead. But that's not the reason I came after you."

"It's not?" Blaster asked pitifully, looking at each stump in turn. "Why then?"

"Because you killed my friend."

"Boater? The fat man? You shot my hands off for an old geez?"

Renn nodded. "Yup."

"You gonna kill me?"

Renn looked him up and down. "Don't you think I should?"

Blaster looked at his stumps, and then down to his leg. It smelled to high heaven. When his eyes came back up, there was a trace of humor in them, and a half smile twisted one corner of his mouth. "Shit. Maybe you're right. Even Doc

Fesker couldn't put me right now. Not on this slime ball. Do me a favor though."

"What's that?"

"Do it from behind. I don't wanta see it comin.'"

Renn nodded and got to his feet. Moving behind Blaster, he tilted the blast rifle up and squeezed the trigger. The bolt of energy went right through and hit the ground beyond. As Renn released the trigger a cloud of steam rose from the ground and floated gently upwards. Slowly, almost deliberately, Blaster's body toppled over sideways.

Scuz awoke two hours later. It was pitch dark except for the flickering firelight which came from behind him. Uncurling, he discovered the empty bottle in his arms, swore, and threw it away. Turning towards the fire, Scuz squinted his eyes against the light, and said, "Blaster . . . Blaster you worthless bastard . . . where the hell are you?"

On the other side of the fire a man stepped into the light. There was something familiar about him, but Scuz couldn't quite remember what. "Blaster's dead."

"Dead?" Scuz asked, looking this way and that, "How'd he die? And who the hell are you anyway?"

Renn smiled. "The first answer is that I killed him. The second answer is that I'm a friend of Boater's." It took Scuz a moment to process the words and make sense of them. Then his hand dived for the slug gun in the cross-draw holster. At one time he'd been very fast indeed, and now, even though his reactions were slowed by alcohol, he was still faster than most. So fast he actually managed to get his gun clear of the holster before the first slug from Renn's .75 hit his chest and nearly blew him in half. The second slug made the mess even messier.

Renn extracted the clip, fed it two new rounds of ammunition, and searched his emotions for some sign of remorse. He found none. Nor was there pleasure. All he felt was relief. Sliding the magazine into the butt of the .75 he felt it click home. Two down, three to go.

An insect landed on Trap's cheek and he slapped it. Wiping the goo off with his right index finger he looked at it, laughed, and flicked it over the side.

From his vantage point a few feet away, Doc Fesker groaned silently, and cursed the slight irregularity in his tax return which had caused his present state of medical servitude. Why him? Plenty of other people underestimated their income without ending up on a prison planet. It wasn't fair. And his present situation just added insult to injury. Here he was, sitting on a filthy scow, in the company of a congenital idiot, who would soon force him to treat a homicidal maniac. It was obscene. His time was valuable. For one brief moment he considered outright rebellion. He could order Trap to turn the boat around and return to Payout. He rejected the thought as quickly as it came. The request for his services had been made with a blaster pointed at his head. He sighed. No, he'd just have to see it through. At least there wasn't any income tax on Swamp. The thought made him feel better. He found a roll of his latest tobacco prototype in a shirt pocket and lit it up.

Unlike his passenger, Trap was a happy man. The sun was warm, his stomach was full, and he wasn't horny. The first was a matter of good luck, the second stemmed from a good lunch, and the third flowed from the efforts of two homely but cooperative prostitutes the night before. So life was good. Hauling the doc into the swamp was a pain in the ass, but what the hell, Blaster was a buddy, and you gotta take care of your own. In fact, the clearing should be right around the next bend.

Squinting against the glare, Trap cut the power, and edged in towards shore. As the boat lost way, Trap scanned his surroundings for signs of danger. Everything seemed just fine. His long, sharp nose picked up the faint smell of wood smoke, that was to be expected, his sensitive ears heard only the normal sounds of the swamp, and his sharp eyes found no signs of visitors. Scuz should be standing guard, but had most likely passed out, and unless he'd gone belly up, Blaster would be sleeping in. What a pair. Trap grinned, baring two durasteel incisors. Just for the fun of it, he'd give them a little scare.

Mooring the boat to some convenient trees, Trap removed the rotor from the distributor, tucked it into his pocket, and told Fesker to stay put. Waving a negligent hand, the doctor pretended disinterest, but groaned internally. Damn! Without the rotor, the engine wouldn't start. He watched resentfully as Trap disappeared into the jungle.

The jungle was Trap's element. Unlike most of the people confined on Swamp he liked it. He liked the rain, the lush vegetation, everything. Maybe it was because he came from a planet where it was hot and dry, or maybe it was the freedom, but whatever the reason, Trap looked forward to that magic moment when he stepped into the warm humid guts of the swamp. He liked the smell of rotting vegetation, the water dripping from leaf to leaf, the danger lurking just out of sight. It was exciting and comforting at the same time.

Prior to hunting people, Trap had made a living hunting monsters, skins mostly, and unlike other hunters, he used traps. Most people didn't use traps because they must be tended, and tending them required frequent trips into the jungle, and too many trips into the jungle could be fatal. But not for Trap. Somehow the swamp seemed to know him, seemed to sense his love, and sheltered him from harm. Oh he'd had plenty of close calls, but always come out fine and, to his mind, always would.

So, as Trap drifted through the jungle, he seemed more a primal force than a man. As he moved, a part of him reached out to touch the many life forms surrounding him, and somehow sensed an imbalance in the total flow of things. He smiled. Not too surprising, since both Blaster and Scuz were as imbalanced as you could get. Still, there was something else, something he couldn't quite put this finger on, but didn't like. As he neared the perimeter of the clearing, he checked the action on his needle gun, and carefully peered around the trunk of a tree.

There was the clearing, a fire in the middle, barely burning now, garbage scattered around as always, and two sleeping forms, both huddled under blankets. One had an empty bottle only inches from outstretched fingers. The other had one leg slightly elevated on a half empty equipment bag. How sweet. His premonition forgotten, Trap chuckled in anticipation. Tiptoeing across the clearing, he approached Scuz first, the bastard deserved it for sleeping on guard duty, and prepared his canteen. Nothing like a little shower first thing in the morning! He had just started to pour, when the blanket was suddenly whipped aside, and Trap found himself looking down the business end of Renn's .75.

"Surprise!"

To his credit Trap almost pulled it off. He threw the canteen in Renn's face and did his best to whip the needle gun around in time. But fast as he was, the slug from the .75 was even faster, and literally blew his head off. He fell with a soft thump.

Wiping water off of his face, Renn remembered Boater's coffee cup bouncing off his face, and smiled. He tried to stand, but found his legs unwilling to move. He'd been lying there for about six hours and they were very stiff. So he sat and exercised his legs. Finally, when everything was working again, he stood.

"Well, I see you ignored my advice and opted for the life of a hunter."

Renn whirled, the .75 coming up in a two-handed grip, his finger already starting to squeeze, when he recognized Doc Fesker. The doctor was leaning against a tree with his arms crossed in front of him. "And it seems you're good at it, too." Fesker shrugged. "Even I'm wrong once in a while."

A few hours later they were aboard *Fred,* headed for Payout, with Trap's boat bobbing along behind. Renn had just finished telling Fesker about Boater's death, and the events which followed. "So now I've got to find Cyclops and Knife."

Both men were silent for a moment, and then Fesker said, "Three for one is a pretty good tradeoff. Why not just leave it at that?"

Renn shrugged. "I can't. Not after what they did to Boater. Besides, if I don't go after the Clops, he'll come after me."

"Maybe," Fesker agreed reluctantly. "But killing him won't be easy."

"No," Renn said grimly. "It won't be easy."

Meanwhile, many miles behind them, dusk gradually edged into night, and brought with it the small things which eat the dead. Like respectful mourners, they gathered around Trap's body, and then little by little, the swamp took back one of its own.

One rotation later, *Fred* sat bobbing at the rear of Fesker's house as the two men shook hands. "I hope you win," the doctor said simply.

Renn grinned, accepting the other man's outstretched hand. "I do too."

Fesker turned, climbed the short ladder, and disappeared into his house.

Renn double-checked *Fred*'s mooring lines and went

inside the cabin. Spreading a blanket on the table, he laid out the .75, the hand blaster, and the little hide-out gun. A rifle would be a hindrance in the close quarters of the Payout Saloon. And that's where Cyclops and Knife would be. According to Fesker, they arrived at the same time each night, drank steadily for three or four hours, and staggered out. With that in mind Renn planned to arrive towards the end of the evening. If they were drunk, so much the better. He needed any edge he could get.

He cleaned and loaded each weapon, making sure he had a back-up energy pak for the blaster, and extra magazines for the .75. Even so it was still early when he finished. He tucked each weapon into its holster, killed the lights, and forced himself to wait. Suddenly time slowed to a crawl, his belly began to fill with cold lead, and his palms began to sweat.

It was noisy and crowded inside the Payout Saloon. People argued and swore in loud voices, waiters shouted orders towards the bar, and a tired looking whore stood on a tiny stage and tried to sing. No one bothered to listen.

From Marla's vantage point on the floor, the room was forest of human and wooden legs. Above and beside her sat Skunk. As usual, she was preparing to sucker a couple of hunters just in from the bush. It always worked the same way. They'd see Marla, pet her with clumsy hands, and ask Skunk where the dog came from. Skunk would tell them one of three or four lies, and mention Marla's amazing ability to do tricks. Naturally they'd clamor to see the tricks, and Skunk would agree, slyly suggesting a modest fee for each trick. More than a little drunk, and starved for any sort of entertainment, the hunters would agree, and Marla would perform. The whole process made her sick, but she did it anyway, primarily because of the additional freedom it allowed her. Most of the tricks were things like sitting up, rolling over, and fetching Skunk a beer from the bar. However, some tricks required her to make noise, barking three times when Skunk held up three fingers, and so forth. This meant freedom from the durasteel wire Skunk had previously wound around her muzzle. And, by unspoken agreement, the wire stayed off so long as Marla refrained from speech. The sight of Marla talking drove Skunk crazy, since some part of her burned-out brain thought Marla was an animal, and believed animals shouldn't speak. Also, if anyone saw Marla speak, they'd soon realize she wasn't a dog, and would no longer pay to see her do tricks. Of course, some of the saloon's regulars had caught on long ago, but they weren't about to tell the suckers anything, so Skunk was living better than she ever had before.

So Marla endured. She had little choice. There was still some time left to serve on her one-year contract, and Skunk had used some of her new-found wealth to place an explosive collar around Marla's neck. Any time Skunk wished, she could open the little black box strapped to her right wrist, touch the button inside, and blow Marla's head off.

Needless to say Marla planned to kill Skunk at the first opportunity. Skunk knew this, and was very careful. She used an elaborate system of safeguards to make sure it didn't happen. The ironic part was that the attention to detail had forced Skunk off the bottle. Marla hadn't seen her take a drink in months.

There was a sudden flurry of activity by the door, and from the hoarse laughter and crude jokes, Marla knew Cyclops and his cronies had just arrived. The one-eyed man thrived on his notoriety and loved to make an entrance. He often came dressed in some outlandish manner, or in at least one case, dressed in nothing at all. Everyone would laugh, Cyclops would take a bow, and then settle down to some serious drinking.

Of course there were other evenings too. Evenings when Cyclops arrived in a foul mood, his good eye sweeping the crowd like a laser, searching for someone to kill. But from the sound of it Cyclops was in a good mood so everyone else was, too.

People scrambled to get out of their way as Cyclops and Knife headed for Skunk's table. The two hunters who'd been talking to Skunk suddenly took off, and she sighed, resigning herself to the lost income. Marla didn't even bother to get up. Cyclops and Skunk were friends, occasional lovers, and more importantly, kindred spirits. He was therefore a regular fixture at her table.

Bending over, Cyclops gave Marla the usual pat on the head, along with a hideous smile. "Good doggie." Then he sat down next to Skunk and placed a possessive hand on her thigh. Knife made a place for himself to Skunk's right, doing his best to step on Marla's tail, and just missing.

Marla grinned, wondered where the rest of the merry mutants were, and thumped her tail against the floor a couple of times to show how much she liked seven-foot-tall psychotic freaks. Cyclops still thought she was a dog. The first night Skunk chained her to the rail outside, Cyclops had spotted her, and remembered her from the LZ. Which wasn't very surprising, since she was the only thing that looked like a dog on the whole planet. Anyway, he'd assumed she was a regular dog, which Skunk had encouraged, and suited Marla just fine. She sighed. Just another miserable evening. Oh well, maybe the Clops would keep Skunk busy, and she wouldn't have to do any tricks. Putting her head on her paws, she closed her eyes, and left her super-sensitive ears to keep watch.

Renn paused outside the door to the saloon, took a deep breath, shoved the fear down into the black hole from which it had emerged, and stepped inside. The place hadn't changed from the last time he'd been there, except now it was jam packed, and the noise was deafening. Fighting his way over to the bar, he saw Maxwell's work had progressed quite a bit, and wondered how the artist was doing. He ordered a drink, paid for it, and turned around to survey the crowd. He hadn't even started when he heard someone say, "Shit . . . ain't that the guy who went out with Boater?"

And then a mixture of comments as people turned to look. "Damn I thought the Clops did him, too . . ." "Uh-oh . . . there's gonna be trouble . . . let's get out of here." "*Dios mio* . . . he must have the biggest co-jones on the planet. . . ." "Ten to one the Clops cleans his clock . . . whaddya say?" "I dunno . . . he looks pretty hard." "Bullshit . . . nobody's hard enough to take the Clops and Knife, too."

Marla heard the comments long before either Cyclops or Skunk. Suddenly she was wide awake, her body rigid as steel. Renn! They were talking about Renn! He was here. Careful not to show the slightest sign of interest, she produced an elaborate yawn, and looked up just as someone whispered something in Knife's ear, and then backed away. Knife leaned across Skunk and whispered to Cyclops.

From the floor Marla could see only a small portion of Cyclop's face, but there was no mistaking the sudden concern. While completely ruthless, Cyclops wasn't stupid, and didn't relish the thought of a public fight, especially one where the odds were only two to one in his favor. Forcing a smile for the benefit of the onlookers, he said something to Skunk and then rose, with Knife doing likewise. As they moved away from the table, Marla saw Skunk pull her blaster from her thigh holster and place it in her lap. So . . . Cyclops had improved the odds a little more. Careful not to attract any attention, Marla eyed the black box on Skunk's right wrist, and figured her odds. The more she thought about it, the tighter the explosive collar seemed to get, until it was hard to breathe.

By the time Cyclops and Knife stood up Renn had them spotted. As people scurried to get out of the way, Renn scanned the room trying to gauge the size of the opposition. Maybe there were some more and maybe not. He'd have to chance it.

Knife and Cyclops were forty feet away when they came to a stop. Knife stood to the left with Cyclops to the right. Knife wasn't wearing a sidearm, but from his reputation, Renn knew the man was capable of throwing any of six different knives with the speed and accuracy of bullets. He was short and swarthy with a heavy beard and black eyebrows that met in the middle. The bright little eyes which hid under them were filled with animosity.

Cyclops towered over Knife, his one good eye measuring distances, his chrome eye reflecting light. His long arms hung straight down, fingertips brushing the butts of the twin .50's he wore low on each hip. With a flick of his head Cyclops threw his long, greasy hair back behind his shoulders, and smiled. It was not a pleasant sight.

Renn still held his drink in his right hand, while allowing his left to hang straight down. His most obvious weapon was the .75, and to get it he'd have to put the drink down, which would provide Cyclops with plenty of warning. That was the theory anyway. The drink was shaking a tiny bit and he hoped Cyclops wouldn't notice.

Cyclops looked him up and down before breaking the total silence which had fallen over the room. "You should have stayed dead."

As Renn brought his left arm straight up, and fired the hideout gun twice, he remembered Boater's exact words, "Don't try and bullshit 'em to death lad, kill the sons-abitches first, and talk about it later."

He hoped to kill Cyclops first, but decided it was safer to take the left target with his left hand. Two black holes appeared in Knife's chest as Renn dropped the drink and went for the .75.

Marla took Skunk's hand off just above the wrist as she started to pull her blaster out from under the table. With blood spurting from the stump, Skunk dived for the black box still strapped to her amputated hand, hoping to trigger the explosive collar. It was a serious mistake. As Skunk came down, Marla leaped up, and ripped her throat out.

Cyclops had a two-second head start and fired first. Renn felt the heavy .50 caliber slug rip through his left shoulder, spinning him around, and knocking the .75 out of his hand. As Renn fell, Cyclops missed his second shot, but scored with his third, punching a hole through Renn's right thigh.

Cyclops was squeezing the trigger one last time, when the rods lining the back of his good eye detected a flash of light, and tried to tell him about it. The message never got through. A millisecond later Renn's energy beam entered Cyclops' brain, tunneled its way through, and burned a hole in the ceiling. Cyclops fell like a huge tree, crashed through a table, and hit the floor with a heavy thud.

For a moment there was complete silence in the room, until the wizened little barkeeper peeked over the top of the bar, and said, "Well I'll be damned. Someone get Doc Fesker. The drinks are on me."

Chapter Eight

Renn walked out of Doc Fesker's place exactly one month after the fight in the Payout Saloon. His wounds had healed, his clothes felt two sizes too big, and his legs were a bit shaky. Still, it felt good to go outside again. Marla was padding along at his side, the sun was warming his back, and the air had a faint fragrance to it.

Things had changed. The main street was bone dry, and the town seemed half empty. Although this was only one of the six yearly so-called dry periods it was the longest, and therefore the best for hunting. So most hunters were out in the bush. Which reminded Renn of their own situation. Looking down at Marla, he said, "Damn, we'd better get a move on or we'll miss the whole season."

"There's no hurry," Marla cautioned. "You need time to regain your strength. Besides, *Fred*'s loaded and ready to go."

And it was true. During his month-long recovery, Marla had taken charge of his affairs, selling the boat he'd taken from Trap, and appropriating everything found in Cyclops' quarters. Two men had tried to stop her, and both wound up dripping blood on Fesker's new rug. The doctor was still grumbling.

The stolen skins had already been sold, but Marla found a hoard of money and other valuables hidden under a loose floorboard in Cyclops' quarters. She gave the valuables to the Hunter's Association in hopes they could be returned to their owners, but kept the money. A quick tally showed there was more than enough to fund a hunting season. In fact they could've taken a year off, but Renn wouldn't hear of it, insisting they couldn't afford it.

By then he was sitting up in bed, while she was curled up in a nearby chair. "We need to get off this slime ball, Marla. I want to clear my name, and you want a new body. Yeah, yeah, I know. It can't be done and all that stuff. Maybe. But money talks . . . and that's why we're going hunting as soon as we can. If there's some way out of here we're going to find it and money will help."

Marla disagreed, gently suggesting that he should be more realistic, and put his energy into building a life on Swamp.

Renn heard her out, but finally shook his head, saying, "I just can't agree, Marla. But let's back up for a moment. First, we've been talking like we're partners. Are we?"

Marla felt a lead weight drop into her stomach. Was he hoping she'd say "no?" Should she say "no" for her own sake? After all, where the hell was this relationship going? Where *could it* go? She knew she wanted something more than friendship, but that was impossible, so why prolong the torture?

As though reading her mind, Renn reached out to stroke her fur. Marla hated to have people pet her, but there was something about the way Renn did it that was different, that made her feel good. "I'm sorry, Marla. That wasn't fair. Let me rephrase the question. I'd like you for a partner . . . so how 'bout it?"

For some reason Marla found she couldn't speak, and nodded instead.

"Good. And while we're on the subject of 'us,' there's one more thing I'd like to discuss. My last medical bill."

"Damn it," Marla said, her eyes flashing as she sat up, "Doc promised me he wouldn't tell."

"Whoa," Renn said holding up a hand. "He didn't. I finally figured it out for myself. And if I wasn't so incredibly stupid, I wouldn've figured it out a long time ago. Doc doesn't do anything for free. You indentured yourself to Skunk in order to pay for my treatment. And while you were living with that bitch . . . I sat around feeling sorry for myself."

"Jonathan . . ."

"No, I'm not finished yet. I was an idiot and I apologize. There. Now I'm finished."

Although she had accepted his apology, and his gratitude, she was left with one nagging question,—did he *really* want her around? Or was it his way of paying a debt? She couldn't be sure. Nonetheless, there was a chance that he did—and a chance was better than nothing. With that decision made the rest was easy. She accepted his dream of escape—outwardly at least—and worked to make it real. And in return he gave her affection and friendship. Perhaps it wasn't perfect, but it sure beat hell out of nothing at all.

So they were partners and folk heroes to boot. Maxwell had incorporated the killing of Cyclops into his mural, Renn had become a living legend, and people took pride in talking with Marla. Her explosive collar now hung over the bar where it would fuel conversations for years to come.

So as Marla and Renn made their way down the boardwalk, everyone had a kind word to say, and everyone hurried to get out of the way. This was partly out of respect, and partly out of fear. Gaunt though he was, the .75 still hung low on Renn's right hip, and no one would ever forget the way Marla had killed Skunk.

Moving carefully, his legs still a bit unsteady, Renn followed Marla down a short flight of stairs into the street. It seemed strange to stand where water usually swirled and rushed. Now, instead of the boats Renn was used to, a rusty old crawler stood rumbling in the middle of the street. Whatever its original power plant, it now boasted a diesel engine, and looked old enough to date back to the first survey. Marla had hired it to save him the hike to the river, which was as close to Payout as *Fred* could come during the dry season.

With Marla anxiously looking on, Renn climbed slowly into the crawler's cab, and took a seat. Marla followed with a single leap and took the seat beside him. There was a horrible grinding as the driver found and then engaged first gear, followed by a sudden roar as he stepped on the accelerator, and they lurched into motion. Then, with worn treads squealing in protest, and noxious black smoke belching from the mouth of a rusty pipe, they moved down the street and out of town.

As the crawler jerked and bumped along, Renn marvelled at the swamp's magnificent transformation. Healthy new growth had sprung up to replace that which had died and rotted away during the rains. Exotic blossoms had appeared turning the normally drab jungle into a riot of color. Like the flowers of earth, these played a role in the parent plant's reproductive cycle, though a slightly different one. Here the flowers were used as decoys, luring insects and birds away from tasty reproductive parts, thereby helping the species survive. Whatever the reason, the flowers were pretty, and lifted Renn's spirits.

The crawler jerked to a halt a few minutes later. "It's just a short ways from here," Marla said, "How do you feel?"

Renn smiled. "A helluva lot better than I look. Let's go."

As Renn climbed down, Marla thanked the driver, and asked him to wait for a few minutes. By prior arrangement he would be paid from their account with the Hunter's Association. It was a complicated way to make a simple payment, but paws aren't much good for handling money, and Marla didn't want to focus Renn's attention on her obvious shortcomings. Besides, she told herself, it's what you do that counts. It sounded good. But as Marla jumped down, and hurried to catch up with Renn, she wished she believed it.

To Renn's amusement he found himself slipping into the ways of the swamp. His hand hung near the .75, his ears listened for unusual sounds, and his eyes took nothing for granted. Good. Cyclops might be dead, but the swamp was very much alive, and dangerous as hell.

As Marla fell in beside him, the jungle turned to marsh, and before long the marsh turned to swamp. As they squished their way towards the river, the familiar water smells assailed Renn's nose, and there, pretty as a picture, sat *Fred*. Thanks to Marla's efficiency he was spic and span from bow to stern.

Two guards suddenly materialized between them and the boat, recognized Marla, and waved. Both were middle-aged women, and to Renn's surprise, identical twins. They were heavily armed and looked quite competent. Marla handled the introductions. "Jonathan, I'd like you to meet Pat and Peg. Don't ask me which is which."

"It don't matter," one of the women said cheerfully, "long as *we* know the difference. Glad to meet you Jonathan."

"Likewise," the other twin agreed. "You did good killing the Clops. We got enough problems without trash like him."

"It's a pleasure, ladies," Renn replied gravely. "As for killing the Clops, well, I was damn lucky and had lots of help." He indicated Marla. Cyberdogs don't blush, but they can feel warm inside, and Marla did.

Quick to change the subject, Marla said, "Thanks for taking care of *Fred*. Your pay's waiting at the Hunter's Association."

"It was our pleasure," the first twin said. "You've got a real nice boat there."

Meanwhile her sister had gone aboard *Fred*, and now

returned carrying two packs. They spoke in unison. "You take care out there."

"We will," Renn assured them, and waved as they headed for the road, and the waiting crawler.

Once the twins had disappeared from sight Renn and Marla went aboard and prepared to cast off. This was the moment Marla had both dreaded and looked forward to for weeks. The idea of going off alone with Renn, of having him all to herself, made her spirits soar. Yet she knew life in the swamps would provide Renn with daily reminders of just how limited her abilities were. She couldn't use weapons, or clean the boat, or tie a knot, or cook a meal, and even worse, didn't need to. Even the ritual of eating, and the human contact which went with it was denied her. For some reason nobody wants to sit around and talk while you pop open a hatch in your back, aim your receptors at the sun, and suck up some rays. Fortunately she didn't have to do it very often.

Meanwhile Renn was inspecting the boat. Starting in the bow, he gradually worked his way back, sticking his head into every storage compartment as he did so. Finally he reached the stern, and straightened up. "Nice job, Marla. Even Boater would've been pleased!"

"Yeah," Marla thought to herself, "I'm just great when I can get people to do things for me, but let's see how you feel in a few days."

In spite of Marla's fears, the first few weeks rolled easily by. Renn made the chores look easy, and, much to Marla's surprise, she found there were things she could do. By hanging one leg over the tiller, and sitting on her haunches, she could steer. And while she couldn't tie knots, she became quite adept at undoing them with her teeth. So it was a pleasant time, made more so by the fact that Renn could only hunt for a few hours each day. Then his wounds would start to ache, forcing him to stop. So they spent long lazy afternoons cruising, or just taking it easy, lounging around the decks, and dashing inside to escape the occasional showers, which came more frequently as the next rainy season approached.

Gradually, bit by bit, they each told their life stories. Hours passed as they talked and laughed, getting to know each other, while living in the past, until some thought or comment would shatter the spell and remind them of Marla's imprisonment. And even though they tried to avoid such episodes, they were bound to happen, and Renn knew that Marla sometimes cried herself to sleep.

As the days passed, Renn grew stronger and stronger, until he could once again put in a full day's work. And though Marla couldn't help with some things when it came to hunting, she was the perfect partner. They worked as a team. Marla would slip through the jungle, her enhanced senses picking out targets of opportunity, while Renn came along behind, shooting whatever she flushed from the undergrowth. Renn was hesitant at first, afraid she might be ambushed by some monster before he could get there. But he soon learned not to worry. It was a rare monster that escaped notice by Marla's infrared vision, amplified hearing, and keen sense of smell. And the one or two that did quickly fell victim to her slashing teeth.

They were so efficient in fact, that they piled up more skins in a few weeks than Renn and Boater had gathered in months of hunting. As a result they decided to build a shed in which to store the skins while they went out to hunt for more. They could've constructed a lodge like Boater's, but chose not to, deciding *Fred* was sufficient for their needs. After what had happened to Boater, Renn favored a floating and therefore mobile, home.

So, after looking at a number of potential sites, they chose a small island, one of many located towards the center of a large lake. By building low to the ground, using lots of camouflage, and being careful not to leave any signs of their visit, they made the shed almost impossible to spot. Once it was complete, they filled it half full of skins, locked up, and took off for some more hunting.

But the rainy season was in full force so they wound up doing a lot less hunting, and a lot more sitting inside *Fred*'s snug cabin. For hours on end a lead-gray sky would dump water on the planet below, beating the roof of *Fred*'s cabin like a drum, and then, just when it seemed the rain would never stop, the downpour would cease suddenly, as if someone had turned off a gigantic faucet. Then a thick mist would slowly rise, making it hard to see more than a few feet away.

It was such a time when they heard the sounds of distant combat. The sounds were muffled by jungle and mist, but there was no mistaking the rattle of slug throwers on full automatic. At first Renn thought it was a hunter, someone new and inexperienced with more ammunition than brains. But he soon changed his mind. For one thing, it sounded like several weapons were being fired at once. He turned to Marla for confirmation. "Am I losing my mind . . . or is someone fighting a war out there?"

Marla's head was cocked to one side, as she stared into the mist, and turned her audio receptors up to max. "No . . . I'd say there's six . . . maybe seven auto slug throwers . . . and some kind of heavy duty handgun. The guy with the handgun fires twelve times . . . probably a full magazine . . . reloads and then does it all over again."

Renn's mind was racing as he steered *Fred* in towards the shore. What the hell was going on? If this was some kind of territorial feud between a couple of hunters he wanted no part of it. On the other hand, if some poor bastard was fighting the likes of Cyclops and his gang, then he'd want to lend a hand. Unfortunately, there was only one way to find out.

Renn moored *Fred* to a convenient tree, and grabbed his blast rifle, an extra energy pack, plus a fistful of magazines for the .75. Then, with Marla ranging ahead, he slipped into the jungle. Water squished and gurgled under his boots, plants made a swishing sound as they slid along his skins, and the gunfire grew louder. Ahead he caught glimpses of Marla, weaving in and out of the mist, like an elemental wolf spirit fleeing the light of day.

Abruptly, everything changed. At first Renn thought he'd stepped into a clearing. Then he realized it wasn't a clearing at all, but a broad swath of flattened jungle. Except for adult trees, every piece of vegetation had been pounded flat, and then trampled into green paste. If he hadn't known better, he would have assumed some sort of huge machine had rolled through the jungle, leaving a path the size of a super highway behind. But a glance at the ground showed otherwise. Thousands, maybe even millions, of long three-toed feet had flattened everything in sight. They looked like roo tracks, but that couldn't be, since roos were loners. Still, tracks didn't lie, and here were a zillion tracks, all telling him that roos like to come together and tromp jungles. And from the sound of the gunfire, some poor bastards had managed to get in their way.

He moved quickly, staying towards the edge of the roo path. If he ran into trouble the jungle would offer some cover. Because of the ground mist, he couldn't see more than ten or twenty feet ahead, so he damned near tripped over the bodies. Roos all right. A cluster of six or eight. They'd been riddled with automatic fire. He moved on, and found more dead roos, some in clumps of four and five, others strung out in lines of fifteen or more. Gradually, a picture was emerging. The hunters would run for awhile, stop and make a stand, and then be forced to run once again.

Now he was running too, or trying to, constantly fighting the accumulations of mud, which quickly built up on his boots. Up ahead, he saw something in the mud. It wasn't roos. Quickly looking left and right, he decided to take a chance, and dashed out into the middle of the churned up muck. Damn! Human bodies . . . or what was left of them. Razor-sharp teeth had left little more than a few broken bones, scraps of cloth, and pieces of light body armor. Body armor. Renn thought to himself, hunters don't wear body armor, they wear skins. He picked up a large piece. The camo pattern looked familiar somehow, but it couldn't be. It *looked* like standard marine issue! Imperial Marines on Swamp? Stampeding roos, Imperial Marines, what next? The poor bastards had apparently tried to make another stand and were overrun.

Renn started off once again, making for the side of the trail, unlimbering his blast rifle as he ran. Now the gunfire was a long rippling roar from just ahead. And there was something else, a horrible gibbering sound, as thousands of roos screamed in unison. The sound made Renn's blood run cold.

Suddenly Marla materialized at his side, yelling, "Quick, over here."

Seconds later they were crouched behind a tangle of fallen trees, looking out on a scene straight from hell. In front of them was a seething mass of roo monsters. They filled the clearing to overflowing. And slithering all around and in between them were their snake-like tails, separate now, and eager to be in on the kill.

Facing this churning mass of hostile flesh were five men and two women. They stood back to back on a small rise, their weapons spewing death, mowing down wave after wave of ravenous monsters.

One, a huge black man wearing the tattered remains of a section leader's uniform, was firing a heavy tri-barreled machine gun as though it were a machine pistol. As the weapon's recoil shook his body into a blur, the front rank of roo monsters danced and fell, but was soon replaced from behind. Renn could see the marine's mouth open and his lips move as he screamed defiance at the oncoming horde. His voice, however, was completely lost in the hammering roar of gunfire and the gibbering demands of the roos.

Suddenly a roo tail wrapped itself around the section leader's right leg, and slithered upwards towards his throat. Seeing this, a blonde woman took careful aim with a large-caliber hand gun and blew the thing's head off. The section leader didn't even notice.

No doubt about it, this was a last stand. The situation called for a brilliant plan. But Renn didn't have one so he did the only thing he could.

Resting his blast rifle on a convenient log, he turned to Marla and yelled, "Cover my back!" She nodded, and a second later he opened up with the weapon. He started with the rearmost rank of roo monsters, and picked them off with almost mechanical precision. It was tempting to just hose them down, but then he would probably wound more roos than he killed and draw attention to himself right off the top. He hoped to kill quite a few before they realized what was happening. So it was aim— fire, aim—fire, aim—fire.

As they were hit, the roos would jerk, fall, and lay kicking in the mud. If uninjured, their symbiotic tails immediately went after a new host, and often wound up in fights, as two or more snakes tried to link up with the same roo. This added still another strange element to the scene. As auto slug throwers beat out a hellish rhythm, roos fell, their skins shifting to match the mud, their tails slithering this way and that, while a wispy white mist drifted slowly upwards, now revealing, now concealing, the insane orgy of death.

It went on and on. Just as Renn had hoped, it took the

roos awhile to figure out what was happening, but when they did, it seemed as if they were controlled by a single mind. Suddenly they divided their forces into two. The first half continued to attack the seven humans, or was it six now, Renn couldn't tell, while the rest turned, and headed straight at him.

Seeing this, the marines were heartened, and fought even harder. But Renn had little chance to notice because the gibbering horde was almost on him. There was no need to aim now. He held the firing stud down and simply swept the blast rifle back and forth across the oncoming wall of flesh. Bodies were cut in half, limbs amputated, and still they came. They were only yards away when the blast rifle's energy pack registered empty.

Dropping the rifle, Renn drew the .75, shifted it to his left hand, and used his right to pull the hand blaster. As the roos swept around him Renn alternated the two weapons, firing one and then the other, each shot killing or maiming a crazed monster.

As the surviving roos circled Renn, and turned inwards, Marla was there to defend his back. Fangs and claws tore futilely at the metal and plastic of her body while she ripped the creatures apart. But even as she killed them, Marla knew the roos would win. Any moment now they'd overwhelm her with sheer numbers. And then they'd take Renn from behind. No! she thought. That mustn't happen. A new wave of roos hit and Marla fought with renewed vigor. She became a whirling dervish, a killing machine that ripped and tore, slashed and cut, on and on.

And then the battle was over. As if responding to some invisible signal the roos turned and ran, disappearing into the jungle, leaving a whole host of tail-snakes to slither after them. Apparently they'd had enough.

Marla looked at Renn and saw that he was bleeding from a dozen small wounds. But that didn't concern her as much as the dull preoccupied look in his eyes. He released the empty magazine from the .75 and inserted a fresh one like an automaton. It was as though his spirit had gone somewhere else and left his body to carry on alone. There were roo monsters piled three and four high around him. Some were still twitching. He holstered the .75 and used the hand blaster to shoot each one in the head.

"Jonathan?"

Renn turned as if surprised to see her. He smiled, and suddenly life flooded back into his face. "There you are Marla . . . is everything all right?"

Marla heaved a silent sigh of relief, and looked back along a scarred flank. "I guess so. There's nothing a little plastic and some wire mesh won't fix up." She looked up at Renn. "You, however, are leaking."

"And that's for damn sure," a basso voice said, as the big section leader stepped out of the clearing. Turning slightly, he cupped his hands and yelled, "Hey Doc, get your ass over here. This guys leakin' red stuff all over my boots." Turning back to Renn the marine stuck out a massive paw and said, "Section Leader Marvin Jumo, Imperial Marines. Next time I play baby sitter to a bunch of biologists . . . I'll bring an armored division."

Renn laughed. As they shook hands Renn took an instant liking to the big marine. He had intelligent brown eyes, high cheek bones, a flat nose pounded even flatter no doubt in countless bar room fights, a huge grin, and teeth so white they positively sparkled. "Jonathan Renn at your service, and may I present my partner, Marla Marie Mendez."

"Glad to meet you both," Jumo said, accepting Marla's raised paw without the slightest hesitation. "Real glad. If it wasn't for you, I'd be meeting my ancestors right now, and from what Pappy said, they're some mean sonsabitches."

The conversation was interrupted by the arrival of another marine, this one as little as the section leader was big. She had a small pixie face, short brown hair, and an incredible load of gear. An auto slug thrower was slung over one shoulder, an ammo carrier over the other, and the straps of a class two med kit were gathered in her right hand. Jumo pointed at Renn. "There's your patient, Doc . . . go to it."

Doc nodded, her bright little eyes quickly sorting Renn's wounds by severity, as she dumped the slug thrower and ammo carrier on the the ground. She opened the med kit and pointed to a fallen tree trunk. Renn obeyed her silent orders to sit down.

"The doc don't talk much," Jumo said with a smile, "which works out just fine . . . cause I do."

"Truer words were never uttered," a male voice said. Turning slightly, Renn saw a pleasant looking man in tattered camos step out of the clearing. He had Euro-asian features, and thick black hair, which was parted in the middle, and combed straight back. Good-natured intelligence gleamed in his brown eyes. His right arm was encased in a bloodstained sling.

Jumo made a face. "Look who's talking. This is Doctor George Chin. Chin, I'd like you to meet the folks who saved our bacon. That's Jonathan Renn over there, and the short furry one is Marla Mendez. Don't mess with her . . . she bites."

Marla laughed in spite of herself. She'd have killed most people who called her short and furry, but something about the way Jumo said it made Marla feel included, different but accepted. She wasn't even embarrassed as Chin bent to shake her paw. "It's a pleasure, Doctor Chin. Welcome to Swamp."

Straightening up, Chin gestured towards the nearest pile of corpses and said, "They gave us one hell of a welcome, all right. "What's the deal? Are they always like that?"

Renn raised one eyebrow. "That's a good question

Doctor, one I was planning to ask you. We've never seen this particular species behave like this, but isn't that your job? Studying the local fauna?"

Chin looked sheepish, and then glanced at Jumo who smiled and shook his head. The sound of approaching voices gave Chin a perfect excuse to run off and greet the newcomers.

Renn got the distinct feeling the scientist had something to hide, and whatever it was, Jumo was in on it, too. For a moment Renn considered asking Jumo what was going on, but quickly rejected the notion, sensing he'd never get anything out of the marine that way. So he tried another tack. "No offense, but aren't you folks traveling a bit light? There's a lot more than just roos to worry about here, you know."

"Like dangerous criminals," Marla added dryly.

Jumo nodded soberly and tactfully ignored Marla's remark. "Roos? Is that what you call 'em? Well, I guess the name fits. They do look a bit like homicidal kangaroos. In answer to your question we didn't plan to land. As you probably guessed, we're from the space station. This was supposed to be a low-level photo recon, but we had a power failure, and went down like a rock. What's left of the shuttle is a few miles thataway." Jumo pointed east.

Renn nodded, wondering why a photo recon mission would carry a team of marines, but knowing it wouldn't do any good to ask.

"I'm still not sure what the problem was," the marine said, "since both our pilots were killed in the crash. Anyway, we were still pulling survival gear out of the wreckage when the roos hit us. We weren't very well prepared, so we ran." He shrugged. "Turns out that wasn't a very good idea."

Renn knew Jumo was right. They should have stayed with the wreckage and used it as a fort. And from the expression on Jumo's face, Renn got the distinct impression someone else had given the orders to run.

"They picked us off one at a time as we ran," Jumo continued. "That's how we lost Sanchez and Goldman. Then we made a stand about a half mile back. That slowed 'em down . . . but cost us Corporal Burns and Lieutenant Costello."

Doc looked up from bandaging Renn's leg and said, "Silly bitch."

"Keep it zipped, Doc," Jumo said sternly.

Doc shrugged as if to say, "So sue me," and went back to work.

Renn remembered finding the pathetic remains in the middle of the roo path, and knew who'd given the orders to run. Lieutenant Costello. Well, she'd paid a heavy price for her mistake. Too bad Sanchez, Goldman and Burns had paid it too.

Further conversation was forestalled by the arrival of two more marines supporting a woman between them. There was a fresh bandage around her right thigh. Chin brought up the rear.

Marla's heart sank. Even smeared with mud and patches of dried blood the woman was beautiful. She had blonde hair, bright blue eyes, high cheekbones, and full red lips. And Marla could tell that, in spite of her baggy camos, she had a nice figure as well. A single glance at Renn confirmed her worst fears. He was looking at the woman with an expression of mixed hunger and adoration. It made Marla sick. Anyone could see the blonde hair was permatreated. But, she told herself resignedly, so what. Every thing else she's got is real . . . and that's more than you can say."

The two marines eased the woman down onto the tree trunk next to Renn. "Thanks guys," she said cheerfully. "You make a great taxi." Then she turned to Renn and stuck out his hand. Renn noticed she had the firm grip and short fingernails of someone who works with their hands. Not what you'd expect from a person who spends the day peering into a microscope, or running programs on a computer. Her voice was warm and friendly. "Hello. I'm Vanessa Cooper-Smith."

"*Doctor* Vanessa Cooper-Smith," Chin added playfully. "And even though she looks like a holo hostess she's got a few smarts."

"More than *he* does," Doc added getting to her feet.

"Doc . . ." Jumo cautioned, but stopped when Chin waved a negligent hand.

"Jonathan Renn. It's a pleasure to meet you," Renn said. He wanted to say more, but was suddenly aware that he hadn't been around women for a long time, and was afraid he'd make a fool of himself. Well, that wasn't quite true. There was Marla, but outside of his fantasies that didn't count. He suddenly realized he hadn't introduced her.

"Dr. Cooper-Smith, may I present Marla Marie Mendez. Marla, Dr. Cooper-Smith."

The scientist lifted an eyebrow as she nodded in Marla's direction, as if to say, "What have we here?" Renn missed it, but the little byplay cut through Marla like a knife. "It's a pleasure, Marla. I hope you'll call me Vanessa. Thanks for your help."

Marla nodded stiffly, not trusting herself to speak. Neither made an attempt to shake "hands."

"Much as I hate to interrupt these pleasantries," Jumo said, "I think we should get out of here. With all this meat laying around we could have uninvited guests any minute."

Chin and Vanessa looked towards Renn, who nodded his agreement. "The section leader's right. This much food is going to attract some ugly customers." He shook his head regretfully. "To bad we don't have time to skin 'em. There's a fortune in skins laying around out there."

Vanessa wrinkled her nose at the thought. "If you'd be

kind enough to act as our guide, I'm sure we could compensate you for the loss."

"Oh goody," Marla said sarcastically. "She's going to compensate us for our loss. How generous."

Renn frowned, and Marla realized her comment had backfired on her. "Come on Marla . . . I think that's a very generous offer. Vanessa will too—once we tell her what all those skins were worth."

Everyone laughed, but Marla knew it was a battle lost, and there was nothing she could do to make things better.

Renn stood, released the dead energy pack from his blast rifle, and inserted the back-up. "Marla and I have a boat moored nearby. I suggest we go there to regroup. Then we can figure out what to do next."

"Sure," Marla thought to herself. "Let's give these imperial moochers half our supplies. Then they'll lift, leaving us here to starve." *Fred* was *theirs*, the one place where she was safe from hurt, where she had Renn to herself. Now *they* were about to invade it, and *she* would take over. On one level Marla knew her thoughts were full of self-pity, but was too busy wallowing in it to care.

Marla kept her feelings to herself, and Renn's suggestion met with universal approval. So after a little organizing by Jumo, they gathered their few possessions together, and followed Renn into the jungle. Vanessa said her leg felt much better, so she walked beside Renn, the two of them talking and laughing. Next came Doc and Chin, followed by the privates, Issacs and Ford. Jumo and Marla brought up the rear. Was this arrangement an accident she wondered? Or a carefully thought out strategy? They were criminals after all, and for all Jumo knew, they might have friends waiting in ambush or god knows what. So she wouldn't blame him for taking what precautions he could. And he'd done a good job. By placing Renn in front, with three heavily armed marines right behind him, and keeping her in the rear where he could keep an eye on her, Jumo had effectively divided the potential enemy forces in half.

If the big marine had such thoughts, he concealed them well, apparently intent on watching their back trail, talking a mile a minute at the same time.

Meanwhile Marla listened to the laughter that floated back from Renn and Vanessa, made perfunctory replies to Jumo's chatter, and thought her own dark thoughts. Things were changing. She could sense it. And when things changed it was usually for the worse. A light breeze suddenly came up, and the leaves and branches around her began to bob and sway, as if nodding in agreement. Slowly at first, and then with increasing force, it began to rain.

Chapter Nine

They buried the dead marines during a heavy rain. As ranking noncom, it was up to Jumo to say the words. "I don't know if these people believed in God or not. We didn't talk about things like that much. But I know Waller and Ho loved to fly . . . and they were damned good at it. They'd do anything to leave the station and rack up a few hours. This time it got 'em killed. And Sanchez, well she liked men, tall, short, fat, skinny, she didn't care, long as they could sing in Spanish, or were willing to learn. Goldman was, well, he was different. He spent most of his spare time reading micro spools. I don't know what it said on 'em, but whatever it was made him laugh a lot, and then we'd laugh too. And Corporal Burns, well, there wasn't anyone that could handle a flamer like him. Too bad he didn't have one when he needed it most. I didn't know Lieutenant Costello very well, her being an officer and all, but I know she loved the green hills of New Britain. Anyway, if there's a god out there, I hope you'll take good care of them. They were marines."

It took only a few hours to bury the dead, but it took three days of hard work to clear an LZ for the shuttle. It turned out that Chin was good at electronics. He managed to piece together a transmitter from the piles of shuttle junk Renn and the marines brought him. This made Renn a little suspicious, since Chin seemed to be a lot better at electronics than he was at biology, but he decided to keep his thoughts to himself.

Five hours after Chin's first transmission, a shuttle roared overhead. Help had arrived. Renn and Marla watched with detached amusement as everyone else jumped up and down with excitement.

Chin dashed into the cabin as the roar of the shuttle died away and turned on the transmitter. "Chin to shuttle, Chin to shuttle, you just passed over our position, repeat, just passed over our position." Since they had no receiver he said it over and over again, hoping the shuttle crew would home in on the signal.

Outside, all eyes were on the sky. The dense layer of clouds made for poor visibility, but they looked anyway, hoping to see the shuttle return. And return it did, dropping out of the clouds with a mighty roar and pushing a tidal wave of displaced air before it. As the shuttle came to a stop and hung suspended on its repellors, the jungle foliage swayed this way and that, while the muddy water of the channel was pressed completely flat. A black rectangle appeared in the bright metal of the shuttle's hull, and moments later, a bright orange dot fell towards them.

It became an orange blob, then an orange rectangle, and then a parachute suddenly blossomed over it to slow its descent. As the parachute drifted slowly towards the ground, the pilot waggled his wings, goosed his engines, and disappeared into the clouds.

Seeing that the chute would hit about two miles to the north, Renn, Jumo and two marines took off to get it.

Marla felt good. The air drop would ease the demands on their supplies, plus it should be only a matter of time before the survivors were rescued. And the sooner the better. Though friendly as always, Renn was increasingly preoccupied, and Marla knew why. Dr. Vanessa Cooper-Smith hung on his every word, oohed and aahed over his knowledge of the swamps, and took full advantage of her considerable assets.

Renn was attractive, but Doctor Cooper-Smith's interest

seemed forced somehow. Why would a woman like Vanessa be so taken with a criminal? A criminal condemned to life on a prison planet? It didn't make sense. Or was Vanessa so in love she couldn't think straight? Well, either way the sooner she left the better.

The search party returned two hours later carrying an orange trunk. It was about six feet long, three feet wide, and constructed of heavy plastic. Inside was a treasure trove of survival gear, food, medical supplies, and best of all, a small transceiver.

Minutes later they were communicating with the space station via the tiny satellite, which the shuttle had dumped into geosynchronous orbit over their position.

Once the casualties were mourned, and the survivors cheered, serious planning got underway. Marla assumed they would simply land, pick up the survivors, and take off. She soon learned it wouldn't be that easy.

Having already lost one of their two shuttles, plus their best pilots, those in charge were reluctant to take any more chances than they had to. They wouldn't be able to get another shuttle for some time, and since the remaining craft was also their only lifeboat, they were understandably cautious. So, to safeguard the shuttle, a temporary LZ would have to be built.

A small island was chosen about a mile from *Fred*. Energy weapons were used to clear away the jungle. The shuttle's weapons could have accomplished the same thing in a few minutes, but that would have meant an extra trip, an idea quickly vetoed by station management. So, every tree, shrub, and plant was leveled. Then the whole mess was set on fire. At first the wet vegetation refused to burn, but by the judicious placement of some volatile fire weed, and the addition of some kerosene from *Fred*'s stove, they finally got a roaring blaze.

Meanwhile Vanessa had earned Marla's grudging respect. When it came to clearing brush the blonde scientist pitched in with a will, often working shoulder to shoulder with Renn, and never complaining. And if that wasn't bad enough, Marla had to sit around and watch. Without hands she couldn't help much. So she watched from a distance as they kissed, silhouettes against the dull red flames of the fire. With the kiss came a dull ache deep inside her, which, unable to ease, she did her best to ignore.

So she watched the dense black smoke boil upwards towards the sky, instead. Fortunately the clouds were low, and unless someone was very close, they wouldn't see the smoke. Though he hadn't said much, Marla knew Jumo was concerned about Swamp's other residents, and she really couldn't blame him. There were some very nasty customers out there, gangs like the one Cyclops had run, who would regard the scientists as a crop ripe for harvesting. So Jumo posted sentries and scattered electronic sensors over the approaches to the camp.

These were quite primitive as sensors go, being the sort of broad spectrum devices included in standard survival kits. Unlike the more sophisticated types, these had no intelligence of their own, and would respond to almost anything. Hearing noise, or sensing body heat, they sent a signal to a small control panel in *Fred*'s cabin. The glowing red dot would show the location of the sensor, but not the nature of the potential threat.

As a result Marla spent a good deal of her time venturing out into the rain, checking on sensors which had heard a dead tree fall, or sensed the passage of a roo monster. This was not a pleasant duty, but Marla took pride in it, since she could do it better than anyone else. The fact that Vanessa was afraid to go into the jungle alone made it even better.

So Marla welcomed the morning of the fourth day, and the shuttle which came with it. By nightfall the Imperials would be gone, and things could return to normal. The shuttle hovered as it played its energy weapons back and forth across the still smouldering surface of the small island. Everything the blue beams touched turned to molten soup. Here and there the molten muck overflowed exploding into steam as it hit the surrounding water and quickly condensed into mushy rock. As soon as the surface of the island glowed red, the energy beams snapped off, the shuttle waggled its stubby wings, and lifted towards space.

The rain poured down all afternoon, sending up sheets of steam, and gradually cooling the surface of the island until it formed a hard crust. When the shuttle returned, the uninvited guests would leave. Marla couldn't wait. So when Renn approached, and suggested a walk, it seemed as if things were finally getting back to normal.

They chose the well-beaten path to the wrecked shuttle, not because it was especially pleasant, but because it was the easiest the follow. When they stopped using it the path would disappear in a matter of days. "They won't try to salvage the shuttle will they?" Marla asked.

Renn frowned. "I don't think so. Why?"

"Because it's a potential gold mine," Marla answered patiently. "The durasteel alone would fetch a good price back in Payout, not to mention the seats and other stuff."

Renn remembered the toilet Doc Fesker had salvaged from a similar wreck and laughed. "Don't forget the toilet."

It was Marla's turn to frown. "I don't get it."

"Never mind," Renn replied. "Salvaging the wreck is a damned good idea. Should've thought of it myself. But first we've got a unique opportunity, and I think we should grab it."

"What kind of an opportunity?" Marla asked, immediately suspicious.

Renn didn't answer right away. They'd just stepped into a small clearing. The shuttle had cut a swath of destruction through the soft flesh of the jungle, which now lay in a twisted heap, a memorial to its own destruction. But the swamp had already started the process of healing itself. New growth was poking its way up through the mud, eager to reach the light and carve out a niche for itself in the new order of things.

Renn made a mental note to take compass bearings. In a few months the wreckage would be covered with new growth and almost impossible to find. Feeling her eyes on him he looked down. "How would you like a little vacation from all this?"

For a second she wondered what he was talking about, and then it hit like a ton of bricks. "Go up there? What the hell for? It'll be that much worse when they dump us off again."

Renn shrugged. "Maybe . . . but I could use a little R & R, and whether you admit it or not, so could you. Among other things they've promised to test your systems and perform any maintenance they can."

The prospect was more attractive than Renn could know. Marla's body had taken a lot of abuse over the last few months, and she'd been concerned about maintenance. Still, the whole thing sounded like something Vanessa had cooked up to prolong her relationship with Renn. If so, Marla wasn't about to tag along and watch. "Thanks, but no thanks. I suspect it's you they want anyhow. I'll wait here."

"You're wrong Marla," Renn lied. "They invited us both." Actually Vanessa had invited him, and he'd insisted Marla be allowed to come as well. Vanessa had reluctantly agreed. Now Renn used his winning argument. Or at least he hoped it was his winning argument. "Look at it this way, you get a free tune-up, and we get our pick of supplies."

Marla's ears perked up. "Really? Our pick of supplies?"

Renn nodded. "That's right. In payment for all those roos we didn't get to skin."

Marla was tempted. Chances were they could recover the

supplies their guests had used up, and then some. Even if that meant watching Renn and Vanessa play kissy face it might still be worth it. Besides, she could tell that Renn really wanted her to go. "OK, you're on. But I still think there's something funny going on here. Why all this gratitude? Why not just say 'thanks,' and lift?"

Renn shook his head in mock exasperation. "Marla, Marla, you're so cynical. I'll admit it seems a little too good to be true, but let's go with the flow and see what develops."

They returned to *Fred*, spent some time cleaning up, and moved him into a narrow side channel. Then they doubled up his mooring lines and used some cut brush to camouflage him. When they were done Renn figured the odds against anyone stumbling across *Fred* were about a million to one. As he and Marla made their way to the LZ, Renn found he was looking forward to the upcoming excursion. At the very least it would provide a welcome break from life on Swamp, and who knows? Maybe it would offer some other form of profit. At the very least he'd have some more time with Vanessa.

An hour later, a very nervous shuttle pilot touched down onto the steaming surface of the makeshift LZ, and swore steadily as his passengers took their own sweet time climbing aboard. Lt. Fitz wasn't ugly, in fact women found his even features and thick brown hair quite attractive, but they wouldn't have recognized him right now. His skin was parchment white, his eyes wide and dilated, his lips pulled back into a tight smile. One hand hovered over the big red emergency boost button, while the other babied the stick. The problem was that Fitz didn't have much experience. As a result he was scared shitless. Waller and Ho could fly anything anywhere, and if this planet had killed them, then it was a bad place to be. Like all the station personnel, Fitz was trained for a variety of back-up jobs, and shuttle pilot was one of them. Why couldn't he have been back-up cook? Or back-up librarian? This was his third trip to the surface and he hoped it would be his last.

"Well, we're aboard . . . what the hell are you waiting for, Lieutenant?" The voice belonged to Chin. He couldn't wait to leave, plus, he held Fitz in rather low regard anyway.

Fitz swore. He'd been so wrapped up in his own thoughts he'd missed the ready light. "OK asshole," Fitz thought to himself, "if it's speed you want . . . try this." His right hand slammed down on the emergency boost button and the shuttle took off like a bullet. Every passenger except Marla passed out. Though immobile under the additional G's, she was completely conscious, but wished she wasn't. It was the damned motion sickness again. At least her bionic body would save her from the humiliation of throwing up all over everyone.

Thanks to his flight suit, Fitz had no trouble coping with the additional G's. As the shuttle achieved orbit he dumped emergency power, and heaved a sigh of relief. But his troubles weren't over. Moments later Chin came to and gave him a royal ass-chewing. Fitz just kept mumbling, "Yes sir, sorry sir," until the enraged civilian finally gave up and killed the intercom.

Meanwhile Fitz saw a spark of reflected light up ahead. The station. Good. With a grunt of satisfaction he flipped some switches, tapped a series of keys, and leaned back to enjoy the ride. The on-board computer would take it from here, thank God. No way was Mrs. Fitz's son going for a manual approach. If they wanted that kind of bullshit they could damned well round up a regular pilot.

As the computer worked out a leisurely but safe approach, Renn took the opportunity to inspect the space station. It filled the viewscreen on the forward bulkhead. It seemed small by the normal standards of the human empire.

Of course this was a research station, not an orbital factory complete with residential areas. Renn had seen all sorts of space stations during his travels, ranging from the ominous bulk of Imperial weapons platforms, to airy creations, more sculptures than habitats. The one floating towards them fell somewhere in between. The outermost part of the station consisted of two large tubular hoops set at right angles to each other.

Each hoop was thousands of feet across, and perhaps fifteen feet in diameter, suggesting they were probably hollow. Spinning within the framework of the hoops was a large globe, its surface a patchwork quilt of solar receptors, antennae, cooling fins, and other assorted gear. Renn assumed that the hoops would be used for docking and storage, while the spinning globe would function as the station proper. The spin would provide those inside with artificial gravity.

His theories soon proved correct. He felt a gentle bump as the shuttle made contact with one of four docking platforms spaced around the circumference of a single hoop. One for each shuttle, plus two for emergencies or visitors. There was a clanking sound as the shuttle was mechanically locked into place, followed by a series of dull thuds and faintly felt vibrations.

Outside robo hoses emerged from their metal lairs, slithered towards their assigned fittings, and pulsed with temporary life as a variety of fluids flowed through them and into the shuttle they served.

Inside Renn heard the hiss of equalizing pressure as the shuttle's main hatch cycled open. There was momentary confusion and a lot of good-natured joking as everyone released at once and floated into each other. But since the station personnel were experts at zero G the confusion was soon sorted out and they all lined up to leave the shuttle.

Though quite experienced at weightlessness himself,

Renn stayed back, waiting for the others to clear out. For one thing, he knew Marla would need some help, and for another, there was the question of the shuttle. Should he steal it or not?

With their minds firmly fixed on showers and the other amenities the station had to offer, both scientists and marines alike were in a hurry to disembark. In fact, Vanessa was the first one out the hatch. He and Marla were being left to fend for themselves. That suggested a high level of either trust or stupidity. Renn thought it was trust, but there was no way to be sure.

Trying to look bored he scanned the shuttle's spartan interior for signs of electronic surveillance. He didn't find any. And why should he? The station had no reason to distrust its own personnel and didn't normally invite convicts up for dinner, so security should be minimal, especially aboard the shuttle. Furthermore, they had no way to know he was an experienced pilot, a pilot with a blaster tucked under his left arm, and a derringer in his boot. Yes, it would be easy to lock the hatch behind them, immobilize the incompetent idiot in the control room, and blast off.

But where would they go? Like most of its breed, the shuttle wasn't equipped with a hyperdrive. It was designed for in-system use only, and was in many ways more a plane than a space ship. It would therefore take multiple lifetimes to reach the nearest civilized planet, assuming he had a limitless supply of fuel and food, which he didn't.

"You coming Jon?" Jumo was upside down, looking back from the main hatch. He grinned, white teeth sparkling.

Renn waved. Did the bastard know what he was thinking? If so he didn't seem too worried. The marine waved back, executed a neat somersault, and disappeared.

Renn turned to Marla and found she was grinning. And like most canine smiles, this one looked more like a leer than a smile. "You were thinking about stealing this tub weren't you? Naughty, naughty. Life as a criminal has warped your mind."

Renn laughed as he stripped off his belt and looped it around her middle. "Look who's talking." Grabbing a handhold, he released his harness, and reached for hers. As she floated free he grabbed hold of his belt and used it as a handle. Zero G isn't easy without hands.

Doing her best to ignore the sick feeling in her nonexistent stomach, Marla felt both humiliated and pleased at the same time. She hated her own helplessness, but enjoyed the attention, and took special pleasure in the fact that he'd anticipated her situation. The fact that he'd been considering an escape was frosting on the cake. Maybe Vanessa's hold on him was weaker than she'd thought.

Holding onto Marla with one hand, and pulling himself forward with the other, Renn made his way through the main hatch and into a circular passageway. In the absence of gravity there was no "up" or "down" in the normal sense of those words. Nevertheless, a section of the hoop's inner curve had been left clear of the pipes and conduit which covered every other surface, making it a good candidate for "down." It also boasted a generous supply of handholds and was clearly intended as a sort of sidewalk.

Pulling himself along, Renn followed the arrow-shaped green decals, each proclaiming "STATION ACCESS" with boring regularity. He noticed the light seemed to come from everywhere at once and had an artificial yellow glow to it. Renn assumed the warmer light was an attempt to relieve the sterile feel common to so many scientific installations. If so it seemed to work.

Every thirty feet or so they passed through sets of airtight double doors. Open now, they would automatically seal in case of a pressure loss, and could also serve as emergency airlocks.

A beeping sound came from behind him, and a half second later a globular maintenance bot shot by, used some compressed air to correct its course, and then vanished around the next curve.

Meanwhile, Marla knew Renn was towing her around like so much baggage, but was too sick to care.

A few minutes later they reached an intersection where the green "STATION ACCESS" decals made a right turn. Renn did likewise, pulling Marla in close so she wouldn't bump into anything. About fifteen feet later they arrived in front of another lock. Unlike the emergency locks they'd passed through earlier, this one was larger, and had seen lots of heavy use during the station's assembly phase. It cycled open at the touch of Renn's palm. No fancy security measures here. Anyone with a warm body could get in.

Pulling himself inside, Renn waited for the outer door to close, and the inner door to hiss open. As it did, a flashing light appeared above it. "ARGRAV AHEAD." They were about to enter the station proper and, therefore, artificial gravity.

It felt strange to step out of the lock and into gravity. One moment he was weightless, swimming effortlessly through the air, and the next it felt as if he weighed a ton. But the sensation passed, and since the argrav was less than Swamp normal, Renn found he had an extra spring to his step.

Meanwhile, Marla's self-confidence and equilibrium had returned along with the gravity, and she felt ready to tackle just about anything. Anything except a large multicolored alien like the one that had just stepped out of a side corridor. It stood about six and a half feet tall, was covered with colorful plumage, and regarded them with large saucer-like eyes as it fiddled with the black box hung round its neck. It opened its maw experimentally and sound came out of the box. "Testing . . . testing one, two, three, damned contraption. Can you hear me?"

"Quite well Far Flier, thank you," Renn replied, using the traditional Finthian address, appropriate when addressing one of slightly higher rank, on occasions when both parties are far from their ancestral nesting grounds.

"You know us then," the Finthian replied, obviously pleased.

"I cannot claim full knowledge of your honorable race," Renn said solemnly. "But I have visited the beautiful hanging cities of your home world, and while there, I was systematically cheated of almost every credit I had."

The Finthian cackled with laughter. "Truly you know us well. They call me 'The one-who-flies-to-knowledge,' but most of the staff just call me 'Honcho.'" He gave them what might have been the Finthian version of a grin. "That does mean 'boss' doesn't it?"

Renn and Marla looked at each other, and then back at the alien. It didn't make sense, but apparently the Finthian was in charge. "That's what it means all right," Renn answered.

"Good. I'd hate to think they were calling me 'bird brain,' and getting away with it!" Overwhelmed by his own joke, the Finthian once again broke into cackling laughter.

It took the alien a while to recover, but when he did, he stuck out a claw-like hand and said, "Sorry about that. You are Jonathan Renn . . . and you are Marla Mendez."

After he had shaken both their hands, the Finthian said, "Welcome my friends, and thanks for all your help. Without it many more would have died. But enough of that . . . you must be tired. Follow me and I will escort you to your quarters." With that he turned and headed down an evenly lit side corridor. His walk could only be described as a waddle.

Marla looked at the alien's swaying tail feathers, and then at Renn. They both smiled and managed not to laugh as they followed the Finthian down the hall.

After many twistings and turnings they arrived at the

station's core. It consisted of a vertical passageway connecting all the decks. Clear plastic surrounded the passageway, and inside Renn saw powered lift tubes, plus an old-fashioned ladder. It was meant for emergencies, but later he'd learn the marines had standing orders to use it instead of the lifts. Jumo had a number of favorite expressions, including, "a soft marine is a dead marine."

"We're going one level down," Honcho said, waiting for the next platform to arrive then stepping aboard. Since there was room for only one person at a time, Marla went next. Then it was Renn's turn to step onto a slowly descending disc, wait for a moment, and step out into a comfortably furnished lounge a few seconds later. The lounge was circular in shape. There were five or six people sitting around, including Doc, Lt. Fitz, and Private Ford. They smiled and waved. The others watched Marla with the open curiosity of people touring a zoo. Marla growled, and they all turned away.

Renn started to say something, but thought better of it, deciding they deserved whatever they got.

Choosing to ignore the whole episode, Honcho gestured expansively and said, "This is the lounge, church, and night club all rolled into one. As you can see crew quarters line the outside bulkhead, but they're pretty cramped, so the lounge is in use all the time."

Looking around, Renn saw the alien was correct. The circular lounge was surrounded by doors, and since they were quite close together, the compartments beyond couldn't be very large.

Honcho led them to a door which bore the number "23" and touched the lighted panel set into the bulkhead beside it. As the door hissed open he looked down at Marla. "You'll have the emperor's suite. If he shows up you'll have to move."

"Of course," Marla replied with mock gravity. "I wouldn't think of inconveniencing the emperor."

"And for Citizen Renn we have the Galaxy suite, which for reasons unknown, is one full inch wider than any other sleeping compartment aboard."

"I will cherish the extra space," Renn said gravely, adding a half bow. The door slid open at the Finthian's touch. Renn saw the compartment was not only small, but pie-shaped to boot. A standard bunk took up the far bulkhead, with storage above and below. Closed compartments lined the other walls hinting at a variety of concealed conveniences.

"The mess deck is one level down," Honcho said. "If you feel up to it we'd like you to join our staff meeting at 1600 station time. That's about four hours from now." The Finthian was already waddling towards the lift tubes when he said, "Get some rest, I'll see you later."

Feeling awkward under the barely concealed scrutiny of the crew—people they didn't know—Renn and Marla nodded to each other, and entered their cubicles. Their doors closed behind them.

Renn found his compartment smelled of disinfectant, as though it had been recently scrubbed, which he realized it probably had. As he stretched out on the bunk he wondered who'd lived in the compartment before him. One of the ill-fated shuttle pilots? Lt. Costello? There was no way to tell, but he had the vague feeling of knickknacks only recently gone, and a personality other than his own. "Some people have even worse luck than I do," he thought as he hit the light switch next to his head. The air conditioning made a soft whirring sound as he quickly fell asleep.

As the door started to slide open, Renn came fully awake, rolling onto the deck, his blaster up and ready. He lowered it the moment he recognized Vanessa silhouetted against the outside light. She stopped in her tracks, recovered, and stepped inside. The door slid closed behind her as Renn turned on the lights. "Does Jumo know you have that?" she asked, indicating the blaster.

Renn shrugged. "Who knows? He didn't search me so apparently he doesn't care. I'm sorry if I scared you but my reactions are still tuned to life on Swamp."

She smiled. "It was my own fault. I should have buzzed you first, but the lounge was empty, and I wanted to slip in while no one was looking." She touched a button and a slender chair unfolded itself from the wall. She sat down.

Renn took a seat on his bunk. "Would they care?"

She shook her hair back and away from her face. "No, not if we're having sex, but that isn't why I came."

"Too bad. It sounds like fun."

Vanessa smiled. "There'll be plenty of time for that if you agree to my proposal."

Renn forced himself to look disinterested. "Proposal?"

"Yes," she said, her eyes big and round. "We've done everything we can from orbit. To complete our research we need more information. Information which can only be gleaned on the surface. Yet conditions are so bad on Swamp it takes all one's energy just to stay alive. The marines are good, but they don't know the local ecology, and a lot of us could die before they learn. That's why we need your help."

"And Marla."

She shrugged her shoulders impatiently. "And Marla. So what do you say?"

Renn ignored her question and asked one of his own. "You've never asked what I did to end up on Swamp. What if I'm an ax-murderer or something?"

Vanessa smiled. "Are you?"

Renn laughed. "No."

"Well then. Will you do it?"

Renn did his best to hide his growing excitement. "Well

it sounds interesting, but didn't you leave something out? No offense, but what's in it for us?"

Vanessa laughed. "You're right! I left out the best part! What's in it for you is a full pardon! When our studies are over you could leave Swamp!"

"The others have agreed to this?"

She shook her head. "Not yet, but if you're willing, I'll propose it at the staff meeting. I think Chin will support, as will Jumo, he knows what it's like down there, the only problem is convincing Honcho."

Renn tried to look thoughtful, while his heart tried to beat its way out of his chest. A chance to get off planet! Would he do it? Hell yes, he'd do it! Out loud he said, "Well I can't deny that I find your proposal very attractive, but I need to discuss it with Marla. Assuming she approves, the rest'll be up to you."

Vanessa clapped her hands in excitement. It reminded him of a little girl getting her way. "Leave everything to me. Just be sure you attend the staff meeting." And with that she got up, gave him a quick kiss on the lips, and slipped out the door.

Once outside, Vanessa gave a quick look around, didn't see anyone, crossed the lounge and entered her own compartment.

Marla's door was open only a crack, but it was enough to see Vanessa leave. With the aid of her supersensitive hearing, she'd heard the scientist's arrival, the mumble of conversation and her subsequent departure. While she hadn't heard their actual conversation, the visit told its own story, and it hurt. Even when Renn showed up a half hour later, and told her about Vanessa's proposal, it did nothing to lessen the pain. It did, however, confirm the validity of her earlier suspicions about Vanessa. Maybe she liked Renn, but she was also using him, and doing so in a very calculated fashion. Of course Renn was getting something too. OK, fair enough, Vanessa uses Renn, and he uses her. Everybody ends up happy. Hah! Everybody, that is, except Marla. So they received pardons, so what? Renn and Vanessa would have each other, but what would she have? A lifetime in a dog's body that's what.

She was still feeling sorry for herself an hour later when the staff meeting began. Except for the skeleton crew on watch, everyone else had gathered on the mess deck. Like everything else the mess deck was circular in design. A bulkhead divided it in two. One side was open, and occupied by the tables and chairs in which they now sat, while the other was sealed off, devoted to recycling, hydroponics, and food preparation.

Glancing around, Marla recognized Jumo, Chin, Doc, Issacs, Ford, and of course Vanessa, who looked like she'd just stepped out of a fashion holo. There were about fifty others present as well, a mixture of marines, scientists, and technicians. Two of the scientists were Finthians like Honcho. Why Finthians? She made a note to find out.

Honcho stood, adjusted his translator, and glanced around the room. "Well, it looks like we're all here, no small accomplishment in itself. As you all know by now we have some visitors with us today, people to whom we owe a great debt of gratitude. There are some empty chairs among us, and if it weren't for Citizens Renn and Mendez, there would be many more. We invited them here for some much deserved R & R. I hope you'll do what you can to make their stay as enjoyable as possible. On my home world we would now honor our guests with a ritual sky dance, but since there's only three of us here who know how to fly, and space is somewhat limited, human applause will have to do."

Everyone laughed and applauded vigorously. Finally Honcho held up a taloned hand for silence, and said, "At this point our guests are free to leave if they wish, while we discuss such boring but important matters as the continuing maintenance problems with the waste recyclers."

Vanessa stood among amused chuckles. "Honcho, I've got a proposal to make, and since it involves our guests I'd like them to stay."

Having dealt with other members of Honcho's race, Renn thought he detected the slight stiffening of the shoulders, and the ruffling of neck feathers which indicates annoyance among Finthians. Maybe Vanessa had done similar things before, or perhaps Honcho felt she was stepping on his prerogatives, either way it didn't bode well. But if the scientist was annoyed, there was no trace of it in his voice. "Of course. And that being the case, perhaps you would like to make your proposal now?"

Was there the slightest note of sarcasm in the Finthian's tone? Renn thought so, but Vanessa seemed unaffected. "Thank you, Honcho," she said, getting to her feet, and turning towards her audience. "As you all know our first attempt at a field study was a total disaster. True, what happened to the shuttle was a freak accident, but after spending some time on the surface I feel sure we would've had serious problems anyway. When you're spending all your time just staying alive, it's hard to get much work done." She nodded towards Jumo. "And even with the help of our valiant marines, I'm afraid that's the way things are. As Honcho said earlier, if it weren't for Jonathan Renn, we wouldn't be here now."

Marla almost enjoyed the slight, reinforcing as it did her low opinion of Vanessa. She noticed that Renn wore a frown. Good. Maybe Vanessa would submarine herself. Meanwhile the female scientist was still talking.

"Our project is entering a critical phase. In order to confirm our theories field studies are an absolute must. As you know there's only so much we can accomplish from up here, yet as we've learned, it's damned hard to carry out our work down there. So here's my proposal. We hire Citizens Renn and Mendez to act as guides for our field team. Through their expertise we'll be able to avoid a lot of problems and get the job done. Thank you for hearing me out."

"Thank you, Vanessa," Honcho said calmly. "Questions?"

"Yes, I have a question." The speaker was a burly man with a full beard and a shaved head. He wore the light blue coveralls of the scientific team.

"Go ahead, Burt."

"Well, not meaning to offend our two guests, but what about their status? It's no secret they're criminals. Can we trust them?"

"A fair question," Honcho agreed. "Vanessa?"

Vanessa stood once more. Marla watched in reluctant admiration as she turned on the charm. "They may be criminals, Burt, but I think we can trust them. First, let's take a look at their track record. They risked their lives to save us from the roos, and could have killed us any number of times after that, but didn't. Second, I suggest we offer them a full pardon upon completion of our field studies, a reward which should guarantee their loyalty."

At this point Chin came to his feet and said, "I agree with Vanessa. We need their help, and I for one trust them to give it."

Then Jumo stood, white teeth flashing as he said, "I agree. If I didn't, my friend Renn wouldn't be walking around with a blaster tucked under his left arm, and a derringer in his boot." There was general laughter as he sat down. Renn felt a little silly as he remembered his plans to steal the shuttle. Jumo had been two steps ahead of him all the way, anticipating both the temptation and the final decision.

These last two endorsements came so quickly, and easily,

that Marla wondered if Vanessa had lobbied the two men ahead of time. Apparently the same thought had occurred to Honcho, because he said, "Thank you for the spontaneous demonstration of consensus. Are there any other comments?"

"Well," Burt said apologetically, "I don't want to seem negative or something, but do we have the power to pardon criminals?"

Honcho stared at him for a moment, which though somewhat disconcerting, was the Finthian equivalent of a thoughtful look. "That's a good question, Burt. The answer is 'no,' not specifically. However, as the individual that Vanessa sometimes allows to act as team leader, I have certain broad powers which should be sufficient. And even though I sense a certain amount of maneuvering here, I think her idea is basically sound, and I agree." He turned towards Renn and Marla. "How about it you two? Would you agree to Vanessa's proposal?"

Renn, his excitement almost bursting through his chest, nodded in the affirmative. Marla, her feelings a confused mix of elation and sadness, did likewise.

"In that case," Honcho intoned solemnly. "It's my pleasure to welcome you to our team."

Chapter Ten

"You lied to us." Marla made the words a half growl. She and Renn were sitting at a small table across from Honcho and Vanessa. The lights in the conference room were turned down to enhance the series of holos they'd just seen.

"Not true," Honcho replied calmly. "We left some things out, but everything we told you was true."

"Really?" Renn inquired mildly. "You're supposedly performing biological research on native lifeforms."

"And we are," Vanessa assured him. "Remember Burt?"

Renn remembered the burly scientist with the full beard and shaved head. "Yeah, the guy who wondered if we were such a good idea."

Honcho cackled and Vanessa smiled. "Well Burt's a research biologist, a damned good one by the way, and he really *is* studying native lifeforms. He went crazy over the roo specimens we brought him. However, it's true that some of us are doing research in other areas as well."

Renn had arrived expecting a lecture on the scientific team and the biological research it hoped to perform. But Honcho had talked about artifact planets instead, indicating that Swamp might be such a world, and admitting that biological research was not the team's main purpose. Boater's ruins immediately came to mind, but Renn said nothing, waiting to see where the advantage might lay.

So Renn listened with considerable interest as Honcho told how most of the artifact worlds were discovered during the early years of space exploration, how they were empty of intelligent life, and how the similarities between artifacts found on various worlds left no doubt as to their common place in a single culture. And he admitted that science still had no answers for the big questions. Where did the Builders go? Was there a war? Some sort of interstellar disease? Unfortunately time, weather, and geologic upheaval had erased most of the answers.

But every now and then someone would stumble onto a handful of artifacts protected by luck and happenstance from the ravages of time. They would become an overnight sensation, appearing on every holo cast in the empire, proudly clutching this or that artifact while telling exaggerated tales of the hardships they'd endured to obtain it. Usually their finds had little or no material value. Most were bits of cryptic writing which defied translation, pieces of enigmatic machinery, works of what could be art, or might be the scribblings of the insane. There was no way to tell the difference. While these objects were highly valued by the scientific community, they held little but passing interest for most, and were quickly forgotten until the next overnight sensation came along.

Of course every now and then someone would stumble on a valuable find. New technology, precious stones, things which could be sold for a nice profit. People remembered those, and as a result, numerous scientific as well as private expeditions set forth each year, searching for new and unexploited sets of ruins. The more principled scientists deplored the damage done to valuable archeological sites by the private expeditions, while their less principled brethren competed for the right to lead such endeavors.

Now Honcho's lecture was over. "So," Renn said, "what makes you think Swamp is an artifact planet?"

Honcho's saucer-like eyes regarded them solemnly. "I think Swamp is an artifact planet because of what I see there," he pointed to the holo of Swamp taken from the

space station, "and I feel it here," a claw-like finger tapped
his chest."

"What Honcho means," Vanessa added, "is that we have
two lines of evidence to support our hypothesis. The first is
empirical evidence such as this." She did something to a
small remote, causing Swamp to stop rotating and grow
bigger, until a large cylindrical section of equatorial swamp
floated above the table. She did something else to the
control, and most of the holo went dark, leaving three red
blotches. "The red zones represent potential archeological
sites. It took months of observation, spectroanalysis, infrared photography, and a lot of informed guesswork to narrow
our choices down to three." She looked at Renn, ignoring
Marla as if she weren't even there. "And even after all that
effort we'll be lucky if one of them pans out. But they're the
right size, shape, and density to qualify as productive
sites."

"And the nonempirical evidence?" Marla inquired, curious as to what sort of nonempirical evidence they would
consider valid.

Vanessa frowned in the way adults do when a child has
spoken out of turn, but Honcho preempted her reply. "I'm
the nonempirical evidence. Or something in here is." He
once again tapped his chest. "For some reason even *we*
don't understand, Finthians seem to have a natural affinity
for the builders, and the artifacts they left behind. A few
years ago a human archeologist noticed that Finthians
seemed to find a lot more artifacts than anyone else did. At
first he doubted his own theory, suspecting himself of
professional jealousy, or even a touch of xenophobia. But
his feeling was so strong he decided to put it to the test. So
he tabulated all known finds along with the race of those
credited with the discovery. It turned out that Finthians had
found two sites for every one turned up by humans or
members of other races. Subsequent studies showed that

this trend held up even when variables such as education and experience were factored in."

"Like Honcho said," Vanessa added, "no one knows why or how Finthians do it. The most popular theory posits some sort of racial memory. There are an unusual number of artifact sites inside Finthian space, and perhaps the two races are somehow linked, by bonds so ancient that conscious memory of them has been forgotten. In any case the decision was made to take advantage of this special sensitivity. That's why Finthians were not only included in our staff, they're in charge."

"A fact Vanessa frequently chooses to ignore," Honcho added dryly. "In any case, perhaps you can see why we must maintain a cover story. If word got out we'd have all sorts of people flocking here, not to mention the potential problems with your friends on the surface. Wholesale looting might ensue, leading to the loss of priceless scientific knowledge."

"Or priceless new technology," Renn added sourly. "I doubt that our government, or yours, is funding this project out of the goodness of their hearts."

Honcho nodded agreeably. "Quite true. But that doesn't lessen the validity or importance of our scientific mission."

"Given Swamp's unique potential," Marla asked, "then why make it a prison planet?"

"A damned good question," Honcho said soberly, "and one which we can't answer. A review of the original survey shows enough preliminary evidence to warrant an investigation but none took place. In the rush to identify and populate prison planets, they did some pretty sloppy follow-up, and apparently Swamp's potential was glossed over. It was years before someone stumbled across the data, realized its importance, and took steps to let us know. And, by the time we got the proper authorities to do something about it, prisoners were already in residence. Taking them off isn't practical so we decided to work around them."

"Which," Vanessa added, "brings us to you. With your knowledge of Swamp to guide us, we've got a good chance of reaching the red zones and investigating them."

"Well I've got some good news for you," Renn said with a grin. "There *are* extensive ruins on Swamp, and while I can't be sure they're the kind you're looking for, it sounds like they'd be worth a peek."

Honcho and Vanessa were silent for a moment as they processed this new piece of information, and then they went simultaneously crazy. The Finthian gabbled excitedly as Vanessa whooped with joy and dived across the table to throw her arms around Renn's neck. As Vanessa's lips met Renn's, Marla shook her head in disgust, and pattered off towards her quarters. Why should she watch them play kissy face when she could take a nap?

Three days later they landed on Swamp. Everyone felt better when a nervous Lt. Fitz closed the shuttle's main hatch and lifted. Not only was the shuttle vulnerable on the ground, its comings and goings were like a huge ad saying, "Easy pickings! Come and get 'em!" Fortunately, however, the shuttle managed to land and take off again without incident.

Fred was just as they'd left him, and it took three trips just to get staff, supplies and equipment from the LZ to Boater's ruins. There were fourteen people altogether, including, Renn, Marla, Vanessa, Honcho, Chin, Jumo, and eight marines. Five of the marines were greenies from the station, while three were veterans of the shuttle crash, including Doc, Issacs and Ford. It was a lot of people, more than Renn thought wise, but Vanessa and Honcho insisted. They were accustomed to expeditions which employed hundreds of skilled laborers and a small army of robots.

At least Jumo was sympathetic. He listened intently as

Renn told of the underground passageways and outlined the safest avenues of approach.

Fred meanwhile sat bobbing in the channel loaded down with excited scientists. The ruins were not only sitting right in the middle of the number two red zone, they were classic examples of Builder design, or at least that's the way it seemed. Subsequent study would either confirm or deny it. In the meantime they entertained themselves by scraping away at the artifical embankments and shooting holos of everything in sight.

All except Honcho. He was everywhere at once, delighting in the symmetry of the canal one moment, and marveling at the fine texture of its artificial banks the next. They'd almost lost him. In spite of Renn's advice to the contrary, and Jumo's obvious concern, the Finthian had insisted on performing his own aerial survey. Everyone turned out to watch. With the exception of Renn, none of them had ever seen a Finthian fly. Oblivious to their curiosity, Honcho unfolded the large wings tucked away behind his arms, and waddled down a secure section of trail. Some of the marines made whispered bets as to whether he'd make it. Due to his somewhat portly figure the odds stacked heavily against him. However a few seconds later Honcho was airborne and quite graceful, too. But moments later an adult lifter spotted the scientist while circling upwards and damned near got him. Fortunately, Jumo hit the monster with a lucky shot. Meanwhile, Honcho crash landed in a swampy area and ended up neck deep in mud. Even after hours of grooming his plumage was still a mess. Undaunted, the plucky scientist continued to dash this way and that.

The rest of the scientists were equally eager to get out and prowl around, but first Renn, Marla, and the marines would have to secure the area, and that would take some doing. A quick inspection by Marla confirmed that the ruins were thick with monsters, and since most of the marines were inexperienced, Jumo picked Issacs, Ford and Doc to take part in the initial sweep. That left the other five marines to guard the scientists and the boat.

Marla took the point as they entered the jungle. All her senses were cranked up to max and working well thanks to the free tune-up she'd received on the station. Of course a real tune-up would require a qualified cyber tech and a fully equipped lab, nonetheless, Chin and some of the station's technicians had succeeded in repairing quite a bit of the minor damage she'd suffered during her early days on Swamp. So she felt better than she had in a very long time. And best of all she was doing something useful while Vanessa sat on the boat. Her fear was plain to see and Marla couldn't help gloating.

The jungle was hot and moist. White ground mist drifted upwards as the warmth of the sun gradually found its way down to the jungle floor and released the moisture trapped there. Broad leaves made a swishing sound as they slid along her sides, and her paws made little sucking noises as she moved. The smell of rotting vegetation hung heavily on the air, along with the rich fragrance of exotic flowers, and the slightly acidic odor of roo urine.

As she pushed deeper into the jungle Marla was careful to avoid the game trails which criss-crossed the island. While the trails would make travel easier they could also make it a good deal more dangerous. There might be more of the slug-like things lurking below or an ambush waiting around a bend. So it might be slower to go through the jungle but it was a whole lot safer.

So far so good. No sign of anything too scary. Lots of roo tracks, they'd already replenished themselves since Renn and Boater had hunted here, but nothing unusual. She cleared her throat self-consciously, and said, "Come ahead. Lots of roo tracks . . . but otherwise clear."

Chin had placed a voice activated mic around her neck

and coupled it to a tiny transmitter. She didn't need a receiver having her own built-in version. At first she'd refused to wear the transmitter, hating anything which even looked like the explosive collar Skunk had forced her to wear, but Renn had sweet-talked her into it. Good communications could save lives he said, and since one of those lives might be his, he'd appreciate her cooperation. She'd relented.

Having heard her report via the tiny plug in his ear, Jumo answered, "We read you loud and clear, Marla. We're moving up." There was no need to wave the others forward, since they, too, were equipped with radios.

They advanced in a long open line. Each person found their own way through the thick undergrowth but kept the others in sight. Renn hoped to drive the monsters towards the other end of the island while killing as many as they could. It was a ruthless way to get the job done, but no worse than hunting, and absolutely necessary. Burt and the other biologists were still trying to figure out why the normally anti-social roo monsters had gathered in a large herd and then preceded to run amok. There were numerous theories which dealt with mating, overpopulation, and intermittent tribalism. But none had been proved. So, until the scientists came up with something solid, the only safe roo was a dead roo.

"Contact." The laconic voice belonged to Doc. Renn saw blue light stutter to his right, but made no move to help, mindful of Jumo's instructions not to.

"If you need help we'll come running," the section leader had said, teeth flashing. "But if you can handle it yourself then do so. Otherwise we'll bunch up and make a tempting target for any human types that might be hanging around. Watch your field of fire too. If you shoot one of ours *you'll* do all the paperwork."

So Doc handled it herself, hosing the undergrowth with

lethal energy, and sending up a mist of steam and smoke. They were armed with energy weapons at Renn's request. Slug throwers made too much noise and would be used only in the case of emergency.

"Roos. Two dead. One got away." Renn smiled at Doc's report. Short and to the point.

The hunt went on for another three hours, and by the time Renn called it quits, the team had bagged forty-eight monsters of various kinds. Both Honcho and the less experienced marines were fascinated by the dead creatures, and peppered Renn and Marla with questions.

Once the impromptu biology lesson was over they had to dispose of the bodies before the presence of all that meat brought unwelcome visitors. Renn hated to waste all those skins, but if things went well, he'd soon be out of the hunting business and it wouldn't matter.

The carcasses were loaded aboard *Fred* and taken out into the lake, where they were dumped off. The water was soon seething with hungry diners.

By the time *Fred* returned to shore it was almost dark. Since *Fred* couldn't accomodate the entire team, Renn led them to the great hall, where Boater's crude furniture sat undisturbed. Vanessa and Honcho pronounced the site acceptable and were soon aiming their flashlights into dark corners and gabbling happily.

It took a number of trips to get everything off *Fred* and up to the camp. But once the folding furniture was set up, and the lamps lit, the great hall was almost homey. People made giant shadows on the walls as they got up and moved about. Chin and a marine named Red drew kitchen detail and set about making dinner. It consisted of standard rats supplemented with seasonings brought along for that purpose. Much to Renn's amazement it wasn't too bad.

Having cleaned his plate, Renn waited until everyone else had finished, and drifted over towards Vanessa. She was busy laying out her sleeping bag. She smiled at his approach. "Hi, Jonathan. This is absolutely incredible! Every once in a while I pinch myself just to make sure it's real."

Renn laughed. "I'll bet that's the first time anyone's talked about Swamp that way."

She wrinkled her nose. "Beauty is in the eye of the beholder. These are the most complete ruins I've ever seen, and that's what counts. Honcho says we'll be famous." As she said it, her eyes were bright and excited.

"I'm glad you're happy," Renn replied. "How 'bout a walk?"

Her expression changed as she looked out into the dark. "Out there? You've got to be kidding."

Renn smiled. "It's safe enough if you know what you're doing. Besides, we won't go far. What do you say?"

Vanessa looked doubtful. "You're probably right, but I'm beat, and tommorow's a big day. How 'bout a rain check?"

Renn shrugged. "Sure. I'll see you in the morning."

As he walked back to his gear, Marla watched from a shadow, and smiled. Maybe something was going *her* way for once.

Morning brought a bustle of activity. People woke up and wished they were somewhere else. Tired guards turned in too tired to care. Breakfast was opened, complained about and eaten. And then, when Jumo was satisfied that all was ship-shape, a planning session was held.

Drawing on Renn's memories, and the little bit that Honcho had glimpsed from the air, Chin used his portable comp to sketch a plan of the ruins. Then hard copies were printed out and given to each member of the scientific team. Honcho and Vanessa divided Chin's map into quadrants, and then divided the quadrants between themselves. Each would use a holo cam to carry out a survey of their particular quadrants. Later the holos would be shown and discussed. All possible sites would be identified and prioritized. Then those with highest priority would be investigated first.

Once the quadrants had been assigned, three teams were formed. Two were survey teams, headed by Honcho and Vanessa, and the third was a defense team headed by Jumo. Each survey team was assigned a guide, Renn for Honcho, Marla for Vanessa, as well as two marine guards. The rest of the marines fell into Jumo's team. One was still asleep, having stood the last four hour night watch, and the other three were split between *Fred* and the main camp. Onc on *Fred,* and two at the main camp. Everyone would be armed and in continual radio contact.

As she set off with Vanessa, Marla wondered how the assignments had been made. Why had she been chosen to accompany Vanessa rather than Renn? Was it chance, or had Vanessa requested that arrangement? There was no way to tell, but one thing was for sure, Vanessa usually got her way.

Meanwhile, Renn was a little hurt at being assigned to Honcho, and a bit amused as well. It appeared the ruins had taken his place in Vanessa's love life. He'd hoped for something more, but never really believed it would happen. Ah well, easy come easy go.

As the day progressed Renn found the whole process quite interesting. In spite of the way he babbled constantly, and seemed to dash this way and that, the Finthian was actually quite systematic. Once Renn had checked the area for monsters, and the marines had taken up good defensive positions, Honcho would enter, holo cam in hand. First, he recorded every square inch of the surface area using long practiced swoops of his camera. Since the images could later be computer manipulated in thousands of ways, *how* he shot the footage was less important than the *way* he shot it. The key was to leave nothing unshot and to record as many different angles as possible. The resulting images could be digitalized and manipulated in whatever way Chin chose. The final holos would not provide an academic record of how things looked before they were disturbed and a data base from which all sorts of computer extrapolations could be run.

Meanwhile Renn was gathering his own impressions of the ruins. Although he'd wandered through them with Boater he hadn't really examined them. Basically they were shaped like a long narrow rectangle. What he thought of as the great hall was located at one end of the rectangle and underneath. Sitting on top of the rectangle were six circular structures, each an island festooned with thick jungle growth, and each having a personality of its own.

Of the three which fell within Honcho's area of investigation, one was entirely featureless, while the other two had distinct personalities. Most of the things which made them different were constructed of the same smooth material as everything else, but at least one was made of metal, and it drove Honcho wild with excitement. "Look Jonathan, metal! Isn't that wonderful? And not a speck of rust or vegetable growth on it. Why's that Jonathan? And look at the shape. By all that flies, what a strange shape. Oh my, oh my, Vanessa will be so excited."

Grinning at the Finthian's antics, Renn began to circle the structure. It was about ten feet tall. It was hard to see through the thick growth around it. Nothing . . . nothing . . . wait a minute, what's that? There was a curious darkness behind one particular section of vegetation. Using his machete to hold some vines aside, Renn leaned forward to take a better look. There was darkness all right, the darkness of an unlighted stairway! "Honcho," Renn said using his throat mic, "come around to the other side. There's something I'd like you to see."

"I'm too busy, Jonathan. I'll work my way around there in a few minutes."

"OK," Renn replied. "In the meantime I guess Ford and I will just see where these stairs lead."

Renn heard an indignant squawk over the intercom and seconds later the Finthian stood by his side. "I don't see any stairs. If this is some sort of human joke, I don't think it's very funny."

Renn used his machete to push the vegetation aside, and this time Ford stepped in to help. A tall narrow doorway was revealed with steps beyond. Squawking his happiness, Honcho jumped up and down, waving his holo cam in every direction. "This is wonderful! A way in! I had feared we might have to force our way in, and that could do a lot of damage. Vanessa, Vanessa. Can you hear me?"

"I think so," Vanessa said from the far end of the ruins. "Did you say something about stairs?" There was excitement in her voice, and something else, resentment perhaps?

"I certainly did," Honcho replied happily, and went on to describe what they looked like. But the stairs went temporarily unexplored. Honcho insisted that the video survey be completed prior to entry. "We must proceed in an orderly fashion," he said sternly. So the spot was marked, and the survey continued.

Everyone was exhausted by the time evening came. Climbing up, over and around the ruins was hard work. Nonetheless a sense of excitement filled the hall as dinner was prepared and consumed. Everyone wondered the same things. Where did the stairs lead? What would they find inside the ruins?

But where everyone else was filled with excitement Vanessa was strangely silent. Her quadrant was interesting, but devoid of anything like Honcho's stairs, and she seemed less than happy. And when Vanessa was unhappy she tended to take it out on those around her. Especially Marla. The two of them were no longer speaking.

Meanwhile Honcho ate alone, talons clicking on the keyboard of his Finthian computer, his huge eyes locked on the tiny screen. He'd dumped the holo cam memories into his computer. Now he was sifting images, comparing them to others he'd recorded light years away, and mumbling to himself. Finally he uttered a chirrup of satisfaction and stood up. "That was an excellent dinner, whatever it was. How can I help?"

"You feathered con artist, you know damn well it's too late to help," Chin replied, gesturing towards the spotless eating area. "But since you offered we'll save the breakfast mess for you."

"You're too kind," Honcho replied solemnly. "Shall we review what we've got so far?"

His offer met with enthusiastic agreement all around. Those who weren't on guard formed a semicircle around Honcho. Many were still sipping their coffee, or munching on one of the rock-hard fruit bars masquerading as dessert.

Meanwhile Honcho and Chin set up a holo projector and linked it to the Finthian's computer. Then Honcho cleared his throat and waited for the buzz of conversation to die down. "All right. Thanks to everyone's efforts we accomplished a great deal today. Our initial survey is complete, which means we can now turn our attention to those sites which seem most promising." Cheers and applause followed, to which Honcho held up a restraining hand.

"Though it's true that I deserve all the credit, it would be more seemly to pretend that my associate Dr. Cooper-Smith, along with my company of loyal slaves played some small part in this accomplishment." For a moment boos and a variety of friendly insults filled the air. Vanessa smiled weakly but didn't join in.

As soon as the noise died down, the Finthian scientist

turned serious. "As you know, Jonathan found a door and some stairs which seem to lead down into the interior of the ruins. This seems like the place to start. However, Jonathan, Marla, and Section Leader Jumo have all pointed out that there's a good deal of danger involved. Jonathan knows from personal experience that there are passageways under the ruins, and under the surrounding jungle as well, which harbor some very unpleasant lifeforms. Therefore, we will enter with great caution. As for the ruins themselves, well, they're everything we'd hoped for and more. And while I normally avoid any sort of hypothesis this early in a survey, this is no ordinary survey, and our time is severely limited. Therefore, I'm going out on a limb. By the way, while that expression is common to both our races, it seems far more appropriate to mine."

Honcho's joke was met with lots of laughter, during which Renn happened to notice Vanessa. She wasn't laughing. Instead she was looking at Honcho with something approaching anger. Renn had a feeling that whatever the Finthian was about to announce hadn't been shared with her.

Honcho gestured towards the ruins around them. "To make a long story short, I've got a theory about these ruins. At first I thought they were a series of structures all located in close proximity to each other. But after looking them over, and running some computer comparisons I don't think so anymore. No, I think they're all part of a single structure, a structure which may have once been hundreds of feet tall."

Honcho was silent for a moment giving them time to absorb what he'd said. Chin was the first to break the silence. "But if this structure was hundreds of feet tall, then there should be all sorts of debris marking where the top portion fell."

A long, slow grin split Honcho's face, giving Renn a

glimpse of the Finthian's predatory ancestors. "Not if we're standing on the roof."

There was another long silence while everyone took it in. Meanwhile Honcho walked over to his computer and tapped a couple of keys. A holo snapped into existence. It was a line drawing of a tall building with six circular structures on the roof. "I'm just guessing of course, but it may have looked something like this. Then thousands of years ago there was some sort of cataclysm. Eventually we'll have to get some geologists in here to figure it out, but something changed the planet's climate, and probably created the equatorial swamps as well. Based on the time lines we've established elsewhere, that probably happened long after the Builders disappeared. In any case, this structure was so strong, it withstood the initial cataclysms, plus the thousands of years of erosion and flooding which followed. Perhaps a good portion of the polar ice caps melted down causing the water level to rise thereby creating lowland swamps. Perhaps it was something else. But whatever it was buried the first few hundred feet of this building in mud."

Renn noticed that Vanessa's expression had gone from anger to thin-lipped hatred. Apparently her fellow scientists revelations were as big a surprise to her as everyone else, and her dreams of academic glory were fading fast. The way things were going she'd be nothing more than a footnote in Honcho's final thesis.

Honcho touched a series of computer keys and a line of darkness moved upwards to consume all but the top of the building. When the line stopped, it rippled slightly, dropping a little on one side. Honcho picked up a black wand and an arrow popped into existence about six feet out from his hand. Pointing it to the side of the building that was slightly more exposed, he said, "My guess is that we're sitting right here, in what was once a top floor office, or comparable space. We've been entering and leaving this space via a huge window. The reason we didn't realize that is the lack of a casement or other structure which would suggest a window. Perhaps they used some sort of transparent forcefield to keep the weather out." As he talked, the arrow bounced from place to place. "In any case I think those six circular structures on top are housings which contained various kinds of building equipment. You know, air conditioning, communications gear, that sort of stuff. If so, the metal artifact I found today may be some sort of antenna, and Jonathan's stairs would provide roof access for repairs. Of course, it's all guess work for now. So, unless Vanessa has something to add, I suggest we wrap this up and get some sleep. Tommorow we'll investigate Renn's stairs, and perhaps they will tell us more. Vanessa?"

"I have nothing to add," Vanessa replied bitterly. "I think you covered it all."

If Honcho understood her tone, he gave no sign of it, nodding solemnly, and urging everyone to get a good night's sleep.

As the meeting broke up, Marla caught Renn's eye. He shrugged and replied with a grin. For some reason she found that to be quite reassuring.

Everyone was up bright and early the next morning eager to get breakfast out of the way and investigate the stairs. Even the marines seemed caught up in the excitement, vying to accompany the scientists, and groaning when Jumo assigned them guard duty.

Marla fell in beside Renn as the scientific party made its way towards the top of the ruins. "You plan to go first, don't you." She made it a statement rather than a question.

Renn looked down and smiled. "Good morning to you too, and yes, I plan to go first. I'm the only one who's been in the underground passageways before."

"I'm coming with you."

"The hell you are."

"Don't be stupid, Jonathan. My enhanced senses will give us an edge. Besides I'm smaller and that might come in handy. And there's one other thing, too."

"What's that?"

"Otherwise, I'll bite you in the ass."

Renn laughed and slapped her on the back. "God forbid! You win! I guess it's you and me just like always."

"That's good enough for me," Marla thought to herself as she padded along. "That's good enough for me."

Half an hour later they all watched as the marines cut away the vegetation which blocked the door. "Careful," Honcho cautioned them. "Just the vegetation. Don't touch anything else. And that goes for you as well," he said sternly, turning to Renn and Marla. "If you see any loose artifacts laying around don't touch them. It's important to record their exact position and condition before they're moved. Otherwise important information about their relationship to the things around them can be lost."

Having already heard this lecture twice in the last fifteen minutes, Renn and Marla nodded dutifully, and exchanged winks. Next it was Jumo's turn to lecture them. "Now remember we'll be in radio contact the whole time. If you lose radio contact then return immediately. Don't try to explore. That can wait till you get some help. Understood?"

"Understood," Renn replied.

"Yes, daddy." Marla added with a sly grin.

Jumo laughed. "Well, get to work then."

Renn had a powerful flashlight taped to the barrel of his assault weapon. He turned it on. The assault weapon was a short ugly looking thing which wasn't too accurate but could throw out a curtain of lead. Remembering his earlier experiences Renn had chosen the auto slug thrower over his usual blast rifle. If they ran into trouble the noise created by the slug thrower might give them an edge.

Marla paused in the doorway, and said, "Last one in's a roo's rear end," and disappeared. Everyone laughed as Renn stepped through the door. His flashlight threw a large circle of light onto the wall, and then the steps, as he pointed the rifle downwards.

"Marla?"

"I'm on a landing one flight down. Nothing so far. Watch your step."

As Renn started down the stairs he understood her warning. The risers were unusually high, reinforcing his earlier impression of a tall skinny race. Marla's synthetic eyes glowed red as she looked up to greet him. We've got company."

"Details!" Jumo's voice snapped over the intercom.

"Droppings, a faint odor, and distant scrabbling sounds," Marla replied.

"Watch your step," Jumo cautioned in her ear, "and haul ass at the slightest sign of trouble."

"Will do," Renn agreed. "OK Marla, let's go down one more flight." She hugged the right hand wall as she decended the stairs. Her durasteel claws made a slight clicking sound as she took the steps in a series of small jumps.

Renn followed, noticing that all traces of daylight had disappeared. The circle of light generated by his flashlight seemed to float down the stairs ahead of him like a ghost seeking its tomb. The air was colder now, seeping slowly upwards and bringing a foul odor with it, as if the ruins were somehow alive and breathing. Renn pictured himself descending down a monster's throat into its bowels, knowing at any moment it might awaken, sense his presence, and swallow him.

Suddenly a gibbering noise came from up ahead and his blood turned ice cold. There was a burst of static followed by Marla's voice. "We've got company Jonathan. Run!"

"What about you?"

"I'm fine damnit. Run!"

"Both of you, get the hell out of there!" The voice was Jumo's.

Renn heard a snarling sound from below as Marla tore into the oncoming monsters. He flicked the safety off and ran down the stairs. The gibbering horde came up to meet him.

───── Chapter Eleven ─────

Renn took the stairs two at a time, his light washing the walls white. Then he saw Marla, and beyond her a seething mass of bodies held in check by her slashing teeth. They had sleek dog-like heads, elongated bodies, and three sets of legs apiece. They were the same kind of underground creatures he'd run into before. Then there was no time for thought. He squeezed the trigger and the rifle made a stuttering roar.

The front rank staggered, tried to turn, but couldn't because of the mob behind. Trapped, they surged forward and almost overwhelmed Marla. She fought like a thing possessed. Renn was just about to order a retreat when Jumo appeared beside him. He sensed others behind and knew they couldn't help because of the narrow stairwell. He and Jumo were so close that when the section leader fired, hot gases from his ejection port burned Renn's arm. It was worth it. Jumo's weapon doubled the sound causing all of the creatures to turn. Some made it, but many died, the bullets cutting them down in swaths. Suddenly they were gone. Their weapons made pinging sounds as they cooled and wounded creatures whimpered pitifully.

Jumo stared after the vanishing horde. "Damn. I swear to god this is the worst pus ball in the whole damn galaxy." He turned to Renn. "I thought I ordered you to get the hell out of here."

Renn nodded soberly. "So you did. But I got confused in the dark and ran in the wrong direction."

Jumo regarded him disbelievingly. "Shit. You got confused and . . . shit." He turned to the marines on the stairs behind them, the beam from his flashlight revealing their grins. "What the hell are you grinning about? Get down there and finish off the wounded. What, I've gotta do everything?"

There was a whole chorus of "Yes-sir's," but the marines were still smiling as they squeezed past Renn.

"What have we got?" The voice belonged to Honcho. The somewhat bedraggled looking Finthian had followed the marines down.

"Oh terrific," Jumo said disgustedly. "Doesn't anyone listen around here? Did you hear me say, 'all clear, come on down'?"

Honcho produced a sly Finthian grin. "I got confused and went the wrong way."

Jumo just looked at the scientist for a moment, his jaw working wordlessly, and said, "Shit." Then he turned and walked away. A series of single shots rang out from the chamber beyond as the marines finished off the wounded.

"Marla, are you all right?" Renn knelt beside her. Her fur was ripped here and there, and her muzzle dripped greenish blood.

She looked into his eyes. "I'm fine thanks to you, but just for the record, I agree with Jumo."

"Traitor." Renn used his sleeve to wipe some of the blood off her face.

"Very interesting." The voice was Honcho's. The Finthian scientist was busily examining a dead monster. The light from his small flash roved this way and that, before coming to rest on its chest. "Jonathan, have you seen anything similar to this species during your time here?"

"Nope," Renn answered. "These things look completely different from anything else I've seen. Plus they don't change to match the background."

"Look at this," Honcho said, beckoning him over.

Renn knelt down to take a closer look. The scientist's flashlight moved back and forth to illuminate the creature's brown chest. And then Renn saw them, nipples! Two rows of them. A mammal! What was a mammal doing on a planet where everything else was oviparous?

"Burt will be most interested," Honcho said. "I'll ask Jumo to stabilize a couple." The Finthian waddled off in Jumo's direction.

Renn knew specimen bags came in various sizes, each equipped with a canister of stabilizing gases. Put a specimen inside, seal it up, trigger the canister, and presto! Canned whatever. The specimens looked horrible through the cloudy plastic, but Renn supposed it was better than dissecting them on the spot, or hunting more later.

"Hey, Section!" The voice belonged to Ford. "Looks like we've got a swimming pool over here!"

Renn and Marla wound their way through the dead bodies and towards the bobbing lights. For the first time Renn realized they were in a large open area. If Honcho was correct, than this was the top floor of a fairly tall building. Why would anyone put a swimming pool on the top floor of a building?

One of the marines turned on a portable flood, and the sudden glare hurt Renn's eyes. The marines were gathered along a high wall. It looked to be four or five feet tall. Uncomfortably high for humans but just about right for tall, skinny builders. Stepping up Renn saw the wall formed a large open square about a hundred feet across. Remembering this was the top of floor of a high-rise building, or more accurately, a balcony, Renn realized the open area had once been an atrium. Not any more. Looking down, he saw jet black water twenty feet below. From the stains on the far wall he deduced that the water was sometimes much deeper. During the rainy seasons, no doubt. The water rippled gently as a tiny breeze found its way down the stairs, over the wall, and skittered across its surface. Renn shivered. Something about the black stillness of the water scared him. He felt a sharp pain in his right ankle. "What the . . .?"

Looking down he saw Marla. She'd nipped his ankle. "How about me you big lug? Did it ever occur to you that I'd like to look, too?"

Renn laughed. "Sorry." Grasping her around the middle he heaved her up so she could rest her front legs on the top of the wall. As he did, she suddenly realized she'd asked for his help without worrying what he might think. It was a new high, or a new low, she wasn't sure which. She looked down at the inky water and nodded.

"OK, put me down before you get a hernia or something." He put her down.

"Thank God. If I didn't know better I'd think you were putting on weight." He felt another sharp pain in his ankle and said, "Stop that!"

"Interesting." The voice was Honcho's. He'd just worked his way around the circumference of the wall.

"What do you make of it?" Marla asked. "Ford says it's a swimming pool."

"Well, as far as I'm concerned, Ford is welcome to take a dip," Honcho allowed thoughtfully. "But I doubt that's what the builders had in mind. My guess is that we're standing on a four-sided balcony over what was once an open space. If so the water isn't supposed to be there. Chances are it corresponds with the surrounding water table."

Renn was secretly pleased to have his own hypothesis confirmed. "Maybe a public gathering place of some sort?"

"Possibly," Honcho said, "That would explain it's size. But there's no way to be sure. Maybe they liked big bedrooms."

"So what's next?" Marla asked.

"I think it's time to consult our friend Dr. Chin. Why should he lounge around while we do all the work?"

Two hours, and numerous trips to the surface later, the area was flooded with light. Chin was sitting at a makeshift table heaped with electronics. The tiny comp screen washed Chin's face with green as agile fingers tapped out a quick rhythm on the keyboard. Multicolored wires snaked their way across the floor to climb the wall and disappear over the top. Chin had circled the wall dropping a variety of instruments into the water like a fisherman with more than one line.

Meanwhile, Marla and the marines had explored the rest of the floor. They found three staircases. Two led downwards and were blocked by water or cave-ins. The third also led downwards but ended in a tunnel. Common sense, plus a trail of blood and droppings, indicated this was the escape route used by their six-legged attackers. Two marines were posted at the entrance, and lights were placed fifty feet down the tunnel so they could see anything which approached.

Marla and the marines also found a whole row of flooded shafts. She thought they were some sort of lift tubes or elevators, but Honcho simply shrugged, saying it was too early to tell. He pointed out they could also be garbage chutes, ventilators, or ceremonial pathways to planetary gods. Marla agreed politely, but thought Honcho was making the whole thing too complicated. After all, why would anyone with sufficient technology to build tall buildings, run up and down the stairs? She felt sure Honcho would come up with all sorts of reasons, but didn't want to hear them.

"Well folks, here's everything you ever wanted to know about what's down there," Chin said modestly. They all gathered around to look at the print-out which Chin's equipment had produced. Peering between Honcho and

Jumo, Renn saw a grid on which there were large expanses of blue cross-hatching, and blobs of white. "For the uninitiated," Chin said, "the white blobs are objects with sufficient density to bounce a signal off, and the shaded areas represent open space."

Renn was struck by the fact that the white blobs, or solid objects, were symmetrically arranged towards the center of the room. In fact, if the atrium weren't flooded, and he looked over the wall, he'd be looking straight down at them. All of which suggested that the balcony, and the open space around the objects, was intended for viewing. Evidently Honcho agreed, because he said, "From the looks of it, those white blobs in the center of the next floor down were pretty important. One gets the feeling that the builders liked to stand around and look at them. Anyone feel like taking a dip? I'd volunteer, but I'm not really built for it."

A lively discussion ensued. Jumo felt that one of his marines should make the dive, but Renn objected, pointing out that the marines were stretched thin guarding *Fred*, the camp, the entry point to the ruins, plus the underground tunnel which the monsters used. Marla and Honcho weren't built for the task, Chin was too valuable, and Jumo should be available to lead his marines. Furthermore, Renn argued, he'd done quite a bit of diving on Terra, and could anyone else say the same?

Jumo finally gave in, the expedition's single set of diving gear was brought from camp, and Renn made ready for his dive. Ready, but not eager. The water had a dark ominous look. Doing his best to ignore the water, and all that its flat reflective surface might conceal, he gave his gear one last check. The face mask-light combination seemed to fit fairly well though he wouldn't know for sure until he got into the water. The rebreather unit on his back fed him rubber flavored air like it was supposed to, the weight belt around his waist felt just about right, and his swim fins were a size too small, but better than nothing. His only weapon was a force blade strapped to his right thigh. They'd forgotten to bring a spear gun. Well, hopefully he wouldn't need it. So far there were no signs of life on any of Chin's electronic sensors. There were two lines fastened to his harness, one in case of trouble, and the other for any interesting artifacts he might run into along the way.

As Renn climbed to the top of the wall and prepared to enter the water, Marla prowled restlessly back and forth along the edge of darkness. She didn't like this one bit. In her opinion it was a job for the marines, but she didn't dare say so, especially since Renn might resent her interference. So she swore silently to herself and hoped it would be over quickly.

"Remember . . . three tugs on either line and we'll pull you up, pronto," Jumo said sternly.

Renn nodded, grasped the mouthpiece firmly between his teeth, and jumped feet first. It was a long drop to the water and he hit with a tremendous splash. The water was shockingly cold. As he sank towards the bottom Renn noticed the water was surprisingly clear. A million tiny bits of mineral matter reflected his light back at him, but except for those, the water seemed very clean. Good. He'd expected the murky, sediment-laden stuff of the swamp, and this would make the job a lot easier.

Rolling forward he pulled his arms in and kicked towards the bottom. The water was damned cold, and the two lines were an annoying encumbrance, but otherwise it was almost fun. He'd always enjoyed diving, the sensual flow of water across his skin, and the tiny bit of danger that always went with it. But here the potential danger outweighed the pleasure and put him on edge. Renn did his best to keep a good look-out, but outside of the mineral motes and the darkness beyond, there was nothing to see. Then the floor suddenly rose to meet him. Its surface was covered with a softly undulating carpet of whitish sediment which billowed up and around him as the tip of one fin scraped along the top of it.

The objects should be somewhere to the right. Turning, he kicked towards the center of the large room. His light glided over the sediment. Wait . . . what the hell was that? Something had broken the perfect symmetry of the floor. He executed a tight turn and went back, moving slowly this time, so he wouldn't miss whatever it was. There . . . At his touch the sediment seemed to leap off the object as if happy to get away. It swirled for a moment, glittering in the light, and then drifted away to reveal a triangular skull. A few wispy bits of flesh and skin still clung to white bone.

Renn felt something heavy drop into his stomach, and whirled through a 360-degree turn, almost tangling his lines. Judging from the skull, the dead thing had been fairly large, which meant that whatever killed it was even larger, and might see him as a fitting dessert. But there was nothing to see. Just glittering motes which danced before his eyes. Clenching the rubber mouthpiece between his teeth, Renn turned and kicked towards the center of the room. A tiny trickle of water had found its way into his mask and was collecting at the bottom. Suddenly he wanted to finish the dive as soon as possible.

Moments later, something loomed large in front of him. An artifact. It had no discernible shape, was about half his size, and thickly covered with white sediment. Only the surface layer floated away at his touch. The rest formed a solid crust inches thick. He saw something from the corner of his eye and whirled, reaching for the force blade. He felt foolish. Just another artifact. Swimming right he found three more. Then, circling around behind those, he found four more standing back to back with the first row. He couldn't tell what the objects were, but knew they were different from each other. For example, the one right in front of him was more horizontal than vertical. It stood on three short pedestals.

He approached the artifact and put both his hands underneath it, bent his knees, and lifted. Nothing. Backing off he pulled his force blade and flicked it on. It vibrated slightly in his hand. Kicking down towards the base of the artifact he used the force blade to attack the sediment. The blade seemed to vibrate more as it cut into the encrusted material. A cloud of sediment rose to surround him. Renn completed the cut by feel and turned off the force blade. The sediment was already starting to settle as he slipped the blade into its sheath. Placing his arms under the artifact, Renn flexed his knees, and tried again. For a moment nothing happened. Then the artifact broke free, jerking upwards a bit before falling back. Good. The thing was heavy, but not too heavy to lift.

Pulling down some more line, he tied it around the object, checked his knots, and jerked on his lifeline three times. The response was instantaneous. He shot upwards like a rocket.

Meanwhile, hundreds of feet away, something long and sinuous completed its long journey through underwater tunnels, and slid into the cool water of the pool. The water tasted like home. Though completely blind, the thing had other senses, including a keen sense of taste and the ability to detect even the smallest vibration in the surrounding water. It paused. Something was moving where all should be still. Though not very intelligent, the thing was nonetheless cautious, for there were other even more dangerous denizens of the deep roaming Swamp. But the source of this disturbance was too small, too puny to be one of those, and must therefore fall into the other category. Food.

With a powerful sideways swish of its body, the thing slid upwards through the water, mouth open to expose razor sharp backward curving teeth. The day's hunt hadn't gone well. It was hungry.

Not knowing if Renn was in trouble or not, everyone grabbed into his lifeline, and pulled with all their might. As yard after yard of dripping line came over wall, Marla ran this way and that, desperately wishing she could help. Even Chin left his equipment to lend a hand. If he hadn't, maybe he'd have seen the long white shape arrowing up across his tiny comp screen. But he was pulling on the line instead and cheering with the others when Renn burst up through the surface of the water. Seconds later he was hauled dripping over the side. As Renn removed his face mask and mouth piece they bombarded him with questions. Was he OK? What was it like down there? Should they haul in the other line?

So no one saw the long coil break the surface of the water and dive from sight. The thing was puzzled. Somehow the food had escaped its grasp. But such things had happened before. The solution was patience. If one waited long enough, food that disappeared upwards often returned. Having completed its long dive, the thing allowed itself to sink into the upper layer of sediment. Billions of tiny particles exploded upwards, and then one by one, drifted gently down to cover the thing with a soft blanket of white.

The excitement was almost palpable as Jumo and Chin rigged the collapsible A-frame. As they worked, Honcho was everywhere, getting in the way, and providing a running commentary on their efforts. Once the frame was assembled, Jumo produced a blast rifle, dialed up a narrow beam, and drilled a series of holes in the floor. Renn watched as the holes in the A-frame's base plate were lined up with the holes in the floor, bolts were inserted and then melted into place. Now the A-frame was ready to go. Metal squealed on metal as the structure was swiveled out and over the water.

"All right slaves," Honcho said happily, "let's see what sort of fish Jonathan has hooked!" As Renn towelled off, Jumo and Chin fed the line through the pulley at the top of the A-frame, and Honcho waddled back and forth in excitement.

"Grab on," Jumo instructed, and everyone did. Even Marla got into the act, grabbing the far end of the line with her teeth, and backing up. The pulley squeaked under the strain, but inch by inch, foot by foot, great loops of dripping line piled up at their feet.

Far below the artifact broke contact with the floor, and swayed slightly, giving off a small avalanche of sediment. Then it began to jerk its way upwards. Stirring at first, then sensing that the movement had nothing to do with food, the thing returned to its state of patient watchfulness.

Up above they all gave one last heave on the line and the artifact broke the surface. Honcho's feathers went every which way as he jumped up and down with excitement, reminding Renn of an antique feather duster. A feather duster with a loud voice. "All the way slaves! Take it all the way!"

Pulling in concert they hauled the object up and out of the water until it swung just below the apex of the A-frame. "All right Honcho," Jumo grunted, "lock the line."

Honcho flipped a lever on the side of the A-frame which engaged a brake on the pulley. Renn felt the tension go off the line as the brake locked it into place.

Jumo wiped his hands on his pants as he eyed the dripping artifact and the supporting A-frame. "You think it'll fit?"

Renn nodded. It looked as if the artifact would just barely fit through the top part of the A. A quick measurement by Honcho confirmed his guess.

"Well then let's give it a try," Jumo grabbed the line and they all followed suit. "On three," Jumo said. "One, two, and three!" They all heaved as hard as they could. Since the line was locked in place this had the effect of pulling the top of the A-frame towards them. With a screech of unoiled metal the A-frame swiveled on its hinged legs. As the A frame tilted towards them, the artifact came with it, swinging neatly through the top part of the A with only inches to spare. The artifact jerked to a halt as the A-frame hit the stops built into its base, and hung there, swinging gently back and forth. The pulley lock was released, and moments later the artifact was gently lowered to the floor.

By now it was evening, and time to return to the camp. Ford was sent up to the surface for a couple of long poles. By placing these side by side on the floor, and connecting them with short pieces of line, Renn made a sling. The artifact was placed in the sling upside down pedestals up. Then with a man on each end of both poles the artifact was carried to the surface. By the time a second trip had been made to retrieve Chin's electronics, it was dark. The A-frame and other heavy duty gear were left below for future use.

The artifact and Chin's gear were painstakingly hauled to camp. As they entered, the first thing Renn saw was Vanessa, sitting in a camp chair reading a micro spool. She didn't even look up when the marines entered carrying the artifact between them. It didn't take a genius to figure out that she wasn't too thrilled with Honcho's success.

After dinner was made, eaten and cleared away, Honcho began work on the artifact. It was a long, slow process. Working with infinite care, he used a variety of brushes to clean off as much sediment as he could, and then went to work with a collection of small tools. Gently, he chipped away at the encrusted sediment, often mumbling to himself, the clink of his tools echoing softly between the walls.

Renn watched for a while, but grew increasingly sleepy, and decided to lay down for a little nap. The next thing he knew, it was morning and Jumo was nudging him awake. "Come on Jonathan. It's time to get up."

Yawning, he sat up, and then clawed for the .75. There was a tunnel creature sitting not ten feet away! Their laughter stopped him. He took another look. It was the most incredible piece of sculpture he'd ever seen. Every line was perfect, somehow capturing not only the look of the beast, but the feeling too. It seemed to live, to breathe, as if any moment it might come out of a trance and move towards him. But it was different somehow. For one thing there was a half smile on its dog face, similar to the one Marla often wore, and there was something else a look of wisdom in its eyes. But how could that be? The tunnel creatures were among the most vicious on Swamp!

"We don't know," Honcho said simply, answering Renn's silent question. The Finthian looked drawn and haggard. He'd worked through the night, unable to stop. Each additional patch of cleaned sculpture had demanded another, and so on, until the whole thing was laid bare.

"Not even a guess?"

Honcho grinned wearily. "You know damned well I couldn't resist a guess." He gestured to the sculpture. "I haven't got much to back it up, but based on the fact that these things are mammals, while everything else on this planet is oviparous, you've got to ask yourself if they originally came from off planet. And if they did come from off planet, then it seems logical to think the Builders brought them here, and thought them important enough to immortalize through sculpture. Take a look at those feet."

Renn did as Honcho asked, and saw that the first two sets of feet were clearly prehensile. He knew without checking that the creatures they'd killed earlier had elongated claws on their front feet.

Honcho nodded knowingly. "That's right. Tool users. It seems this particular species was sentient at one time.

Apparently they de-evolved into their present state. "The question is why?" Honcho stared at the sculpture as if willing it to answer.

"They got left behind?"

Honcho looked up and frowned. "What did you say?"

Renn shrugged. "Maybe they got left behind when the Builders took off. Perhaps they were dependent on the Builders in some special way, and when the Builders left unexpectedly, they couldn't make it on their own."

Honcho smiled. "Not a bad theory. I think I'll write it up and take credit for it."

"So what else is new," Vanessa said, getting up from her chair, and stalking outside. Marla was forced to scurry out of her way.

Renn barely noticed Vanessa leave. He was getting caught up in the intellectual puzzle. If the first artifact recovered suggested an intelligent race descended into barbarity, then what would the other seven reveal? Renn wanted to know, and judging from the look in Honcho's huge eyes, he did too.

So two hours later they were underground once more. Chin assembled his electronics, while Renn stripped, and prepared to dive. Meanwhile Marla fussed around the edges. She felt Renn had done his share, and that someone else should take a turn. But Renn was stubborn as usual, insisting that he was the logical choice. He knew where the other artifacts were and what to expect. Besides, he'd be better equipped this time. With Jumo's help, he'd jury rigged a cutting torch from a mini-welder, and cobbled together an adjustable sling. Together they'd simplify the whole process of cutting the artifacts loose and getting them to the surface.

Chin dropped his instruments into the cold water and ran a preliminary check. Renn eyed Chin's findings as he made the final adjustments to his diving rig. There they were, seven white blobs, and no sign of anything new. He gave Marla a thumbs up, attached both lines to his harness, and climbed up onto the wall. The water looked flat and black. Renn felt a sudden chill which had nothing to do with the cold air, but shook it off. He'd been down there before and emerged without a scratch. He stepped into space and dropped feet first into the water.

Far below the thing sensed the shock wave caused by Renn's entry, and stirred slightly. So, the food had returned. The thing had no sense of time. Seconds or days might have passed. It made little difference. The food had gone away and returned. And that was good. The thing was hungry. A vast, empty need ran the length of its body and demanded satisfaction.

As before Renn saw nothing but glittering sediment. Kicking strongly he headed for the center of the room and the waiting artifacts. His light touched them first and, moments later, so did he. He unwrapped the sling, slipped it around an artifact, and made it fast. Next he used the torch to cut through the encrusted sediment around its base. Suddenly a cold current of water touched his neck. He spun around, eyes probing the darkness. Nothing.

Just nerves. He turned back to the artifact and clipped the cargo line to the sling. Something hit his lifeline with incredible force. The lifeline jerked him upwards and then let go as razor-sharp teeth sliced it in two. Looking up Renn saw a huge mouthful of backward-curving teeth coming straight at him. Renn ducked behind an artifact and felt the water boil around him as the monstrous thing slid by. He tried to follow the thing's head and just barely escaped as it darted in from behind. Suddenly a huge coil of the thing's snake-like body materialized around his waist. As it began to tighten he saw the head turn on the end of a long serpentine neck and dart his way. If he didn't do something fast he'd wind up as snake food. He went for the force blade. Damn! It was out of reach below the fat coil of hard flesh which was wrapped around his middle.

Desperate fingers scrabbled for the cutting torch and found it still clipped to its lanyard. He triggered it. Nothing. The head was still coming. Damn and double damn, he'd forgotten the safety. Clumsy fingers released the safety and hit the trigger again. A foot long lance of blue energy leaped into existence and boiled the surrounding water. He saw the thing's head jerk back. Good, he'd bought some time. Then he felt his eyes bulge as the thing squeezed even harder.

The thing was puzzled and a little frightened. What was this food which fought back in strange ways and created heat? Why wouldn't it die as food should?

It was hard to breathe. Renn's vision began to blur as he applied the torch to the thing's flesh. Skin, muscle and bone seemed to melt away. Dark blood spurted out to stain the water. The thing writhed in agony but managed to hold on. Gritting his teeth, Renn directed the torch back and forth across the width of the thing's body, determined to cut it in two. He was about a third of the way through when it suddenly let go.

Whipping itself around in a tight circle the thing came straight at him. Gasping for air, Renn felt the floor under his feet and held the torch straight out. The monster kept on coming. Then, just when it seemed the creature would swallow his arm—lance and all—the thing swerved.

Acting on impulse, Renn bent his knees and used the floor to push off. As he hit, Renn threw his arms and legs around the thing's snake-like body, and hung on. It wasn't easy. The thing tried to throw him off, snapping from side to side, and looping this way and that. Twice it tried to bite him, but couldn't bend enough to reach something only six or eight feet back from its own head. Renn continued to work his way up towards the thing's skull. Having failed to cut the creature in two he'd try for its brain. If its brain was somewhere else, then maybe he could destroy the thing's mouth. Inch by inch, foot by foot, he moved slowly upwards.

Something hit his right leg and hurt like hell. The damned thing was trying to scrape him off against the artifacts! The rubber mouthpiece was suddenly jerked from his mouth. With his air supply gone so was his time. He couldn't reach back to get it without letting go, and that would mean certain death. Gritting his teeth against the pain Renn doubled his efforts to move upwards. Moments later he found himself clinging just below the thing's flat head. His lungs were on fire, his vision blurred, and his thoughts painfully slow. Mustering every remaining ounce of strength, Renn aimed his torch at what he hoped was the creature's brain case, and hit the trigger. A lance of blue energy disappeared into the thing's skull. Brains boiled. Convulsions rippled the length of the creature's body. It went limp. Renn let go and grabbed for the mouthpiece. As he sucked cold, sweet air into his lungs, the thing fell, throwing up a long wave of sediment as it hit the floor. Soon its flesh would rot away and be eaten by a host of tiny scavengers. And then it would join its victims beneath a shroud of white.

—— Chapter Twelve ——

Renn made six more dives over the next two days. Chin maintained a sharp lookout via his sensors but saw no signs of life. Perhaps the water was too cold for other monsters, or the passageway too hard to find, or who knows. Whatever the reason the pool remained empty and Renn worked undisturbed. They had it down to a science now, reeling the artifacts in like dead fish, and hauling them back to camp.

Meanwhile Honcho worked day and night. Under his careful hands the sculptures were reborn, gradually emerging from sedimentary cocoons to new life. They were a varied lot, alike only in their absolute perfection. The first statue was still the only one corresponding to a known life form. Although Honcho had cleaned up five more, and each was quite interesting in its own right, none corresponded with the alien races encountered by man. Some were probably sentient, since there is a high degree of correlation between tool-use and sentience, and these had prehensile limbs, or were depicted as having tool-like artifacts. Others were less clear having physiologies too alien to understand via a piece of sculpture. So the sculptures evoked all sorts of questions, the primary one being what were they to each other? And or, what were they to the Builders? One of the most popular theories was that they represented subject or member races within the Builders' empire. Honcho pointed out that while that was one of the possibilities, it was more than a little anthropocentric and was therefore less likely to be accurate.

So they vied with each other to create new theories. Jumo came up with one of the most original during dinner one evening. He was standing in front of the statues, chewing his last mouthful of food when he asked, "How do we know the Builders were nice guys? For all we know these statues might be a menu, you know, the eight foods Builders like best!"

Honcho smiled. "Not a bad theory, although I wouldn't want to snack on any of them myself. They're too weird looking."

Now it was the fourth day, all the artifacts had been raised, and things had settled into a routine. Vanessa was sulking as usual, Marla was on a security patrol with Jumo, and Renn was just goofing off. A privilege everyone agreed he'd earned. His leg was a little sore, but otherwise he felt pretty good. He was sipping his third cup of morning coffee when the chipping sounds suddenly stopped. He noticed because the clink and clatter of Honcho's tools had long since become a natural part of the background. No one could figure out how the Finthian scientist managed to keep going without sleep, but somehow he did. Maybe he was finally taking a break.

Then Renn heard an inarticulate squawking noise. The sound had a distressed quality. Renn jumped to his feet, dropped his coffee, and hurried toward's Honcho's make-shift work area. As he approached, Renn noticed that Honcho wasn't wearing his translator. That would account for the squawking noises but not his obvious distress. Honcho's eyes bulged with pent-up emotion, his neck feathers fluffed out into a stiff collar, and his hand trembled as he pointed towards his latest effort. Turning Renn felt his heart leap into his throat. The half-cleaned sculpture was a perfect replica of a Finthian male!

Needless to say the Finthian sculpture stirred up a great deal of discussion. It even brought Vanessa over for a narrow-eyed look. Glancing from Honcho to the sculpture and back again, she nodded knowingly, and said, "Well this certainly supports the thesis that there's some sort of special link between the builders and the Finthian race."

And it was true. The sculpture seemed to prove some sort of ancient linkage between the builders and the Finthians. Curiously enough, this seemed to trouble Honcho rather than please him. He stopped working, retreated to a distant part of the hall, and sat there for two days refusing all conversation, and consuming nothing but a little water.

As the Finthian scientist faded into the background, Vanessa came forward. She picked up the work where he'd left off, finishing the Finthian statue, and completing another as well. As she worked, Vanessa spoke steadily into a small recorder fastened to her belt, and occasionally paused to take holos of work in process. She was half way through the last statue, a strange insectoid looking lifeform, when Honcho emerged from his self-imposed isolation.

Looking over what she'd done Honcho nodded his approval. "Good work Vanessa. Nicely done." He caught Jumo's eye. "Call everyone together please. Guards excepted of course. I'd like to hold a short staff meeting." As Jumo hurried off, the Finthian scientist selected a meal pak from his private supply, and triggered the heating element. Seconds later he ripped the top off and began to eat. Renn averted his eyes, disliking the sight of the poached grubs which Honcho so eagerly forked into his mouth. By the time everyone had gathered around he was polishing off his second meal pak. "Care for some grub, anyone?" Honcho held up an especially ripe specimen on his single pronged Finthian fork. "No? Well you're quite right. Something about the way they make these damned meal paks dries 'em out. Nothing worse than a dried out grub."

The humans tried to look sympathetic, wincing only slightly as Honcho placed the last grub in his mouth, and then popped it with his beak. "So it seems I owe you an apology. I know that by human standards I've been somewhat distant over the last few days. I assure you however that such periods are a normal reaction to stress among my people, and quite healing. Why you humans run to each other during such times will forever escape me. In any case, the source of my stress was the discovery that there is indeed an ancient link between my race and that of the Builders." Here Honcho turned away as if ashamed. "I'm afraid my reaction was quite unscientific. Leaping to unscientific conclusions has always been one of my greatest weaknesses, and when I saw my race represented in what might very well be a subordinate role, well, I allowed my emotions to momentarily prevail." Now he turned back, large saucer-like eyes turning to each of them in turn. "You humans are not alone in your feelings of superiority." Honcho shrugged a very human shrug. "So it became necessary to retreat within for awhile and deal with my emotions." He smiled. "The funny part is that after other more objective minds have examined our find, they may very well decide my assumptions were grounded in fact, and conclude that all of these races were somehow subservient."

"But their judgment will have to wait. I called you together because I think we've taken this effort about as far as we can. What started out as a survey has turned into a full scale dig, only without the tools and personnel required to do a good job. I fear that before long both our supplies and our good luck will begin to run out." Renn saw Jumo nod in agreement, and knew without looking that Marla agreed as well.

"So," Honcho continued, "Rather than wait for that to happen, I propose we transport the artifacts to the LZ and put them aboard the shuttle. Then we'll take a quick look at the other two sites, pack up, and lift. After that, well who knows. Our artifacts should stir things up. Maybe even enough to get our superiors off their roosts. On the strength of what we've found, perhaps they'll land enough marines to do the job right."

"Or hire locals to do it," Renn suggested. "There's a lot of tough customers on this planet, they have to be, but the promise of a pardon would raise a small army."

Honcho nodded his agreement. "An excellent suggestion. Given that kind of protection, enough supplies, and sufficient time we could learn a lot here. We've only scratched the surface."

"I agree," Vanessa put in. It was a simple statement, and one which suggested a truce. But Honcho simply nodded, apparently taking her comment at face value. Renn wondered if the Finthian scientist had noticed her recent unhappiness. As Honcho had explained earlier, Finthians considered withdrawal to be a completely normal and routine behavior. Renn smiled to himself. All that drama wasted!

The next five days were a lot of hard work. It took ten trips to transport people, supplies, and sculptures back to the LZ. Then there was the effort involved in setting up a new camp near the LZ. *Fred* was too small to house the entire party, and Renn insisted they build a new camp for reasons of security. Jumo backed him up. Both knew that the longer you use a camp, the longer traces of it will remain. So far they'd been lucky, and escaped notice by Swamp's less pleasant citizens. It was a trend they hoped to continue.

So by the time the shuttle arrived they were bone-tired. They groaned in unison as Lt. Fitz misjudged the landing, and thumped in hard. Then it was more work unloading new supplies and loading artifacts. The moment the artifacts were strapped down, and the hatches sealed, the shuttle blasted upwards. As usual, Fitz heaved a giant sigh of relief as the ship entered space.

Meanwhile, far below, a shifty set of eyes watched the shuttle disappear, and fed that information to a crafty brain. He was a little man, only partly sane, quivering with the intensity of his thoughts. A filthy hand came up to scratch a grizzled chin, and a rasping chuckle issued forth from a toothless mouth. "My, my. What have we here? Funny business that's what. And where there's business there's profit. Oh my yes. And where there's profit there's crazy Dan. Crazy like a fox, I am. My, my, yes. Come, my darlings. Take Daddy to dinner."

With a strong shove the old man pushed off from shore and felt the current grab the hull of his flat bottomed boat. As the boat started down the channel there was a great flapping of leathery wings and two lifters launched themselves from nearby trees. As their massive shadows swept over him, Dan looked up with considerable pride. Where others saw ugliness in their long curving necks and predatory talons Dan saw beauty. They were his friends, his confidants, his children. He'd painstakingly reared them from chicks, protected them from predators, fed their endless appetites, and conditioned them to do his bidding. Now they were his eyes in the sky. His allies. His only friends. They would guide him to the feast, and then, when all was ready, help him consume it.

Another rainy season had started. The big, fat rain drops hit *Fred*'s windows like tiny bombs and splattered in every direction. The cabin was too small to accommodate everyone at once, so half sat inside drying out, while the rest waited their turn in the huddled misery of the open cockpit. It made little difference to Renn. As the only qualified helmsman he stayed outside all day.

Fifteen days passed in a never ending succession of channels, lakes and jungle. What were now officially named "Boater's Ruins," had been designated as "Red Zone Two" on the orbital survey maps. That left "Red Zone One," and "Red Zone three," for investigation. They reached Red Zone One five days after the shuttle lifted. It was nothing more than an extensive rock formation. Some sort of volcanic upheaval, maybe the same one which created the swamps, had upthrust a huge slab of rock honeycombed with countless passageways. As a result it had the same density, reflectivity, and ambient temperature as Boater's Ruins. While interesting in its own right, the rock formation had nothing to do with the Builders, so they departed for Zone Three. Ten days later Zone Three lay just ahead, and Renn was glad, since both supplies and tempers were starting to run short.

Marla was standing in the bow, the rain running in rivulets off her synthetic fur, the breeze filling her olfactory sensors with swamp smells. It smelled no better or worse than any other part of the swamp, but for some reason Marla couldn't explain, she didn't like it. Perhaps because it was a part of her original self, and not an electronic component, Marla had come to trust her intuition a great deal. And as Renn guided *Fred* in towards the bank, her intuition screamed, "Get the hell out of here!" But as usual, her inner voice went unheeded, like her, a victim of circumstance.

As soon as *Fred* was secured, Renn and Marla went ashore looking for a campsite. One was soon found, a small clearing sheltered by a stand of enormous trees, and backed by a jumble of rock. Some of the marines went to work setting up collapsible shelters, while the rest set up a defensive perimeter, and the scientists sorted out their gear. Night fell just as these activities were completed, and with the exception of the sentries, they all fell into an exhausted sleep.

Feeling refreshed in spite of a two-hour turn at guard duty, Renn finished his breakfast quickly, and suggested a quick recon of the area. "Marla and I will just take a quick look around just to make sure we aren't camped in the middle of a roo monster picnic area or something."

"Fine," Jumo agreed, "providing you wear radios, and stay in contact."

"Of course," Renn replied innocently. "We're always careful, aren't we Marla?"

"Always," Marla said with a wolfish grin.

"Shit." Jumo turned away shaking his head in disgust.

They slid into the jungle fifty yards apart, close enough to see each other, but far enough apart so they wouldn't fall victim to the same ambush. Seeing each other was a sometimes-thing. Renn caught glimpses of Marla every now and then when she passed through a small clearing, or paused on top of a rotting log to scan ahead. It felt like their old hunting days all over again.

As she loped along Marla's sensors told her that everything was all right and her intuition told her it wasn't. It said there was danger lurking out there. She sighed. Of course there was danger. The whole damn planet was dangerous. At least the rain had stopped for awhile.

A lone roo monster broke from cover up ahead and scurried off to the right. Renn let it go. This seemed like good country. No one had hunted here for a long time, if ever. Then he saw it, a change in the texture of the jungle up ahead. "Something ahead, Marla," Renn said softly, knowing Marla would hear via her radio.

"Trouble?" The voice was Jumo's.

"Nope. At least I don't think so. Just something up ahead. A clearing maybe."

"OK, but be careful."

Renn scrambled up a slight incline, jumped a small stream, and passed between the last of the trees. As he emerged into the clearing Marla did likewise about fifty feet to his left. The open area was about three hundred feet across and perfectly level. Nothing grew on its surface larger than small plants, which had a withered sickly look. That in itself was strange, since the plant life of swamp was locked into an eternal battle for space, and here was a large patch of ground going largely unused. "You circle left, I'll circle right."

Marla nodded and loped off to the left. Renn moved to the right, observing as he did so that the clearing seemed to be a perfect circle.

"Got something?" Jumo again.

"Just a clearing," Renn answered. "But a strange clearing."

"How so?" Honcho's voice this time.

"Well, for one thing, it seems to be in the shape of a perfect circle."

"And for another, plants seem to avoid it," Marla added, padding along the opposite edge of the clearing from Renn.

Honcho said, "I'll be there in a few minutes."

"No you won't," Jumo said sternly. "Not until Renn and Marla say it's safe."

A few minutes later, Renn and Marla met on the far side of the circle from where they'd started. Both had seen signs that the area was frequented by various kinds of monsters, but nothing unusual. Renn felt a shadow slide across his face. His right hand dipped and came up with the .75. High above two huge lifters circled. He fired twice, more to scare them off than anything, and saw one jerk slightly. A hit! The huge creature screeched in pain, recovered, and headed east. The other monster did likewise, flying alongside the first as if offering protection and comfort. Renn had never seen anything like it. Like roos, lifters were usually antisocial, and didn't spent much time worrying about each other.

"Report!" The demanding voice belonged to Jumo.

"Nothing," Renn answered. "Just a couple of lifters. I

wounded one and they took off. The clearing seems safe enough if Honcho still wants to take a look."

When Honcho arrived Vanessa was with him. Together they circled the clearing and then ordered the marines to dig a slit trench. Griping and grumbling, a couple of marines went to work under Jumo's supervision. Though messy the task wasn't hard. The water-saturated ground was quite soft. Each shovel full made a sucking noise as it came up and out of the trench. Water soon ran in to fill the bottom of the ditch, and before long the marines were standing ankle deep in the stuff. A few minutes later, Ford's shovel made a clanging sound as it hit something hard. "What the hell?"

Moments later Issacs hit something hard as well. For the next few minutes the marines worked like demons. Finally they managed to clear out most of the mud, although the bottom of the trench was still invisible under three or four inches of water.

Honcho's huge feet made a big splash as he jumped down into the trench and felt around under the water. By scooping it away he was able to obtain brief glimpses of a hard gray surface. When Honcho emerged from the ditch he was covered with mud and a big grin split his face. "We'll have to analyze it to be sure, but I'd swear it's more of that duracrete-type stuff the builders used for everything. One thing's for sure, it isn't rock, so onwards slaves! Let's have another trench over there!" Honcho pointed dramatically towards the other side of the clearing. The marines groaned in disgust, picked up their shovels, and trudged towards the far side of the clearing. Later they would find out it was only the first of many trenches yet to come.

That evening, long after the scientists had finished dinner and gone to bed, Dan was still up. Firelight danced over his face and reflected back from the lifter's eyes. They glowed like red coals in the dark. "Poor, poor baby," Dan crooned softly, running grimy fingers down along the neck of the wounded lifter. "Don't worry baby. Daddy loves you, and Daddy will punish the bad people." Grabbing a leathery wing, Dan pulled it gently outwards. The lifter gave a squawk of protest. "There, there, Daddy's sorry."

Fortunately, the slug had passed through without exploding. There wasn't much bleeding since a lifter's wings aren't very vascular, and what there was Dan had managed to stop. He'd disinfected the wound, sutured it up, and briefly wondered when he'd learned to do things like that. Maybe he'd been a doctor once. He wasn't sure. There were lots of memories all jumbled together. It made his head hurt to think about them. The lifter could fly, that was the main thing. He released the wing and watched the lifter tuck it back into place. Outside of the gunshot wound things had gone very well indeed.

Using the lifters as scouts, Dan had located and tracked the scientists with surprising ease. For the last ten days he'd been following them, watching, and waiting for the proper killing ground. Now the time was right. Their camp was well chosen but not impregnable. He'd proved that by entering and leaving it during broad daylight. Slipping between the sentries as though they weren't even there a tiny corner of Dan's disturbed mind saw their uniforms and wondered what marines were doing on Swamp. But it was an unimportant detail, hardly central to the task at hand, and therefore unworthy of his consideration. First, Dan tallied the weapons and supplies, a rich haul indeed, and complete with a fancy boat to carry it away in. Then he listened as a talking bird thing spoke to a human woman about things he couldn't understand. The woman stirred memories between his legs. He made a note to save her for last. He'd use her and then feed her to his pets. Forcing himself to concentrate, Dan counted the people in the camp, assigned them places on his death list, and slipped away unnoticed.

Chuckling to himself, Dan opened a waterproof case, and

withdrew a long-barreled rifle. It was more than three hundred years old. An antique, but a deadly one, since Dan had spent endless hours crafting new parts to replace old, and adding small improvements of his own design. The once plain stock was now an intricate work of art, carved into fanciful shapes, and perfectly shaped to his liking. There was a satisfying click as the powerful scope snapped into place. The action made a snicking sound as he worked it a couple of times. Then with the love of a father for a child, Dan laid the rifle on its case, and selected a twenty round magazine. He opened a box of hand loaded ammo and selected the bullets one at a time. They were designed for long distance killing. Solid slugs with plenty of chemical propellent behind them. Dan chuckled as he thought about the clearing the scientific party liked so well. What a perfect killing ground. Open, outside the defensive perimeter, and surrounded by natural cover. A sniper's dream.

The bullets were slick with their individual coatings of silicon. Each had a name and a personality provided by its creator at the moment of birth. To Dan they were tiny warriors awaiting his orders. One by one he inserted them into the empty magazine. "You first Hercules, and then you Rommel, and you Napoleon, and you Geronimo . . ." The bullets made a clicking noise as he slipped them into the magazine, and gradually the droning of his voice lulled the lifters to sleep.

The second, third, and fourth trenches were just like the first. The marines started right after breakfast on the third day, and soon ran into the same pattern as before. They'd dig down and run into something hard. Then they'd clear the mud away. Honcho would jump in, feel around, and promptly order another ditch. Finally he called a halt. By now it was obvious that the duracrete-like material underlay the entire clearing. "Thanks slaves. You dig a mean ditch."

Unamused, Ford and Issacs mumbled things which

though mostly unintelligible, seemed to cast aspersions on Honcho's ancestry, intelligence, and probable future.

Honcho, Renn, Marla, and Vanessa were about to head for camp, when Chin emerged from the jungle waving a black box over his head. He was flushed with excitement. He skidded to a stop in front of them and said, "A signal! I picked up a signal!"

Vanessa raised an eyebrow. "So?"

Chin shook his head. "No, you don't understand. Not a regular signal. An extremely low frequency signal coming from right here!" He pointed at his feet.

"From here?" Honcho asked in amazement. "Have you been drinking?"

"Yes! I mean no! The signal's coming from right around us. That's what's so weird. Here, listen to this." Chin did something to the dials on the black box and they heard a steady tone. He motioned. "Follow me."

They did as the scientist requested, following him towards camp. As Chin left the clearing, the tone began to drop in volume. Twenty feet from the clearing it was hard to hear, and by the time they reached camp the tone was barely audible. Turning Chin marched back, and as he did so, the tone gradually increased in volume until it was loud and strong once more. "I found it entirely by accident while setting up my equipment," Chin said. "As you just saw, the signal's too weak to pick up more than a quarter mile from the clearing."

The next hour was spent trying to figure out where it came from. The signal was confined to the clearing, and a short distance beyond. It occupied an ultra-low frequency occasionally used by the empire for military purposes, but otherwise largely ignored. What's more, all attempts to locate the transmitter itself had failed. The signal seemed to come from nowhere and everywhere at once.

Having run out of ideas they gathered around Honcho

waiting to see what he'd say. "Well?" Renn asked. "What is it? And please don't give us that 'it's too early to tell' stuff. Go ahead and leap to some unscientific conclusions."

"It's always a mistake to tell members of your race anything," Honcho complained good naturedly. "When you do, it always comes back to haunt you. And *it is* too early to tell." He pretended to examine a filthy talon. "Still . . . one possibility does come to mind."

"Which is?" Vanessa asked patiently.

Honcho gestured broadly. "A landing zone. Complete with some sort of low-frequency homing signal. A signal designed for the final phase of landing. That would account for its limited range."

"Not bad," Jumo said looking around. "In fact, it seems incredibly obvious now."

"Thanks," Honcho said dryly. "I appreciate the compliment." It was the last thing he ever said, because the bullet named "Hercules" entered his head through the center of his right eye, and exited through the back of his skull along with most of his brains.

As Honcho's body fell, different people did different things. Ford died as Rommel punched through his light body armor and severed his spine. Marla became a blur as she ran a zig-zag course for the trees. Jumo spun, and ran the opposite way, instinctively dividing the enemy fire. Renn pushed Vanessa into the nearest trench. Issacs opened up with his auto slug thrower and collapsed in a fountain of blood as Napoleon severed his jugular vein. Renn fell on top of Vanessa as the bullet named "Geronimo" slid along his ribs creasing his armor but doing no damage.

"Damn!" Dan looked up from the telescopic sight. He shouldn't have missed that one. The black marine had escaped, too. The dog didn't matter. "Nice doggie. Pet the nice doggie, Dan." A female voice drifted back to him from long ago. Confusing memories welled up to fill his mind. A jumble of love and pain. No, he must concentrate. The black marine would bring help. "Now, my darlings!" From above and behind there was a mighty flapping of wings as both lifters took to the sky.

Jumo's voice snapped over the radio. "Condition Red. Incoming sniper fire . . . one, two, three friendlies down and two questionable. Report."

"Nothing here Section . . . we're coming your way." It was Red. He and the rest of the marines were in and around the camp.

"Negative," Jumo said. "Stay where you are. I repeat, stay where you are and dig in." Jumo was lying just inside the treeline. Working from left to right he scanned the opposite side of the clearing for some sign of the sniper. Nothing. "Now listen up. We've got one, possibly more snipers out here, and the worst thing you could do is come to our rescue. They'll nail anything that enters the clearing. Their objective is the camp and everything in it. Dig in and don't let 'em have it."

"Roger. We understand and will obey," Red said formally.

"All right. Doc, you read me?"

"It's hard not to. You never stop talking."

"Cut the crap and listen up. Get your shit together and be ready to move when I give the word. We've got people down and some may still be alive."

"I'm ready Section. On your command."

Marla heard the radio conversation only dimly. She was concentrating on a tiny red infrared dot. It had started as a pin prick of heat against the vast backdrop of the jungle. Now the pin prick had become a dot, and as she got closer would soon become a blob. And that blob was going to die.

"What the hell are you doing? If this is your idea of a joke . . ."

"Shut up." Renn was peeking up and over the lip of the

trench. Vanessa was beneath him, almost submerged in the water and mud. His knee guaranteed that she'd stay there. She didn't know what was going on, and he didn't have time to explain it to her. The .75 felt puny in his hand. The sniper—and Renn was pretty sure there was only one—had a large-caliber, scope-mounted rifle and the whole jungle to hide in. If he stood he was dead. But Marla was in the jungle. She'd find the bastard, and when she did, God help him. Renn smiled and Vanessa screamed. She pointed up and behind him. He turned as something huge blotted out the sun.

Time to move. Dan didn't think it, he felt it, and scrambled down from his leafy perch. While his children attacked he would move a hundred yards to the right. From there he could nail them entering or leaving camp. Eventually they'd have to do one or the other. *Wait a minute, what was that? A moving shadow. But shadows don't move, at least not that fast, oh, a doggie! Nice doggie!*

"Always fire two rounds, not just one." Boater's voice rang in Renn's ears as he squeezed the trigger. The .75 roared six times, three sets of two, blowing big holes in the lifter's body. What remained fell on him and Vanessa with a dull thump.

Chin eyed the table full of electronics from the safety of the bunker. Red had shoved him into it and ordered him to stay. But what if some bozo put a round through their radio? The back-up had a bad case of swamp rot. How the hell would they call the shuttle? He wanted to tell someone, but the marines were manning the perimeter defenses, and he wasn't wearing a radio. Chin heaved himself up and out of the bunker. He took a quick look around and ran. Just as he reached the table Doc yelled, "Above you!" Looking up, Chin saw a horrible winged monster diving straight at him.

Marla was a living weapon. The target was a man, a blob of guilty red, holding his confession in his hands. He'd killed, and she was judge, jury, and executioner. She was a blur as she traveled the last twenty yards, and unstoppable wolf thing, its entire beingness centered on the sniper. She didn't understand his outstretched hand, or hear his voice calling, "Here doggie! Come to Dan, doggie!"

Grabbing something off the table Chin threw it at the descending monster. The object didn't even come close, but it did cause the lifter to throw out its wings like giant air brakes, and gave Doc the additional half second she needed. She squeezed the trigger and held on. Doc didn't like auto slug throwers. Even with dampers they tend to ride up. Energy weapons don't do that. Still the slug thrower was doing one helluva job. At first tiny pieces of the monster seemed to fly off, then it staggered, and fell like a rock. Doc followed it down until the slug thrower clicked empty. It hit the middle of the compound with a meaty thud. She smiled. Not bad for a pecker checker.

Jumo and Renn helped Vanessa out of the trench. She looked at the dead bodies and threw up. Politely turning their backs the two men saw Marla emerge from the tree line. As she approached the blood on her muzzle and chest spoke more eloquently than words.

Chin was staring at the dead lifter and shaking like a man with swamp fever. Doc patted him gently on the arm. In her view, he was a jerk, but she felt sorry for him. "Scary, aren't they."

Chin looked up and nodded. "But what's even scarier is that I might have thrown this at the lifter." He held up the radio.

For a long time they just stood there grinning at each other. Doc finally broke the silence. "You know what? I'm just a grunt, but if I were you, I'd use that thing while it still works." Chin smiled. "You know what? I think you're right."

PART THREE

Citizen

—— Chapter Thirteen ——

Shinto flipped a switch and waited while two sets of armored duraplast doors whirred open. Stepping out onto the veranda, he took a deep breath of night air. It had a slightly salty taste picked up from the Pacific Ocean some fifty miles to the west. Behind him one of the twins whimpered. Broken bones most likely. No matter, he'd summon medical attention in a few minutes. First, however, he'd savor the moment. As always, the massive sexual release had left him relaxed. A rare thing in Shinto's life.

In spite of his name, Shinto was not Asian. He was in fact of mostly European ancestry. His name was taken from the Shinto shrine where his mother abandoned him just outside Osaka. He was about three months old at the time. No one knew for sure, but it was assumed she'd left him for a better life among the stars, lifting with other indentured colonists to settle some distant planet. If so, she departed during the very end of the three-hundred-year-long mass exodus which drained off most of Terra's excess population.

Denied a family, Shinto raised himself within the cut-throat subculture of state run orphanages. There he learned to steal, to hate, and to kill. Once released he used those skills to good effect, combining them with the single legacy left him by his mother, a natural presentience. He didn't understand his gift, but knew it was real. It had saved his life many times. On the most recent occasion he'd stepped out of a nightclub and into the sights of a legal assassin. Sensing something was wrong, he pulled Donna in front of him, and felt her jerk as the flechettes hit. His bodyguards killed the assassin, and a few days later, her employer as well. That was two months ago. He still missed Donna. It takes a long time to train a good mistress. Enjoyable though they were, the twins were a poor substitute.

So, thanks to his ruthlessness and presentience, Shinto was a wealthy man. And it took a wealthy man to live in a modern replica of a sixteenth century castle, high in North America's Olympic Mountains. After a childhood spent in the crowded misery of orphanages Shinto needed lots of personal space. And he had it. A hundred square miles of primordial rain forests surrounded him, providing both privacy and a natural barrier between him and his many enemies. He didn't own the forests of course, they were the property of the Imperial government, but he had a long-term lease on them, and that was just as good. He thought of the huge genidogs which prowled the woods below and smiled. Yes, his privacy was assured.

Looking up at the vast canopy of stars that hung overhead, Shinto wondered if his mother was out there somewhere. Would she be proud of him? Happy that her flesh and blood had risen so far? He hoped so. The stars seemed to shimmer for a second before regaining their clarity. He shivered. Others might have dismissed the phenomenon as a momentary change in the atmosphere. But not Shinto. He knew better. Something bad was out there and coming his way. It would destroy him if it could. Suddenly tense and troubled, he stepped into his bedroom and closed the doors behind him.

Renn watched Terra grow larger on the viewscreen. She was blue, frosted with white clouds, and very beautiful. Freedom. It seemed anticlimatic somehow. After the sniper attack, they radioed for the shuttle and broke camp for the last time. While the marines packed, Renn took *Fred* out into the main channel and dropped anchor. Renn used an axe to cut a large hole in Fred's hull. As the water gushed in, he jumped into the sniper's boat and poled towards shore. In a surprisingly short time *Fred* slipped below the muddy surface and disappeared. It hurt to see him go but there was no other way. The ruins and the expedition would have to remain a secret until the scientists could return. Afterwards it was a simple matter to sink the smaller boat along with the sniper's gear. As for the sniper himself, he went into one of Honcho's slit trenches, while his pet lifters made a nice snack for a variety of scavengers.

Shortly thereafter a nervous Lt. Fitz put his shuttle down in the ancient LZ, the first pilot to do so in thousands of years, but probably not the last.

Once aboard the space station, tears were shed, toasts were drunk, and speeches were given. But when all was said and done, Ford, Issacs, and Honcho were still dead. Honcho's body was sealed for delivery to his people and interment beneath his family's sacred tree. Ford and Issacs were buried in space, their bodies placed in eternal orbit around the planet Swamp. All would be missed.

As second in command Vanessa quickly took charge. Her eyes gleamed with excitement as she contemplated things to come. Their discoveries would be front page news, and with Honcho dead, she'd be the center of attention. No wonder then that she seemed somewhat distant during the trip from Swamp to Luna Prime.

A small army of reporters showed up to meet their ship, all clamoring for interviews—interviews Vanessa was only too happy to give. Though careful to credit both Honcho and Chin, Vanessa somehow emerged as the driving force behind the expedition, and the press ate it up. What could be better? An attractive young female scientist lands on a mysterious prison planet, wades through monster-filled swamps, and scores the archaeological discovery of the year! The story dominated the holos and tabs for two weeks before gradually dying away.

By now official wheels were already turning towards a new expedition, and thanks to Vanessa's recommendations, early plans called for cooperation with Swamp's convict population. Renn was glad. Maybe some of the people who deserved a break would get one.

Meanwhile Renn and Marla had managed to stay out of the limelight. Both were mentioned in passing a few times, and even interviewed once or twice, but were largely ignored. And that was good because the last thing Renn wanted to do was warn Shinto. He hoped that Shinto had better—or in his case, worse—things to do than watch junk holo reports.

A hearing was convened to consider their pardons, and, true to her word, Vanessa stood by them throughout the entire process. Just as Renn had feared, there were no clear precedents for such a pardon, and the authorities were somewhat doubtful at first. There were questions as to whether Honcho had sufficient authority to pardon Imperial prisoners, and should the whole matter be referred to a higher court? Based on his previous experience with higher courts Renn almost panicked. Fortunately, however, there was Vanessa's testimony, plus written depositions from Jumo and Chin, all of which argued strongly in their behalf.

And the glare of publicity didn't hurt either. It caused Sir Lucius Griswold, Governor of Luna, and first cousin to the emperor himself, to intercede on their behalf. After listening to their case he pardoned them by executive decree, awarded each the sum of one thousand Imperials, and took Vanessa to dinner. Which was, Renn strongly suspected, the Governor's goal all along.

That night Renn and Marla went out to celebrate their new-found freedom. Their party was a quiet affair, more conversation than celebration. Each felt a need to clarify their relationship. Although Swamp had forced them together initially, a friendship had developed, and then evolved into something more. Something so tenuous and fragile that neither wanted to discuss it. So they steered around the future, discussing the present instead, and agreeing to continue their partnership for a while longer. First they'd solve Renn's problem, then Marla's. Actually they didn't have much choice, since Marla's new body would cost a quarter of a million Imperials, and they were two hundred and forty eight thousand short.

Not that clearing Renn's name would be exactly easy. Assuming Shinto was guilty, and Renn felt certain he was, then the other man would have all the advantages. Included were his wealth, his power, and his small army of personal retainers.

On the other hand, Renn had a few advantages of his own. The first was a matter of attitude. Renn saw Shinto through the eyes of a hunter. A monster like any other monster. A skin who could change his appearance to match the society around him, who could disappear into a jungle of laws and customs, and then strike from ambush at any moment. But Renn knew Shinto's jungle, knew the weapons which would kill him, and had the guts to use them. As the hunter he'd have the advantage of surprise, initiative, and desperation. Yes the odds were at least 50/50. But first he needed information. Lots of it. The shuttle shuddered slightly as it hit a new layer of air. Well first things first. Renn leaned back, allowed his seat to recline, and sent a thought Shinto's way. "Enjoy it while you've got it, Shinto . . . because you won't have it much longer."

Their first week on earth was spent getting organized and finding a place to live. For the first few days Renn practically lived in public access booths, catching up on all the economic and political news, and reading countless articles about Shinto and his various business dealings. A company acquired here, a company sold there, the guy was everywhere. And while not an accepted member of the upper crust, his origins were too humble for that, he had managed to purchase some respectability. His donations to charitable causes, mostly ones associated with children, were well publicized. But after days of reading, Renn knew little more than when he began. By blending in with the background the monster had managed to disguise itself as something friendly, something good.

So he went to work for Shinto Enterprises. It was risky, but every hunter knows that audacity often pays off, and chances were that no one would check. After all he was ancient history by now. So he applied one day and was hired the next. Shinto Enterprises was the largest and best known of Shinto's companies, and Renn assumed, largely legit. It wasn't much of a job, Assistant Warehouse Manager, still it was a step closer to the man and his affairs, and the fact that Shinto was paying him to do it made the whole thing that much better. Renn didn't expect to find incriminating evidence laying around the warehouse, that would be naive, but by checking company records he might be able to identify pieces of what had once been his business. If so, that would be good enough. It wouldn't stand up in court but so what, he had no intention of taking legal action against Shinto anyway. No, that's the way the old Renn would have done it, the soft, fat Renn who'd allowed himself to be framed. This was the new Renn, the survivor, the monster-killer. He didn't need courts, honest or otherwise, he needed information. And once he had it, Renn would serve as judge, jury, and if necessary, executioner.

So as Renn went off to work for Shinto Enterprises, Marla headed for Silicon Alley, a run-down area near the Westerplex spaceport. Dragging along behind her was an old drunk who called himself "Cap." Renn had hired him for protective coloration. Otherwise Marla would spend the whole day answering stupid questions like, "No kidding? You were human once?" That sort of stuff.

So while Marla understood the necessity, she wished Renn could've found someone a little bit more presentable. Cap had bloodshot eyes, a large red nose, and a bad case of body odor. His personality wasn't much better. Cap swore he'd once commanded a deep-space freighter. And although he wore the ragged remains of an old spacer rig, and told hair-raising tales of his adventures in space, Marla was convinced Cap didn't know a hyperdrive from a cup of coffee. Still he was cheap, a bottle of whiskey a day, and she needed an escort. So off they went, Marla urging Cap to greater speed, while he mumbled and grumbled along behind.

They used a variety of public transportation to reach the spaceport. A hover bus, an autocab, and then the most public transportation of all, their feet. Renn referred to it as "revenge on a budget." While Marla didn't think it was funny, she knew Renn was right. Their bare bones single room cost a hundred Imperials a day. Life might be cheap on Terra . . . but living wasn't.

The area around the spaceport was an ugly mess which the local police referred to as the "combat zone." This, however, was not typical of the planet as a whole. Most of the industrial ugliness and squalor had been exported to other planets long ago. Imperial earth had been cleansed, sculpted, and brought under man's control. Now vast parks rolled across the land, rain fell during carefully chosen hours, and nothing offended the eye. Nothing, that is, except the sleazy areas which surrounded the spaceports.

Westerplex was a good example. Like the ancient seaports which preceeded them, spaceports were centers of commerce, places where goods were bought and sold and little thought given to beauty. Spaceports were necessary evils. Entry points for the wealth of the empire. Exits for the debris of earth. Here spacers paused momentarily between ships, and like all sailors before them, ventured out to buy a moment or two of happiness. So in the combat zone there were pleasures of all sorts, legal and illegal, safe and dangerous. There were spacer bars, gaming parlors, navy bars, brothels, drug emporiums, restaurants, aid stations, marine bars, weapons stores and just about anything else a fun-loving human could hope for—including Silicon Alley. A refuge for cyborgs.

As they entered the sleazy ambience of the combat zone, Marla felt she was coming home. She'd spent a lot of time down here in the bad old days. It was a place where she could be herself, where people didn't treat her like a freak, because they were freaks themselves. Off-duty cyberdogs aren't welcome at Terra's more refined entertainments, so she'd come here, determined to find what little pleasure she could. Things hadn't changed much since she'd been away. Oh, a few of the old bars had been replaced by new ones, and half a block had been leveled by a shuttle crash a few weeks before, but on the whole it was the same old zone. The lights still flashed with the same old urgency, the cops still looked paranoid as hell, the robo hawkers still pitched their goods with monotonous enthusiasm, and the place still smelled like the bottom of a recycling vat. But a part of her still liked it. For some perverse reason she was attracted to the forced gaiety, the hidden dangers and the squalor. Unlike the geosculpted symmetry she saw everywhere else, the zone throbbed with life and hidden possibilities.

Cap was no stranger to the zone either. He grumbled, "What's the hurry, damn it; let's stop and have a drink."

"In a moment," Marla promised, scanning ahead. "But only one drink. A drop more and you lose your daily bottle."

"Mutiny, that's what it is," Cap complained sorrowfully.

"Would've thrown you in the brig when I had my own ship."

"Put a cork in it," Marla replied. "Here's the place we're looking for." They'd arrived in front of a featureless durasteel door. It bore no sign or other marking to indicate what might lay beyond. You either knew or you didn't. If you didn't, then you had no business going inside. Marla placed a paw on the black identastrip next to the door and waited. She knew that as she stood there some very sophisticated equipment was busy verifying her status as a cyberdog.

With a whirring noise the large surveillance camera mounted over the door turned to look at her. Its single unblinking eye irised opened slightly. The camera was intended to be intimidating and served its purpose well. "Welcome." The voice came from nowhere and everywhere at once. The camera whirred again as it panned over to Cap. "Who's the biobod?"

"My date."

There was silence for a moment as the camera tilted down Cap's rumpled body. "No offense . . . but nobody would date that."

"Are you going to let me in or not?"

"All right, all right. Don't get your circuits in an uproar." There was a loud click and the door hissed open.

Marla turned to Cap. "You first."

"Why?" his bloodshot eyes were suspicious.

"Because I said so."

"I won't. For all I know it's a body shop." Cap was referring to the illegal practice of killing indigent sentients and selling their organs to biobanks.

"Get serious," Marla replied. "Who the hell would buy a liver like yours? Speaking of which, the drink I promised you is inside." Without hesitation Cap stepped through the door and Marla followed.

Like most bars it was dark inside, but unlike most bars, it was quiet as a tomb. There was no laughter, no ribald jokes, no loud music. Those who came here did so to escape the company of others. They came to be among others of their own kind, beings who understood the pain of exclusion, and struggled with depression. For while it was a rare man or woman on Terra who didn't have some sort of prosthesis or surgical enhancement, no one chose to be a full cyborg—no one in their right mind, that is. Like Marla, most cyborgs had little choice. Some had been born into bodies so twisted almost anything else was preferable, some had escaped dying bodies, and a few, a tiny minority, had given up their bodies voluntarily. Marla was looking for one of these.

It was still early so the place was half empty. What patrons there were occupied the murky booths lining three walls. Each booth was equipped with an elaborate patch panel. By plugging into it customers could access a wide variety of recreational possibilities. Some were lost in intricate mind games, just playing for the fun of it, while others bet large sums on their ability to beat the house. Some were locked in the throes of electronic orgasm, their bodies jerking spastically as waves of ecstasy rolled through their circuits. And unable to find peace any other way, some were completely unconscious, having purchased an hour or two of electronic nothingness.

Marla understood the last all too well. During her time with Intersystems Incorporated, she'd come here often. Especially when she started to think about babies, to dream about them, knowing she'd never have one. Not even the best cyberbod in the world could make another human being. Yes, had they saved some ova, a surrogate mother could've been found, but unfortunately they hadn't done so. A profound sorrow rose up inside her. Gritting her teeth, she forced the feeling down and back.

Heading for the reception desk, Marla was struck by the variety of shapes and sizes that surrounded her. There were wheeled boxes, floating cylinders, various kinds of cyber-animals and other shapes dimly seen. Like herself, most cyborgs were designed for a specific purpose, and form followed function. Many, the majority in fact, were pilots, their brains encased in metal containers of one sort or another, passing a few days or hours while their ships were readied for space. Cyborg pilots were readily acknowledged as the best money could buy. It had to do with their special affinity for the ships they flew. For them a ship was simply a larger body, a larger more powerful extension of them-selves, a feeling biobods would never know. But there were others too, submariners who ran Terra's huge ocean har-vesters, security types like herself, and a dozen more.

As she approached the counter, Marla saw that it was empty except for a beat up looking cashcomp. "I still think your date looks a bit worse for wear, but welcome none-theless. What'll it be?"

Marla looked around. It was the same voice she'd heard outside, but where was it coming from?

"Right in front of you," the cashcomp said in bored tones, sprouting an optical scanner and a single articulated arm. "I'm a robot, so don't waste your time getting emotional. It won't do you any good. There's something wrong with my social interaction program, but the techs can't find it, and my owner doesn't give a shit. So what's your pleasure?"

"I'm here to see Machine."

"Machine doesn't interface with just anyone. Who should I say is calling?"

"Marla. Marla Marie Mendez."

There was silence as the cashcomp communicated with another room, and then said, "All right. I guess you're for real, Marla. Through that door." A door hissed open behind the counter. "But the biobod stays here. Machine can't stand biobods."

"The biobod gets one drink, and one drink only."

"Understood," the cashcomp replied. "I hope he likes whiskey. It's all we've got. There's not much call for alcohol in here."

"Whiskey will be fine," Cap answered eagerly.

"Just one," Marla said sternly. "And wait here. If you're not here when I get back, then there's no bottle tonight."

"Sure, sure," Cap replied. "Ol' Cap ain't never deserted a shipmate and never will."

Leaving Cap to collect his drink, Marla padded around the counter and through the door. A steep flight of stairs awaited her. Although she'd met Machine years before, this was the first time she'd been invited to his quarters. Claws clicking, she trotted up two flights of stairs and emerged into a large loft.

"Down here." The voice had an empty mechanical quality to it, and came from the far end of the loft. Light streamed down through a series of skylights to form distorted squares on the wooden floor. As she approached, Marla saw a high-backed executive-style chair, the back of a hairless head, and beyond that a huge wooden roll top desk. It could've been a replica, but Marla somehow knew it wasn't, and guessed that the desk was a thousand years old at least. There was, however, nothing old about the computer console which rested on it. It was one of the most sophisticated boards she'd ever seen.

Machine's ability with computers was legendary. Somewhere, in some secure place, Machine had a main frame of his own. By all accounts it was an awesome machine so intelligent that it met many definitions of sentience. Most agreed that Machine had designed and built it himself, though no one could say for sure. It was also whispered that Machine's resources were even greater than that. Many claimed he could access the huge computer known as "Earth Central Mainframe," or "Earth Central" for short. If so, he must be very good indeed, because Earth Central belonged to the Imperial government, and the penalty for unauthorized access was death.

In any case Machine referred to himself as an "information interface," and made a living by tracking down facts, in much the same way as a bounty hunter tracks down fugitives. A client would come seeking certain information. A bounty would be agreed upon and the hunt would begin. Unlike bounty hunters, however, Machine rarely left the building. Machine conducted his hunts electronically rather than in person. Of course, Machine wouldn't work for just anyone. He was quite adamant about that. He wouldn't even see a biobod, much less work for one, and often refused work which he thought too boring, or unethical.

The chair spun around without warning. Knowing what to expect, Marla wasn't shocked. Machine's body was a parody of the human form, a life-size anatomical dummy, completely devoid of features. Machine's ovoid head had no ears, eyes or mouth. She knew he had sensors, lots of them, but none were visible. There were no clothes to cover his smooth sexless body. He looked like a store dummy come to life, and for reasons only he knew, Machine liked it that way. It certainly wasn't a lack of money. Everyone knew Machine had once been wealthy, a playboy dedicated to the pursuit of pleasure, a member of that tiny group who already has what everyone else wants. But he'd renounced it all. His name, his wealth, even his body. For years now he'd lived a minimalist existence of his own devising. As always, Marla found it difficult to communicate with something which had no eyes. "Hello, Machine."

"Hello, Marla. You are back from Swamp. I rejoice."

"Thanks. You really shouldn't watch those junk holocasts, Machine, they're all hype."

"Even hype is valid input, Marla," Machine replied evenly. "It is information. And as you know, information is what I sell."

Marla mentally kicked herself for attempting small talk with Machine. He either couldn't or wouldn't participate. "Right, and that's why I'm here. To buy some of what you sell."

"Excellent, Marla. What would you like to know?"

"Everything you can get on a biobod named 'Shinto.' Where he lives, how much he's worth, his favorite color, everything." There was a long silence. Marla waited it out, knowing that Machine was thinking it over. Along with his wealth and physical body, Machine had rid himself of the social niceties, like stalling for time while he thought something over. If he wanted more time he simply took it.

"Shinto is a dangerous man, Marla. I know this without reference to my computer. He would not welcome strangers poking around in his affairs. Computer inquiries can be traced. Can you guarantee my safety?"

Marla considered. What ever else Machine had given away, he still had his sense of self-preservation. And he was right, computer inquiries could be traced, although from what she'd heard Machine was pretty good at protecting himself. She decided on honesty. "No, I can't guarantee your safety, Machine. We'll do everything we can . . . but there's some risk involved."

There was a long silence, during which Marla searched Machine's face for some hint of what he was thinking, and found nothing. Finally Machine spoke. "That is correct, Marla. You cannot guarantee my safety. But life offers no guarantees nor do I expect any. I am glad, however, that time and misfortune have not robbed you of your integrity. That is good. I have defenses which even Shinto cannot penetrate. You shall have what you want. Now we shall talk price."

Marla nodded and sat back on her haunches. So far so good. Now to see if Machine would extend her some credit.

Renn's job was not very difficult. Show up on time, check the computer terminal to see what goods were coming in and what goods were going out. Have coffee with his two human shipping clerks, tell them dirty jokes, and laugh when they told theirs. Ignore the fact that both hated his guts because he'd been brought in from the outside. Assign one to shipping and one to receiving. This was largely a formality because both had a preference. Luko, a short barrel-chested man with hair sprouting from his ears, liked shipping, and, Estaben, a somewhat overripe woman with bad breath, liked receiving. Not just goods, but anything else that might happen along as well.

Both clerks had a small army of robots who did the actual work, many of whom were smarter than they were. So, after their daily meeting with Renn, they'd retreat to their particular loading dock, and screw off for the rest of the day. Renn used the time to learn all he could about Shinto Enterprises.

By asking lots of questions, studying all the records available to his level of management, and reading the trade press, a picture began to emerge. Like many successful business operations Shinto Enterprises had begun to lose its edge. Day-to-day management of the company had passed from Shinto into the hands of bureaucrats who lacked both the vision and the guts to create anything themselves. Most had never even met their employer, and believed the public image his PR people had worked so hard to create. The orphan works his way up by means of superior ability and sheer determination, reaches the pinnacle of success, and stoops to help the less fortunate. Reading between the lines Renn suspected that those at the very top of Shinto Enterprises knew better. But they were probably just as guilty as he was, and remained silent because it benefitted them to do so.

Renn also learned some interesting facts. Although Shinto Enterprises had begun to lose its edge, it was still enormously profitable, too profitable to be real. To Renn's experienced eye it seemed likely that other funds were being pumped through the company's books to cleanse and sanitize them. Of course, he couldn't be sure without seeing the company records, and needless to say, assistant warehouse managers didn't have access to those. He did learn, however that there were two sets of books, one in the company's Westerplex corporate headquarters, and the other at Shinto's residence on the Olympic Peninsula. Renn suspected that both would provide a detailed read-out on Shinto's legal and illegal transactions. After all, even if you're laundering money you must still keep track of it.

Further study uncovered more facts, the most interesting of which was that Shinto had indeed stolen his business, and was probably using it to commit the very crime for which Renn was sent to prison. Shinto had renamed the business "Interstellar Import-Export," and tucked it under Shinto Enterprises as a wholly owned subsidiary. It was all there in the company's last annual report. Renn recognized it immediately. Shinto acquired the company at an auction of confiscated goods, paid the Imperial Government a fraction of its true worth, and immediately sold off the parts he didn't want. Then he staffed the company with his own people and let it run. Another profitable subsidiary. Like Shinto Enterprises, too profitable. According to the last annual report the business had doubled its profits in a single year. Even allowing for more efficient management, and phenomenal market growth, that was too much. So Shinto had stolen his business, and was probably using it for drug smuggling or a similar enterprise. Now Renn knew for sure, and the knowledge filled him with grim satisfaction.

So now he knew Shinto was guilty as hell, but so what? He didn't have anything that would stand up in court. That kind of stuff was locked up in corporate headquarters or Shinto's home. He remembered his earlier bravado. Renn doesn't need courts. Renn the judge, jury and executioner. More like Renn the idiot. All he had against Shinto's money, power, and personal army was the element of surprise. And how far would that get him? Leaning back in his chair, Renn put his feet up and wondered what to do.

A few miles away Shinto sat behind armored glass on the top floor of the Shinto Enterprises Executive Tower. A frown creased his normally handsome features. He took great pride in his face. It was quite different from the original. The original was coarse, homely, and common. This one was cultured, refined, even patrician. Clear blue eyes, a nice straight nose, lips just full enough to be sensual, and a good firm chin. All the work of the best biosculpter money could buy. A biosculpter who had warned him against the effects of excessive sun and unpleasant emotions. So the frown was an unusual indulgence, one which his subordinates had learned to fear, and Shinto used to good effect. And it scared hell out of Signo Amad, his Chief of Security. As a result he sweated heavily as he stood before Shinto's wrath.

"Let me see if I understand this, Amad. We send a man to prison so we can acquire his business. Then, within a year and a half, he obtains a pardon and returns to earth. Lacking any source of income he applies for the job of Assistant Warehouse Manager with Shinto Enterprises. We, for reasons that completely escape me, proceed to hire him. Are those the facts?" The last was said in a voice which was completely calm but as cold as arctic ice.

Amad nodded, his dark skin flushed even darker, sweat dripping from the tip of his blade-like nose. "Yyyess sir. Those are the facts." From years of experience Amad knew better than to make excuses. His only chance lay in complete honesty and a good track record. For the thousandth time he wondered how his employer did it. Shinto had suddenly appeared the day before, obviously upset, and demanding a full-scale security check. "There's something out there Amad, something we don't know about. Find out what it is." How did the bastard know? It was like he had ESP or something. Amad worked his staff through the night, and sure enough, there was something out there. A possible something anyway. A computer cross-check between the content of the news holos and Shinto's personal enemies list turned up Jonathan Renn, one-time competitor, now a pardoned criminal. He'd applied for work under a phony name and made no attempt to disguise his finger prints or retinal pattern. A heavy work load delayed the routine background investigation which would have otherwise caught him. But excuses were not acceptable. Amad knew that. He'd screwed up pure and simple. Now it was a matter of seeing how high a price he'd have to pay.

Shinto reached into his desk drawer and withdrew a dart gun. It was a low-powered affair he sometimes used for target practice in the office. The target was mounted on the far wall just over Amad's shoulder. Shinto brought the gun up and aligned it with the target. Amad was careful not to blink. "So, in spite of all our security precautions, we hired a man with every reason to destroy us." Shinto flicked the gun left and squeezed the trigger. It went *phufut*. A dart sprouted from Amad's cheek. Shinto's sculpted features registered elaborate surprise. "Ooops! Sorry, Amad. I must be losing my touch."

It hurt like hell, but Amad didn't move. If he was very, very careful, he might come out of this alive. "Yyyess sir. We failed sir. We should have been running the computer cross-check weekly instead of monthly. I accept full responsibility."

Shinto squeezed the trigger again. *Phufut*. This time a dart blossomed from Amad's throat. Blood trickled down his neck. "Darn! There I go again!" Shinto said apologetically. "Sorry. As you can see this thing's got me very upset." Shinto focused his eyes on a spot just over Amad's head. "Let me tell you what I think, Amad. I think I'll go to my country place for awhile. It's quiet there and a lot safer." Amad knew this was a reference to Shinto's fortress-like retreat in the Olympic Rain Forest. "Meanwhile, I want you to find Jonathan Renn and kill him. Then you will kill his friends, the two idiots who work for him, and anyone else he's spent time with. Do you understand?" *Phufut*.

Amad jerked in spite of himself as a dart pierced his upper lip. "Yyyess, sir, I understand. It shall be as you say." The dart bobbed up and down as he spoke.

"Good." *Phufuttttttt*. Shinto emptied the magazine. Amad felt the draft as forty seven darts whipped by his ear and thudded into the target behind him. He had a feeling it was going to be a very long day.

As always, Luko plowed his way through the rush hour crowds with all the finesse of a battering ram. Elbowing his way to the front rank of waiting passengers, he smiled as the transcar decelerated towards the platform. He made it a point of honor to be first aboard the transcar each evening, and this had the look of an easy victory. He was in the front rank only a foot or two from where the first door would open. Luko wins again!

Then the old woman behind him gave a mighty shove, and Luko felt himself flying through the air. A half second later he bounced off the front of the transcar and into a duracrete wall. His death made eighteen thousand four hundred and two people late for dinner.

Estaben didn't plan to be a shipping clerk forever. No way. And since the suits at Shinto Enterprises refused to promote her, then she'd have to promote herself. Estaben had dreams of opening her own little business someday, an escort service maybe, or a sex boutique. But that required capital, which is why she moonlighted as "Margo the Whip," at Cicero's House of Pain, deep in the center of the combat zone.

She was headed there when some idiot decided to dive in front of a transcar and slowed the whole damn system. As a result, her first customer was already waiting when she strode into her treatment room and arrogantly cracked her whip. Much to her surprise he didn't cringe and fall to his knees. Instead, he took her whip away from her and used it to hang her from one of the many hooks in the ceiling. She put up quite a struggle but no one noticed since screams of pain were rather common in Cicero's.

A few hours after Estaben's death, Amad waited impatiently across from Renn's hotel. It was dark and warm. Too warm. Sweat was dripping off the tip of his nose again. Amad swore and ran his sleeve along it. Four members of his elite security force had entered the hotel ten minutes before. They should've snuffed Renn and left by now. Where the hell were they? Amad forced himself to give them another five minutes. Shit. Stepping back into a doorway he pumped a round up the spout and attached the silencer to his handgun. It's always best to be careful.

He crossed the street with giant strides and entered through the front door of the hotel. A guest and the desk clerk lay sprawling where they'd fallen. Good. SOP for this kind of operation. Ignoring the lift tube he ran up the stairs to the third floor. He listened for a moment, opened the fire door, and slid into the hall. An elderly man stepped out of his room. Amad dropped him with a bullet between the eyes. Hugging the right hand wall he moved down the corridor while counting off the numbers. Three-twelve, three-ten, three-oh-eight, and there, three-oh-six. The door was open.

Amad went in fast and low, gun up in a two-handed grip. It was a waste of time. His team was there all right, but they were dead. Three looked like they'd been ripped apart by some sort of animal, that damned dog probably, and the third wore a bullet hole between his eyes. A *big* bullet hole, like a .50, or maybe even a .75. A quick check of the bathroom confirmed his guess. No Renn, dead or otherwise. Amad shook his head in amazement. This Renn character was bad news. And his pet dog was obviously not a dog. He'd told them to check on that. Another fuck-up. Well, you win some and you lose some.

A few minutes later Amad was a mile away, ensconced in a public com booth with the privacy shield on. His wife had a smudge of dirt on one cheek. Probably out grubbing in the garden again. He cut her off. "This is it, honey. Here's the code; Alpha, Beta, Alpha. Grab the kids and the satchel. You know where to go."

The smile faded from her face. She nodded once and cut the connection. She knew what to do. A few years back she'd been one of his top operatives. Within ten minutes she'd be out of the house, within twenty it would burn to the ground, and soon thereafter he'd hold her in his arms. A few days later they'd lift and start a new life somewhere else. They were still young, and the satchel full of cash would ease the way. Shinto would be incredibly pissed when he found out, a thought which made Amad smile. He was whistling by the time he hopped into an autocab.

—— Chapter Fourteen ——

It was raining on and off, a fact which wasn't too surprising in a rain forest, but did nothing to make Renn more comfortable. He and Marla were taking a break under the branches of a huge cedar tree. He bit off another mouthful of protein bar, and winced as cold rain drops hit his face. "Damn. And we thought Swamp was bad."

Marla looked up from her resting place on the ground beside him and grinned wolfishly. "He's been on Terra for only two weeks and he's already getting soft."

Renn made a face and took another bite of protein bar. Much to his surprise it tasted pretty good. Kind of nutty. Which also described their situation. Two against hundreds. They'd left the air car in a clearing a few miles back, and were now just inside the boundaries of Shinto's land, about fifteen miles from his mountain hideaway. Things should be easy at first. Although already on Shinto's land they wouldn't encounter much in the way of defenses until the last five miles or so. Otherwise, Shinto's private army would be shooting lost hikers and causing all sorts of problems for the PR department. Besides, a fifteen-mile-deep defensive perimeter would cost a lot more money without adding a lot of protection.

But the last five miles would be real tough. Besides the naturally rough terrain, they'd be up against crack security troops and homicidal genidogs. They'd learned about the genidogs through Marla's cyborg computer expert. "Machine" is a somewhat unusual name, but what the heck, to each his own. In any case, Machine had managed to locate both a blueprint and a security plan for Shinto's fortress. Two years earlier, Shinto hired a general security contractor to update his defenses, and afterwards the contractor squirreled away a copy of the plans in his personal computer. It was a naughty thing to do, and in clear violation of professional ethics, but the contractor thought the plans might come in handy someday. After all, a man like Shinto had enemies, otherwise he wouldn't have a security plan, and they'd pay handsomely for a way into Shinto's fortress. Renn grinned. Not that Machine had paid the contractor a single Imperial! No, he'd stolen the plans right out from under the contractor's nose while that unfortunate individual sat at his keyboard, and worked on another file. All of which justified Machine's rather exhorbitant fee.

Among other things the security plan specified a force of genidogs. While the plan didn't include specs for the dogs, it didn't take a lot of smarts to figure out they'd be formidable opponents, on top of which there'd be human guards, electronic sensors, and a variety of traps.

So, while getting into Shinto's fortress wouldn't be easy, they had a chance. Thanks to his own research, and Machine's added input, Renn had enough information on Shinto to write a book. He knew Shinto liked eastern music, hated mushrooms, adored children, and was slightly claustrophobic. "Know your prey, lad," Boater always said, and it was good advice. It gave you an edge. In this case, however, the edge was somewhat dulled, since the prey knew the hunter was coming.

It still seemed strange to Renn that Shinto's security was lax enough to hire him and then efficient enough to identify him a few days later. But Machine's research revealed lots of strange incidents in Shinto's life—so many, in fact, it almost suggested some sort of precognitive ability. But one thing was for sure, Shinto knew Renn was back. The four killers were proof of that. He was alive, and they were dead, but it could have easily gone the other way.

There he was sitting fat dumb and happy in his room, while out in the hall, killers were preparing to break down the door. Fortunately, Marla chose that particular moment to return. Having dismissed Cap at the back door, she entered the hotel and stepped out of the lift tube just in time to see the killers approach Renn's door. Mistaking her for a dog, they ignored her. That was a serious mistake. She killed the fourth one just as the first three hit the door. Thanks to a strong door, and Marla's attack, Renn had time to grab his .75. It was still close. The second time they hit the door it crashed open. Marla killed the third assailant, a woman, as Renn turned towards the door. The .75 roared, slamming the first assassin backwards into the second, who quickly fell victim to Marla's slashing teeth. After that it was a matter of dragging the bodies into the room, gathering up their belongings, and slipping out the back way.

The rest came naturally. Denied the advantage of surprise, and lacking the funds for a more sophisticated approach, they decided to attack rather than run. Perhaps they could seize the initiative through sheer audacity. Where would Shinto least expect an attack? And where would an attack do the most good? The answer to both questions seemed obvious . . . Shinto's fortress-like home in the Olympic rain forest. If only Shinto would be there. But even if he wasn't, someone would be, and that's all they needed. Once they had access to Shinto's computer, Machine would take care of the rest.

So, armed with a loan from Machine, a loan which the cyborg had pointedly made to Marla and not to Renn, they rented an air car and headed north. Stopping only to purchase back-packing equipment and other gear, they'd arrived the day before. Dropping their air car into a forest clearing, they'd headed for Shinto's fortress. According to

Machine's information, they'd run into the outermost ring of Shinto's defenses in another ten miles or so.

Renn stuck the protein bar wrapper into a pocket and stood. The forty pound pack made it awkward. The pack contained food, gear and ammo. While some of the explosives were a little exotic, parting presents from Jumo, they were quite legal. Rather than support the expense of an interstellar police, the Imperial government relied on a patchwork quilt of local police, combined with bounty hunters and legal assassins to keep crime under control. As a result citizens were allowed a wide variety of weapons. Renn was armed with the same array of weapons he'd carried on Swamp, and while Marla was a weapon herself, he'd found ways to protect her more effectively.

For one thing she wore two small packs which were fastened together to make twin saddlebags. They were constructed of a tough bulletproof fabric which would not only provide her with additional protection, but would also allow her to carry some extra explosives and ammo. In addition he'd made a metal collar to protect her throat. All the gear gave her an exotic look. He laughed as she got up.

"What's so funny?"

Renn struggled to maintain a straight face. "Nothing. You look a little strange that's all."

"Strange? I'll show you something strange, a grown man running up the trail with my teeth in his butt." She growled and lunged towards his rear end. Renn laughed as he ran up the trail. As Marla made a half-hearted attempt to catch him she suddenly realized how natural their relationship had become. Instead of hiding what she was, now she could joke about it, and even take pride in it. The truth was that she loved Renn, and deep down she felt sure he loved her in return, although she knew he had difficulty reconciling his emotions with her appearance. But appearances can be changed. Suddenly she was very frightened. What if Renn was killed? She hurried to catch up.

Shinto flicked a switch, and an entire wall of his cavernous bedroom became a vid screen. Deep in the electronic bowels of his retreat a descrambler took the seemingly random bits fed it by a small geosynchronous satellite, organized them into a coherent picture, and sent it upstairs. Colors swirled briefly before locking up into a shot of the Westerplex spaceport. It wobbled a bit as the camera operator shifted his weight from one foot to another. In the distance, Shinto saw a shuttle warming up on one of the many smaller pads circling the perimeter of the main complex. "OK, Garvin. I'm looking at the Westerplex spaceport. So what?"

Garvin was nervous. As Amad's first assistant supervisor, he wasn't used to dealing with Shinto one-on-one. What if something went wrong? Mistakes could be fatal, as Amad was about to find out. The camera panned over to him, and his voice cracked slightly as he answered. "Amad and his family went aboard twenty minutes ago, sir. The pilot has requested permission to lift in about three minutes."

Garvin's head was round like a melon and filled the whole wall. He had thin blonde hair, green eyes, and a visible tick in one eyelid. Shinto smiled. "Excellent. All is ready?"

"Yes sir. As you requested."

"And you're sure he doesn't know?"

Garvin shook his head. "He suspects nothing, sir."

"Excellent. It seems you're due for a bonus, Garvin. A rather large bonus. Your two-year vigil is about to end."

"Yes sir." Garvin knew Shinto was referring to the fact that while he'd worked for Amad, he'd also been paid something extra to keep an eye on him, submitting regular reports to company headquarters. So when Amad slipped out of Renn's hotel, and contacted his wife, Garvin was right behind him.

"And Garvin?"

"Sir?"

"Pay attention to this. It's the reward for treachery."

"Yes sir." At a nod from Garvin the camera panned back to the duracrete pad. Seen through waves of heat the shuttle seemed to shiver for a moment and then rose towards the sky. Shinto began to worry. What if something went wrong and Amad escaped? He gritted his teeth as the seconds ticked by. Then, just as the shuttle reached five thousand feet, there was a sudden flash of light and it was gone. Gone with it were Amad, his family, and the shuttle's crew. Pieces of burning wreckage were still falling from the sky as Shinto flicked a switch and the wall went gray.

The duraplast doors slid open at Shinto's touch, and he stepped out onto the veranda. He should've felt good, cleansed by Amad's death, but he didn't. For one thing, he hated to kill children, and for another, he liked Amad. The little bastard had guts. But business is business. You can't let the hired help get away with treachery and stay on top. He'd seriously considered allowing Amad to escape but decided against it. Such an act would be widely interpreted as weakness, and that would be very, very bad. No, it was sad but necessary. He had a hollow feeling in his gut like something bad was coming his way. A premonition? No, probably not. He was getting sentimental, that's all. Garvin would find Renn and that would end the whole thing. He looked up, but the light was fading, and more gray clouds had moved in to block the sun.

They had little difficulty locating the outermost edge of Shinto's defensive perimeter. First Marla started picking up routine radio transmissions and then they ran into a large duraplast sign located right next to the trail. It bore an ominous looking skull and crossbones, below which were the words: PRIVATE. KEEP OUT. INTRUDERS WILL BE SHOT ON SIGHT.

Renn looked at Marla and laughed. "That's what I like about Shinto. The man says what he means."

From that point on security would become tighter and tighter until they reached the fortress itself. Assuming, of course, that they managed to live that long. Even though it was getting dark Marla had little difficulty finding the hidden sensors. They weren't much different from those Jumo had used on Swamp. Coarse, stupid things, they'd been scattered around as Shinto's first line of defense. The warmth of their power paks popped out from the cooler background of the forest, making them easy to spot, and once spotted they were easy to avoid.

Renn wondered why they hadn't used more. A thick band of sensors would've been almost impossible to penetrate without setting some off. Stupid though the sensors were, if twenty or thirty went off in one particular section of the perimeter, that would be a pretty good indication of trouble. But the folks in charge of such things had chosen to scatter them widely, instead. Almost as if the sensors were a mere formality. To Renn's way of thinking, that meant they were either very stupid or very confident about whatever defenses lay ahead. He hoped for the first, but feared the second.

Meanwhile it was pretty tough going. Renn figured they were still about four miles from Shinto's retreat, which doesn't sound like a lot, but it is when it's almost straight up. The easiest going was on the trail, but it would inevitably lead them into a series of traps and ambushes, so it was best to stay off it as much as possible. Yet the thick forest to either side made travel there almost impossible. The vegetation did start to thin out as they went higher, but that meant less cover too, and increased the possibility that someone would spot them. So they used the trail when forced to do so, but moved slowly, checking for traps and potential ambushes every inch of the way. Then, whenever things opened up a bit, they went cross-country, occasionally fighting the underbrush, but feeling safer. But either way they had to keep going. If they tried to camp for the night, chances were they'd be discovered. No, tired or not, they'd make their assault on Shinto's fortress tonight, and trust darkness to cover their approach.

In spite of all her fancy sensors Marla fell into a trap so ancient its origins are lost in human prehistory. It happened just as it was supposed to, suddenly, and without warning. One moment she was walking along the trail, scanning the surrounding vegetation for sensors, and the next she was falling like a rock. Had she been a human, or even a real dog, the metal spike would have killed her. As it was, the spike entered two thirds of the way up her side, destroyed her solar cells, and wiped out her radio receiver before coming out through the other side.

Swearing steadily, Renn climbed down the crumbling side of the pit, careful to avoid the forest of sharp spikes which lined the bottom of the pit. Gently, he lifted her off the spike. "Marla? Marla? Can you hear me?"

"Of course I can hear you," she snapped. "That damned spike wiped out my solar cells, not hearing." She regretted the words the moment she said them, but she was scared and embarrassed.

Renn looked hurt as he lifted her up and out of the pit. "I thought you'd been injured."

Back on her feet again, Marla waited while Renn climbed out of the pit. "Jonathan?"

"Yes?"

"It was a stupid thing to say. I was embarrassed that's all. Mighty cyberdog falls into a covered pit and makes a fool of herself. Forgive me?"

Renn smiled. "You're forgiven."

So they kept on going. An hour passed. Marla could no

longer monitor local radio traffic, and the servos for her right rear leg seemed a hair slow, but other than that she felt pretty good. She put on a burst of speed intent on scouting ahead.

Meanwhile Renn found himself plodding along, fighting the fatigue that tried to pull his eyelids down, forcing himself to concentrate. Look right, look left, lift the right foot, put it down, lift the left foot, put it down. Look forward, look back, lift the right foot, put it down. The sequence seemed to go on forever.

Then Marla appeared out of nowhere, nudged him off the trail, and urged him to be silent. Suddenly all his senses were crystal clear, his nerves were wire tight, and the fatigue was gone, washed away by a flood of adrenaline. Fading into the foliage, Renn stood perfectly still. He looked down at Marla for some indication of the problem, but her attention was focused on the trail, so he slipped off the safety on his blast rifle, and held it ready.

The first thing Renn heard was a snuffling sound followed by heavy breathing and the swish of branches along something big. Then he heard a radio, the crackle of a brief transmission, and static. None of which prepared him for the sight that followed. It was a dog, a dog the size of a small pony, and it didn't look friendly. A permanent snarl wrinkled the skin on its long wolf-like nose, fangs appeared and disappeared as it rippled its lips, and red eyes darted this way and that. To Renn's astonishment there was a man riding on the wolf-thing's back. He was dressed in green camos, not as good as Renn's skins, but effective nonetheless. The man was armed with some sort of auto-shotgun. It had a big drum style magazine and a short barrel. Considering the thick underbrush it made sense. There's no need for a long range weapon when you can't see more than fifteen feet.

The genidog suddenly came to a stop and looked right at

Renn. Fortunately, Renn's skins rendered him almost invisible. This confused the animal because it could smell Renn but couldn't see him. It never got a chance to figure things out because a fraction of a second later Renn fired. Even as its master fell out of the saddle, the genidog leaped towards them, and was in midair when Renn's beam sliced through it. The genidog landed with a thump in a pile of its own entrails. Though mortally wounded, it continued to growl and snap. Renn put another bolt through its head and it finally lay still.

Renn looked at Marla and she looked at him. "What the hell is that?" he asked.

"Some extremely bad news," Marla answered thoughtfully. "I've got a feeling we just met our first genidog."

There was a crackling sound off to their left. Then a female voice said, "Unit six . . . base to unit six. Gilda here. Come in six, you miserable sonovabitch."

Renn ran over to the radio and picked it up. A quick check revealed a red transmit key. It was risky, but maybe the heavy static would cover his voice enough to make it work. He pressed the key. "Six to base. Lighten up for God's sake. I just stopped to take a shit."

"You *are* a shit, unit six. Now wipe your ass and get it in gear."

"Yes, your mamship. Unit six out."

Marla looked up and shook her head. "That was close."

"Close, hell . . . that was a disaster. I bought us half an hour, tops."

"So what do we do?"

Renn smiled. "Make every minute count."

A big wolf smile appeared on Marla's muzzle. "Then let's go."

They went. Marla took the point, determined to protect Renn, while he came along behind, watching both sides and their back trail as well. Just to make sure that no one could sneak up from behind them, Renn scattered mini-mines along the path. They were a goodbye present from Jumo, and now seemed like a good time to use them. Each mini-mine was a tiny six-sided bomb that would detonate under the slightest pressure. The mini-mines were designed to wound rather than kill. Every person involved in giving aid was one less person to fight. That was the theory, anyway. But if the mines just let him know someone was coming, Renn would be happy.

Marla smelled the sentry long before she saw him. His cover was excellent, as were his camos, but his deodorant had given up long ago. His body odor was the olfactory equivalent of a neon sign, pointing out his position, and screaming, "Kill me." In order to reach him, however, Marla would have to cross a small clearing, and do so without being seen. Holding her belly to the ground she crept forward. Unfortunately, the guard was paying attention and spotted her right away. "Hey! Doggie! Here, boy."

Marla wagged her tail as she approached him. He held out his hand. "What you doin' here boy?"

Marla pretended to sniff it and grinned. "I'm biting people." As she spoke the sentry saw rows of gleaming teeth. His eyes got big, his big Adam's apple bobbed up and down, and he started to back away. Then he dropped his weapon and ran.

Renn stepped into the clearing his blast rifle ready. "Problems?"

"Naw . . . just a guy who doesn't like dogs."

Gilda was a big woman, so big that when she put her combat boots up on the console, they obscured a good portion of the plot screen. That, and the fact that she had her face buried in a muscle mag, provided Renn and Marla with a period of grace. Had Gilda been watching, she would have seen light after light flash onto the screen as the two intruders tripped entire rows of sensors. Of course there were audio alarms too but Gilda had turned those off. They frequently went off by mistake, and besides, they interfered with the music booming into her stereo ear plugs. Nonetheless all good things must come to an end. Wrapping up a great article on glut enhancement, Gilda glanced up at the plot screen and saw about a hundred flashing lights. A fraction of a second later her huge feet crashed to the floor and a meaty index finger hit the general alarm button. Klaxons went off and people started running in every direction.

Renn and Marla were close enough to hear the klaxons as they went off. Then, before either one could react, there was a series of loud cracks from somewhere behind them. Someone or something had stepped on the mini-mines. Renn whirled just as three genidogs appeared around a curve in the trail. All were riderless, and one was missing a paw. The mini-mines no doubt. While the injury didn't seem to slow him down much, a blaster bolt did, passing through the beast to hit the ground beyond. Renn kept his finger on the firing stud as he swung left, catching the next animal from behind, slicing through it lengthwise until blue energy found and destroyed its brain.

Meanwhile, Marla had rushed forward in an attempt to distract the third beast and soon wished she hadn't. The big animal bit into her right side and lifted her kicking into the air. For a moment she thought it was all over but fortunately the huge beast had sunk its teeth into a saddlebag instead of her. It shook her a couple of times and threw her down.

The genidog died a moment later as an energy beam burned through its heart. Even as it fell, Marla was up and running. Renn was right beside her. Both knew speed was of the essence. Klaxons were blaring, security personnel were running in every direction, and searchlights were probing the tree line. This was their moment of opportunity.

Within minutes the confusion would be over and so would their chances of getting in.

The fortress loomed big and black up ahead, light spilling out from open doors as more and more security troops poured out. Renn ran straight at them, waving his arms, and yelling at the top of his lungs. "Over this way! Come on! There's hundreds of 'em. Hold 'em off while I radio for reinforcements!"

"Yes, sir!" a sergeant replied, leading his squad towards the woods.

Then Renn heard a voice from off to the right. "Reinforcements?" an officer demanded. "What reinforcements? Stop that man! Can't you idiots do anything right?"

Renn sent blue energy burping off into the officer's general direction, and eager to participate, so did a number of security people just arriving on the scene. The officer returned fire, and moments later the night was criss-crossed with a latticework of energy beams, and a hail of lead.

Renn turned and ran towards the fortress. Up ahead a door opened silhouetting a huge figure. "Quick . . . we need help out here!" Renn shouted as he ran towards the door.

But Gilda was suspicious. "Who the hell are you?" she demanded, the "you" somewhat distorted as Renn hit her with a full body block. They crashed to the floor in a tangle of arms and legs. Gilda managed to come out on top. A buzzer added its insistent voice to the incredible cacophony of background sound as massive blast-proof doors began to slide slowly closed.

Gilda's huge fist connected with Renn's jaw. A wave of darkness rose and tried to pull him under. Gilda smiled as he brought his knee up between her legs. "That ain't gonna work on me, buster. Try this on for size." Gilda raised her fist and prepared to smash it down into Renn's face.

Marla growled, and came in from the side, fangs bared.

Gilda rocked backwards, throwing up her arms to protect her face. Renn brought up both feet and kicked with all his might. His boots hit Gilda in the chest, pushing her up and back. Her head hit hard and Gilda was unconscious when the heavy doors cut her in two. Renn turned away. It wasn't a pretty sight.

Struggling to his feet Renn took a look around. Dredging up a mental image of the blueprint Renn saw they were right next to the security control center. There was the lift tube with the stairs which spiraled upwards around it, and the corridor leading to the mechanical section, and, last but not least, the door to the security control center. Ripping open one of Marla's saddlebags, Renn grabbed two gas grenades and stepped towards the open door.

Before he could throw the grenades, a balding tech with an empty coffee cup in his right hand stepped through the door and said, "Who the hell are you?"

"I'm afraid I don't have time for formal introductions," Renn replied. "Could you move over just a hair?"

Responding to Renn's polite tone, the tech did as he was asked, frowning when he saw the grenades.

"Thanks." Renn tossed the grenades through the door. The tech turned to look, and Renn shoved him inside, slamming the door behind him. The grenades hit the floor with a soft thud, rolled for a few feet, and went off with a small pop. The tech dropped his coffee cup and dived for them. Too late. He was unconscious by the time he hit the floor. And so were all the others in the room. Technicians were slumped and sprawled every which way, their screens going unmonitored, the soft mutter of radio traffic going unheard.

Suddenly Shinto's voice shattered the quiet of the room. "Control. What the hell's going on?" No answer. "I said what the hell's going on? Are you asleep down there?" Still no answer. There was a pause, and then Shinto spoke again, fear beginning to color his voice. "Control . . . answer me goddamn it!" Silence.

Renn used his blast rifle to spot weld the control center doors closed. According to the security plan all external doors were controlled from inside the center. As long as the people inside the center were unconscious no one could get in or out of Shinto's fortress. "There . . . that should hold 'em for awhile. Now let's find the slimy bastard."

Discarding his rifle Renn drew the .75 and followed Marla up the spiral staircase. By silent agreement they'd avoided the lift tube, not wanting to enter anything that could become a trap. As they arrived on the main floor, Marla went left while he went right.

The place was huge. The rooms were oversized, as if constructed for the comfort of giants. Compensation for Shinto's claustrophobia perhaps? Whatever the reason, the place was enormous and filled with fine furniture, exquisite works of art, and the very latest technology. Music followed Renn everywhere he went, rooms sensed the heat of his exertions and bathed him with cool air, doors opened at his approach, and entire walls rippled with warm color. Robots hurried up and down side corridors, motors humming, the very picture of domestic tranquility. Everything seemed so normal and quiet that Renn felt silly sneaking around with gun in hand.

Marla rounded a corner and shook her head. "Nothing."

Renn started to answer, but cut himself off as a rather large robot walked up and stopped a few feet away. Like most household robots, it had a vaguely humanoid appearance, but unlike most, was wearing clothes. Unbeknownst to Renn, it was currently fashionable to dress one's robots in fanciful outfits, and this one looked like an undertaker. Maybe it was the clothes, but there was something about the robot which he didn't like—something ominous. The robot's cultured voice interrupted his thoughts. "Good evening. I am known as Bruno. My master sends his greetings, and wonders if you would care to join him in his study."

Renn and Marla looked at each other and then back to the robot. "Shinto sent you?" Renn asked.

"That is correct," the robot answered patiently. "And he asks that you join him in his study."

"It could be a trap," Marla said suspiciously.

Renn nodded. "It probably is. But we could spend a week chasing him all over the castle. Let's see what's on his mind. Maybe he wants to surrender!"

"OK," Marla replied doubtfully. "But let's be careful."

Renn turned to the robot and gave a half bow. "Take us to your leader."

"Please follow me." As the robot walked away, Renn dipped a hand into one of Marla's saddlebags, withdrew two small objects, and stuffed them into a pocket. Sensing the motion, Bruno turned his turret-like head.

"We're right behind you, Bruno," Renn said, watching with interest as the robot headed towards a blank wall. As the robot approached, the wall checked its identity, matched it with a master list, and released a video lock. A door appeared where a blank wall had existed a moment before. Renn felt a little foolish realizing that they'd seen only that which Shinto wanted them to see. And from his memory of the blueprints, there shouldn't be a door in that wall either, all of which proved Shinto was nobody's fool. Given the infinite possibilities of video camouflage, they could've spent hours trying to ferret him out. And given that fact, why had Shinto agreed to see them? Was he scared? Tired of being hunted in his own fortress? Or inviting them into a trap just as Marla feared. They'd have to be very, very careful. Renn tightened his grip on the .75 and followed the robot through the hidden door.

The door hissed shut behind them as they took a

right-hand turn, and followed the robot towards a private lift tube. Bruno touched a panel and brought a platform up from the level below. Marla sat back on her haunches. "I'll wait here. Send the platform back for me when you arrive.

Renn nodded his agreement. If the lift *was* a trap it would capture one, but not both of them. He stepped aboard and heard a slight hum as the platform carried them upwards. It came to a smooth stop, and as they moved forward Renn pretended to stumble, and fell against the robot. Bruno waited patiently while he regained his balance. "Sorry about that," Renn said. "I'm getting clumsy in my old age."

Bruno stepped off the platform with Renn close behind. The robot turned. "We will wait for your companion." Renn nodded his agreement. If Bruno resented the delay there was no sign of it on his metallic features.

Marla arrived moments later, and both followed the robot down a plushly carpeted hallway. It opened up into a huge combination bedroom and study. A fireplace large enough to roast an ox dominated one wall, a vid screen another, while the other two were transparent, one opening up onto a veranda. Shinto stood before it looking out into the night. As they entered he turned to greet them, but remained where he was, hands clasped behind him.

Renn found himself looking at a handsome man with bright blue eyes and a slightly sardonic smile. "So we finally meet. How was Swamp?"

Renn was struck dumb for a moment by the sheer effrontery of the man, and then very much against his will, he started to laugh. Glancing around he said, "Not as pleasant as your country retreat."

The other man nodded soberly. "Which brings me to your presence in my home. Tell me something, Citizen Renn, you were once a businessman, and a good one. Good enough to build a business worth stealing. What are you now, I wonder . . . a businessman . . . or a criminal out for stupid revenge?"

Renn dropped into a nearby chair, but kept the .75 in his hand, pointing it towards the ceiling. "Neither one. I'm a citizen looking for some justice."

"Oh really?" Shinto sneered. "And where, pray tell, do you expect to find that? In the courts that convicted you? In a jury of your peers?"

"Nope," Renn answered evenly, allowing the .75 to come down until it was aimed at Shinto's belly. "I expect to find it right here. In the barrel of my gun."

Shinto laughed. "You and I are much alike, Citizen Renn. More so than you would care to admit. I, too, make my own justice. And when that fails, I buy it. Tell me, Citizen Renn, what are your terms? How much will your justice cost?"

Renn smiled. "Not much. All I want is the master authorization code for your computer."

A frown creased Shinto's handsome brow. "And then?"

"And then I'll make a com call to a friend of mine. He'll use the code to transfer ten million Imperial credits to my account. And once he's done that, he'll take your data bank and dump it into the Earth Central Mainframe."

All color drained from Shinto's tanned cheeks. "The ten million would hurt, but its only a fraction of my wealth, as I'm sure you know. It doesn't please me, but I could live with it. Your other demand, however, is totally unreasonable." Shinto knew, as Renn did, that once the data was dumped into Earth Central, a warrant would be issued for his arrest. In seconds Earth Central would store the data, analyze it, and conclude that Shinto Enterprises was in violation of all sorts of laws. Within minutes a small army of planetary police would be dispatched and Shinto would be taken into custody.

"Yup," Renn replied cheerfully. "It's totally unreasonable, and it's also what I call 'justice'.'"

Shinto looked down at the floor as if studying his feet. His voice was as cold as durasteel. "I'm sorry Citizen Renn. I thought you might be a reasonable man. Capable of putting childish emotion aside and dealing with reality. I respected you, liked your courage, and even considered allowing you to leave here with the ten million. I was wrong. You are stupid. Bruno, kill them." As Shinto spoke, a shield made of armored plastic slammed down from above, protecting him from Renn's .75.

Quiet until now, Bruno came to sudden life, his right arm swinging upwards and transforming itself into a laser cannon. Renn wasn't surprised. Once identified, an Auto Guard is still an Auto Guard, no matter what kind of clothes it wears. And an Auto Guard is an ultra-expensive arsenal of weapons quite capable of dealing with a full section of Imperial Marines.

Marla snarled, and started forward, even as Renn squeezed the tiny black box concealed in his left hand. The demo charge made a loud cracking sound as it cut the Auto Guard in two. The top half of the robot seemed to topple in slow motion, hitting the plush carpet with a soft thud. Some sort of black hydraulic fluid pumped out of severed tubing to stain Shinto's immaculate carpet. Meanwhile, Bruno's bottom half whirred and jerked slightly, as a still functioning servo tried to carry out its last orders.

As Marla skidded to a stop, Renn turned back towards Shinto, and said, "Oops . . . I spoiled your rug. Sorry about that, but when I detected Bruno's antisocial tendencies, I took the liberty of slipping a small surprise into his coat pocket."

Shinto was silent, his eyes locked on Bruno's corpse, his handsome features sagging slightly as he realized there was no way out.

Suddenly Renn's smile was gone leaving only hard lines behind. "I think that's enough of your bullshit. Let's have the code. Or should I have Marla come around that shield and take you apart?"

It was a beautiful day. And why not? He was a millionaire, he'd just finished an excellent breakfast in one of many fine restaurants the ancient Swiss city had to offer, and had enjoyed a nice walk along the beautiful lake. Best of all was the short article on page one of the news fax tucked under his left arm. Renn knew the words by heart and threw it into a recycler as he passed:

PROMINENT BUSINESSMAN FOUND GUILTY

> Citizen Shinto, the well-known philanthropist, businessman, and owner of Shinto Enterprises, has been found guilty of fraud, theft, and tax evasion, and sentenced to life imprisonment on a prison planet. For more details, watch Imperial News Vid at three.

Who knows? Maybe the miserable bastard would end up on Swamp. Smiling at the thought, Renn rounded a corner, and saw the cybernetics clinic. In spite of its function, the building looked more like a classic hotel than a clinic. Cyborgs and people came and went through the huge bronze doors in a never-ending swirl of metal and flesh.

Renn was halfway up the broad stairs fronting the building when the doors burst open, and a young brunette ran out, laughing with joy. Spotting Renn, she waved and then spun like a model, causing her pleated skirt to swing wide, revealing long slim legs. Then she was in his arms, her softness crushed against his chest, her lips meeting his.

And in a bar on a planet far, far away, a man with a horribly scarred face stood before his just completed mural, and proposed another toast. "Friends, this one is for Jonathan Renn and Marla Marie Mendez, wherever they may be. God bless them and keep them."